The POWER to CHOOSE

Sarah Libero

BELLA
B O O K S

2018

Bella Books, Inc.
P.O. Box 10543
Tallahassee, FL 32302

Printed in the United States of America on acid-free paper.

First Bella Books Edition 2018

Editor: Ann Roberts
Cover Designer: Judith Fellows

ISBN: 978-1-59493-602-9

Other Bella Books by Sarah Libero

Consequences

Acknowledgments

I would like to thank Ann Roberts for her help with editing this book. Her insights and ideas improved the story immensely. I learned a lot and her encouragement made all the difference in bringing this book to completion.

About the Author

Sarah Libero is a fiction author, and this is her second book with Bella Books. She was born and raised in Maine. She lived in Massachusetts for several years before moving back to Maine where she currently works as a software developer and lives with her Siberian Husky. Her books take on scenes and places that she is familiar with from around her home state.

CHAPTER ONE

Lisa stopped abruptly in the doorway of the conference room and turned to stare in shocked surprise at the hand squeezing her ass, the fingers working their way into her crack.

"What are you doing?"

The man behind her—her boss—made no effort to avoid a slight collision. His fleshy stomach bumped against her forcefully. Taking a small step away, he raised the offending hand in front of him with a shrug and a smile. "Sorry, it was an accident."

She felt her face flush with embarrassment. The squeeze was certainly no accident, but she wasn't sure how to respond. This had never happened before, and she was caught off guard. She recoiled from her boss and pulled the laptop she was carrying up to her chest protectively.

"An accident?" Lisa tried to determine the best way to get away from him without causing a scene. She knew she should say something more assertive, but her mind went blank. She couldn't think of words to express how offensive she found him.

All she wanted was to get away. "I need to get started on these numbers."

Mr. Mills glanced over her shoulder into the empty corridor before turning his eyes back to her. The smile left his face as he studied her. The client they had been meeting with earlier was long gone, and there was no one around to overhear them.

"No need to be so formal. You can call me Don."

Lisa met his gaze and knew from the look of satisfaction on his face that he was enjoying her discomfort and wasn't sorry in the least. She hadn't been with the accounting firm long enough to know Donald Mills very well, but she certainly wouldn't have anticipated her boss, a respectable married man, treating her this way.

"I need you to have those projections to me by the close of business today," Don said, edging closer. "I'm sure you know I'm a stickler for good service. Let me know if you need my assistance with anything."

Lisa began to back out of the room. She was repulsed by the thought of having to spend another minute alone with Don. The last thing she wanted was his assistance. She could just imagine what he might have in mind.

"Thanks. I'll let you know if I have any questions." Lisa hurried back to her office. Shaking her head in disbelief, she berated herself for the way she had responded. Her boss had groped her, and instead of standing up to him, she had ended up thanking him for his offer to help. She cringed at the thought of his hand on her ass.

Had she done something to make Don think she would enjoy his attention? A disgusting thought, for sure. No one else had seen it happen, and he would undoubtedly deny it was anything but an accident if he were questioned. She wanted to tell him off, or at least tell someone what had happened, but there was no one she could think of to report it to. Don was in charge, and she didn't know her coworkers well enough to share this with them.

She needed to figure this out. Her initial shock was beginning to give way to anger as she recalled the smile on his face when he was watching her. He had a lot of nerve thinking he could touch her like that. Now that she was back in her office, she could think of a dozen things she wished she had said to him.

As infuriating as his behavior was, she didn't want to risk losing her job, so she would keep quiet for now. She had only been with the company since moving to Maine less than a year ago, and Don was one of the founding partners. It wouldn't be good for her career if she made a big deal over something she couldn't prove. It was frustrating to realize there wasn't much she could do other than try to make sure she wasn't alone with him again. She didn't want any future encounters with Don's wandering hands.

* * *

Lisa walked up the stone steps and opened the door to the café. She paused in the entryway to listen to the song the band in the back corner was playing. The air was filled with delicious aromas from the nightly dinner specials. The light scent of garlic along with the smell of freshly baked bread reminded her how hungry she was. It was Saturday night, which meant it was music night at Harvest, the café in the small lakeside town where she had been living for the past several months.

The decision to move to Winchester, Maine, was turning out to be a good one. She liked it here in this eclectic little town next to the lake. The people she'd met were interesting and the area was beautiful. The thriving local music scene meant there was always good entertainment to be found at one of the many local pubs and cafés.

She had lived in Massachusetts for her entire life, and she had been ready to try something different after her mother had passed away. Lisa had been thinking about her mother a lot lately. She missed her mother's presence in her life. She surely would have given her some good advice about how to handle things with Don.

She was looking forward to having dinner with a friend tonight. It would be good to get her mind off her encounter with Don. Fortunately, she had been able to finish up the client's projections fairly quickly the previous day and had submitted them via email, so she hadn't had to deal with Don in person. Now she was trying to forget about work.

She glanced at the upcoming musical lineup among the flyers and announcements on the bulletin board in the entryway. It would be fun to hear the different musicians, and she was planning to come by as often as she could. The restaurant was full and she noticed a few familiar faces while she waited next to the glass bakery case at the front counter for someone to seat her. She didn't know the names of many people in town yet, but she was beginning to recognize some of them as time went by. She was hoping eventually she'd get to meet more of them. She wasn't the most outgoing person and it took her a while to connect with people.

Now that it was late June and the summer season was starting, there were more people in town. Winchester was a popular spot for visitors, but it was far enough off the beaten path to avoid getting overly crowded. Many houses on the lake were owned by people who lived out of state for the majority of the year and came to town for the warmer months. Much to her pleasure, the café had increased their hours for the summer. She wasn't much of a cook, and she often found it easier to come here rather than go to the trouble of cooking.

The owner of the café was a client at the accounting firm where Lisa worked. Her name was Carrie, and Lisa had met her at the office a couple weeks ago when Carrie picked up her tax returns. Lisa looked back into the open kitchen behind the counter and saw her preparing a variety of meats and vegetables on the grill. Her short, dark hair was combed back, and her brow was furrowed in concentration as she transferred food to serving plates. Carrie caught sight of her and waved. She handed her spatula to one of the other cooks and made her way over.

Wiping her hands on her crisp white apron, Carrie leaned against the counter and smiled. "Hi there. How are you?"

It struck Lisa how attractive Carrie's face was when she smiled. Lisa had been a little apprehensive about speaking with her at the office. On previous visits to the café, she thought Carrie was quite stern and intimidating. She was several inches taller than Lisa's five-foot four-inch height, and she looked very muscular under the T-shirts she usually wore. Lisa had found her initial impression was wrong. Carrie had actually been remarkably friendly when she spoke to her at the office. Lisa realized Carrie wasn't harsh, she was focused and determined. It wasn't easy to run a successful business, and Carrie took her work very seriously.

"Hi, Carrie." Lisa smiled back at her. "It looks like you're going to have a busy night."

"Summer is finally here," Carrie said. "I love it. We've got lots of fresh vegetables on the menu, and I think you'll like the vegetarian special tonight."

"I like everything you cook." Lisa was surprised Carrie remembered she was a vegetarian. "This is my favorite restaurant, and it's a stroke of luck for me that it happens to be right here in town."

"Well thank you. I'm glad you like it."

Lisa was about to reply when one of the waitresses approached her. "Would you like a table for one?"

"I'm meeting a friend," Lisa said. "I have a reservation for two."

"Enjoy your meal," Carrie said with a nod, turning back to the kitchen.

"Thanks."

Lisa followed the waitress to a table near one of the windows lining the back wall. A small glass vase in the center held a bouquet of late blooming purple lilacs. It was still light out and there was a lovely view of the lake. She looked out the window and watched the boats go by as she waited for her friend Rachel. The band was taking a break, so the music had stopped for a little while. It was a beautiful evening and the screened porch that extended along the side of the restaurant and across the back was full of diners enjoying the warm night.

The waitress returned with the beer she had ordered just as Rachel arrived. Lisa caught her eye with a wave and Rachel rushed over to join her.

"Hi, Lisa." Rachel ran a hand through her frizzy blond hair. "Sorry I'm late. I forgot how long it takes to get all the way out here from Augusta."

"Don't worry about it," Lisa said. "I haven't been waiting long. It's a nice night to sit and look at the lake. It's a pretty relaxing way to wait, actually."

Lisa had known Rachel since their college days and knew she was always late. They had been college roommates in Boston and had stayed in touch ever since. Rachel was from Maine and had returned to her hometown of Augusta to work as a physical therapist after college graduation. When Lisa had decided she wanted to move, Rachel convinced her to come to Maine. She had visited Rachel occasionally over the years and had always liked the Belgrade Lakes area where Winchester was located, so she had taken Rachel's advice and gone north.

"How's the family?" Lisa asked. Rachel's husband and two teenagers kept her very busy, which meant she wasn't often able to get away for the evening.

"Everyone's good."

The waitress came over and took their orders. Lisa got the vegetarian special that Carrie had recommended, and Rachel ordered a salad and a glass of wine.

"Salad?" Lisa asked.

"I need to lose twenty pounds in the next couple weeks. We're going to the cape and I need to fit into my bathing suit."

"Another diet?" Lisa shook her head. For as long as she had known Rachel, she had always been worried about her weight. "I think you look great."

"Yeah, well, I'm good at starting diets," Rachel replied. "How's your job going?"

Lisa thought about telling Rachel how Don had groped her. While it would have been nice to have some support from her friend, she had already decided she didn't want to think about it tonight. No point in ruining the evening.

"It's going all right. I was super busy all spring, but things will start slowing down now for the summer, so I should have more free time."

The band started up again as the waitress brought Rachel's glass of wine over and placed it on the white tablecloth in front of her. Rachel picked up her glass and took a big sip. "Ah, this is good. Any plans for all this free time?"

"Nothing major on the schedule as of yet. I think it'll be nice to hang out by the lake this summer. I bought a couple of kayaks and I hope you and the kids come over and use them whenever you want."

"The kids would love it, although you need some more people besides us to hang out with. Speaking of which, have you met anyone or gone out on any dates at all since you moved to Maine?"

"No." Lisa didn't want to go into details with Rachel, but it had been a long time since she'd met anyone. Sometimes she worried about the lack of romance in her life, but she had a busy schedule and it really didn't bother her. "I don't know. I don't go anywhere other than the office, and I don't come across many available ladies there."

"We need to fix you up. I'm going to get on it."

"No thanks." Lisa shuddered. "The last time I let you do that it was a disaster. Remember? My date got drunk and then she got sick in my car."

"Oh, I forgot about that." Rachel winced apologetically. "Didn't you say that you come here a lot? Have you met any people here at the café?"

"No one that I think would be interested in me. I've met the owner and she's nice, but I have no idea about her personal life."

"The tall lady back there with the dark hair?" Rachel peered over the table toward the kitchen. "Hmm, she's kind of sexy looking."

"Quit staring. I don't even know if she likes women."

"I thought lesbians were supposed to have a sense about things like that. For the record, I think you're a good catch. You're good-looking, in decent shape, fairly intelligent and you're good with numbers."

"Considering how long I've been single, I must clearly be missing any lesbian vibes." Lisa laughed. "Still, I'm glad to hear that someone thinks I'm a good catch."

In spite of her earlier resolve, her thoughts returned to her encounter with Don. She didn't want to keep dwelling on it. Maybe if she told Rachel what happened, she could get a better perspective on the whole thing and stop thinking about it.

"I did have one person hit on me the other day," Lisa said. "Unfortunately, it was my boss."

"What?" Rachel's eyes widened. "Are you kidding me? Don Mills?"

"It wasn't a big deal." Lisa downplayed the incident. "He grabbed my ass when we were walking out of a room."

"What did you do?"

"Nothing. He said it was an accident." Lisa shrugged. "Hopefully it won't happen again."

"What a pig. You don't grab someone's ass by mistake." Rachel frowned. "You have to report him."

Lisa shook her head. Rachel didn't realize she could lose her job if she started a dispute with Don. Maybe she shouldn't have said anything. "I think I'm just going to stay quiet and make sure he doesn't get a chance to try anything else. I haven't been there long, and I don't want to stir up controversy. I'm sure I can handle it."

"I think you should tell someone."

"Let's just keep it between ourselves for now, okay?"

"If you say so."

Ready to change the subject, Lisa lifted her glass. "This beer is good, I'll have to remember to get this again."

Rachel stared at something over Lisa's shoulder and lowered her voice. "Oh, how sad. The parents of a girl who was killed in a hit-and-run accident last year are sitting at a table behind you. She played basketball and field hockey against our teams, so I used to see them at my daughter's games. Her name was Michelle Nelson and she was an awfully good kid."

"That's terrible. It must have happened before I moved to Winchester."

"Yes. She was walking her dog on a street near her house here in town. A car hit her and didn't even stop to see if she was all right. One of the neighbors found her and it was too late."

"I don't know how anyone could leave a person like that. Did they find whoever hit her?"

"I don't think so." Rachel sighed. "I can't imagine what parents go through when something like that happens. I don't know what I'd do if anything happened to one of my kids."

"It reminds me of the accident that happened when we were in college, when the hockey player my friend Toni was dating hit someone who was crossing the street. Then he took off and left the accident scene."

"I remember that. I wonder whatever happened to Toni?"

"I have no idea."

The waitress brought out their meals. The vegetables and rice in her dinner were delicious. Lisa noticed Rachel looking around at the other diners' plates longingly after she finished her salad.

"Maybe I'll try a piece of that yummy-looking chocolate cake I saw in the case when I came in," Rachel said. "I'll start my diet again tomorrow."

CHAPTER TWO

Carrie woke up with the sun shining in her eyes. It had been a busy night at the café and she'd gotten home late. She needed to get up and get back over to supervise her crew for the breakfast service. They closed at two on Sundays, so she would have plenty of time to relax this afternoon.

She looked out the window through the pine trees at the sunlight sparkling on the lake as she got out of bed and stretched. She loved living here. Her family had lived in Winchester for generations, and her parents had given her this piece of land where she had her house built, right down the road from their place. She wasn't too far from the café, and she had plenty of privacy here in the woods.

When she talked to some of the summertime residents and told them she lived next door to her parents in the same town she grew up in, they usually asked her how she liked it. Occasionally they asked if she ever wished she were doing something more exciting.

She liked living near her parents or she wouldn't be here. Her older brother and his family lived nearby, along with several other relatives. She had gone to college at the University of Maine and had been happy to return home after graduating. Her definition of success was to be her own boss, doing a job she enjoyed with family and friends close by.

It was time to get moving or she'd be late, but her mind kept drifting back to seeing Lisa the night before. There was something about Lisa that caught her attention. Carrie had noticed how pretty she was the first time she had come into the café, but she hadn't talked to her until she ran into her at the accounting office.

Lisa had met someone for dinner at the café last night. Was she on a date or was the woman just a friend? Carrie didn't know what to think and it was probably just as well. The busy season was starting, and she needed to keep her mind on getting things ready for the summer crowd.

* * *

Carrie locked the café door and leaned back with a sigh of relief. She was ready for a break. It had been a busy weekend and they had been cooking nonstop. She was closed on Mondays, which meant she had the next couple nights off. She walked back to the kitchen and did a final check. Everything was washed up and put away, and the stainless-steel counters were cleaned and shining.

"Angie, did you get everything packed up?" Carrie asked.

Angie was one of the other cooks who ran the kitchen. She had been helping Carrie pack some of their leftover breads and desserts to take to the local food bank since they were going to be closed the next day. She was very careful about serving only the freshest food at the café, but she didn't want any leftovers to go to waste.

"It's all set." Angie took off her purple apron and shook out her long, brown ponytail. "I'll drop everything off. We have to make a run into town anyway."

"Thanks," Carrie said. "I guess we're ready to go. Ryan are you ready?"

"Hold on. I'm coming," Ryan called from the back room. He walked into the kitchen and put the empty trashcan back in the corner. He and Angie rented the apartment above the café from Carrie. They had been employed by her for the past five years and they were good tenants. They kept an eye on the place for her and they both worked hard at their jobs.

"I haven't showed you the new ink I got last week," he said proudly. He lifted up his pant leg and showed her the back of his calf. There was a colorful picture of a red-eyed elf with fire shooting from its ears.

"You ran out of room on your arms, huh?" Carrie examined his leg. "That's cool. A demented elf suits you."

"It's the avatar I was using when I met Angie online."

"All right, let's get going." Angie gave Ryan a quick kiss. She turned to Carrie. "See you Tuesday morning, Carrie."

Carrie followed them out the backdoor and locked up. She got into her Jeep and headed for home. Her parents' house came into view as she turned down the wooded road that she lived on. She thought about stopping to say hello, but decided to come back later after she had gone for a run and caught up on a few things at home.

She pulled into her gravel driveway and smiled. Some of the flowers were starting to bloom. One nice thing about her yard was that she didn't have any grass, so she really didn't have much maintenance. She had some blueberry bushes and a few perennials growing here and there, but the area around her house had been left mainly in its natural state with pine trees and rocks surrounding the outer perimeter of the yard. She kept several planters with flowers for color and grew her own tomatoes and cucumbers, preferring to keep things attractive but simple.

She opened the door onto the screen porch and let herself inside, heading immediately upstairs to change into her running clothes. It had been hot and sweaty in the kitchen that morning, and she was eager to go for a run before coming back to shower. At the moment, all she wanted was to get out into the fresh air.

A few minutes later, she was back outside and ready to go. She turned on her iPod and started jogging down the gravel road. Her road branched to a network of camp roads that bordered the cove and wound their way around the eastern side of the lake. She was planning on going for a six-mile loop. The day was comfortably warm, and a light breeze kept the black flies away. It felt good to be outdoors. She could feel the tension of the day fade away as her leg muscles began to pump and she fell into a comfortable stride.

She went around a corner and saw another runner coming toward her from the other direction with a black and tan dog at her side. As she got closer, Carrie was surprised to see that it was Lisa. She slowed and took her earbuds out, hoping Lisa would stop to talk. Lisa's face lit up when she recognized Carrie, and she came to a stop a few yards in front of her.

"Daisy come," Lisa called out. The dog ignored her and ran to Carrie with her tail wagging, eager to meet a new friend. She sniffed Carrie's legs for a moment before returning to her owner's side. Lisa grabbed her collar and made her sit.

Carrie walked closer to them. "Hello there."

"Hi." Lisa held up a finger. "Hold on a sec while I catch my breath."

Carrie waited quietly while Lisa pushed the short, sandy-blond hair out of her eyes and took some deep breaths. She tried not to stare at Lisa's muscular legs and the toned arms revealed by the loose-fitting tank top she was wearing.

"I haven't had a chance to run much lately," Lisa panted. "Don't laugh. I'm sure that my face is as red as a tomato."

Carrie tried to keep a straight face. Lisa's face was actually alarmingly red. "Do you live near here?"

"I live about two miles away, down East Ridge Road. How about you?"

"I live down Sawyer Road, about a mile from here," Carrie answered. "Can I pet Daisy?"

"Sure, she loves people." Lisa loosened her grip on the dog's collar. Daisy jumped forward to greet Carrie as she knelt down to pet her.

"She's beautiful." Carrie stroked Daisy's soft fur and looked up at Lisa. "What kind of dog is she?"

"She's a Gordon Setter mix. I got her at the shelter when I moved here. I still can't believe someone would have taken her there. She's the best dog ever."

Lisa knelt down next to Carrie and started rubbing Daisy's chin. "You're a good girl, aren't you, Daisy? You're my furry little girl."

Carrie became acutely aware of how close they were as Lisa's arm brushed against hers. Her heart rate was already elevated from the run, and it started to increase when she glanced at Lisa, who was looking really good. Her hair was curled with perspiration and her skin was flushed and glowing. Carrie realized she probably still smelled like the grill. She stood up and stepped back quickly.

"So, how far were you planning to run?" Carrie asked, trying to think of something to say to cover her sudden discomfort.

"I think I've gone a couple miles and I might turn around soon." Lisa looked back down the road. "I usually like to go around four miles or so."

Carrie wanted to spend a little more time with her. "Do you mind if I run with you on your way back?"

"I'd love the company. I'll probably slow you down, though."

"I'm not in any rush."

Lisa stood up and they started to jog side by side down the gravel road. Daisy ran a few yards ahead of them, turning back every few minutes to keep a close eye on Lisa. A few clouds were drifting in, keeping the temperature cool for their run.

"Isn't your last name Sawyer?" Lisa asked. "And you live on Sawyer Road?"

"My family's lived here for a long time. My parents put in the road when they got married and built their house. They gave me and my brother each a piece of land along the road for our own houses."

"That's so nice. Do your parents still live here?"

"They do. Right next door to me, in fact." Carrie waited to hear the usual questions about why she would want to live so close to them.

"You're lucky."

"I think so." Carrie smiled.

They went up a long, steep hill, and Carrie noticed Lisa had stopped talking. They both focused on their pace until they made it to the top. Lisa turned to Carrie. "I hate that hill. I always figure if I can make it up something like that without stopping, then I can handle whatever else the day throws at me."

Carrie nodded. "That's a good attitude. Where did you live before you came to Winchester?"

"I used to live in Massachusetts."

"What made you decide to move here?"

"My parents have both passed away and there was nothing holding me there anymore. I guess I was ready for a change. My friend Rachel lives in Augusta. I don't know if you saw her, but she's the one that I met at the café for dinner last night. Anyway, I've always liked this area and she talked me into coming here."

Carrie had seen Lisa's friend last night. So, Lisa had moved here to be near Rachel. It was a good thing she had found that out before she asked Lisa on a date. They reached the turnoff to Lisa's road and continued along their route.

Lisa slowed and came to a stop a short time later when they reached the end of a driveway next to a small house with weathered gray shingles. She put her hands on her knees and bent over, taking some deep breaths while Daisy ran down the driveway toward the lake.

"Thanks for keeping me and Daisy company," Lisa said.

"My pleasure." Carrie turned to head back to the main road. "Well, I hope I see you at Harvest again soon. Bye."

Carrie glanced back over her shoulder as she began to jog and saw Lisa give her a friendly wave. What was it about Lisa that made Carrie keep thinking of her? She shook her head and kept running. There was no point in dwelling on it, because Lisa wasn't available.

CHAPTER THREE

Lisa looked up from her screen and leaned back, giving her shoulders a stretch. It was getting close to the end of the day and she was ready for a break. She had finished reviewing the section of financial records she had been analyzing for the past two days and didn't feel like starting a new section.

She enjoyed the work she was doing. The firm was highly respected in the state of Maine, with offices in Augusta and Portland. She had been thrilled when she landed this job and was able to move to the area. There were several other CPAs in addition to herself, including a few other women. She got along with everyone, although they spent most of their time in their offices focused on their individual assignments. She didn't know anyone here all that well, which was something she would have to put more effort into. At her previous job she had been good friends with her coworkers, and she missed having people to talk to.

She thought she liked everything about her job until Don grabbed her ass. He'd treated her in a professional manner for the most part, but when she thought about it, she remembered catching him staring at her a couple times during meetings. She had no idea where this behavior was coming from and she was determined to discourage it by ignoring any suggestive remarks and avoiding any physical contact.

The notification from her laptop calendar chimed and she looked at it in dismay. It was almost time for her to stop by Don's office. He had sent her a meeting request earlier that day and she had been trying not to think about it because she was dreading spending time with him.

Lisa reviewed her strategy for dealing with Don as she headed toward his corner office at the end of the hall. She had been successful thus far in making sure she hadn't been alone with him, but she couldn't avoid it forever. She was hoping the squeeze from the other day had been a one-time thing. Otherwise, she would do her best to ignore his remarks and evade contact with him. If Don saw she had no intention of responding to any of his overtures, maybe he would leave her alone and she could avoid a confrontation.

Don's door was closed, and Lisa paused to take a deep breath, preparing herself to be ready for whatever might be waiting for her in his office. Before she had a chance to knock, she heard loud voices inside.

"This is bullshit. I knew we couldn't trust him."

"Keep your voice down," Don answered. "You're not going to come into my place of business and start this. If anyone finds out what's been going on, we'll all go down with him at this point. We all have our asses on the line here and I'll handle it."

"Lawrence was supposed to have that contract in place by now. I'm going to lose money if he doesn't come through."

"I'll talk to him. Just keep your mouth shut and don't do something stupid."

"You'd better straighten this out soon, or I'll do it myself."

Lisa stepped back from the door just as it flew open and a man came storming out. He passed by her without a glance and strode down the corridor with his fists clenched.

She turned to see Don standing in the doorway, watching her.

"Have you been waiting long?"

Lisa shook her head innocently. "I just got here."

"Come on in," he said, gesturing toward the chair.

She walked into the office and his body pressed against hers as he stepped toward the door to close it. His hand came to rest on the small of her back and she stepped away quickly. He moved with her and rubbed his body against her breasts, leaning against her shoulder to speak softly into her ear. "So nice to see you again."

"Excuse me. Please don't touch me."

"I was just closing the door. No need to get excited."

Lisa pushed away from him and moved to stand beside one of the chairs facing his desk, putting it between the two of them.

Don's eyes slowly traveled from her legs up to her silk blouse, lingering on her breasts, as she stood there uncomfortably.

"What is it you wanted?" Lisa asked.

"Have a seat."

He walked behind his desk and sat down in the large leather chair, leaning back to fold his hands across his ample paunch. Lisa sat across from him. She had been in here several times before with never any cause for concern. Don ran things here in the Augusta branch and had always treated her courteously. Steeling herself to ignore any suggestive remarks, she tried to maintain the professionalism that had been present at their previous meetings.

"I wanted to check in with you about how you're doing." Don appeared to be past fifty and he hadn't aged well. As she watched, he slid one of his hands down from his stomach into his lap. The height of the desk blocked her view, but she could see his arm moving as he stroked himself. "How do you like your position?"

The only thing she didn't like about her position was spending time with him. Lisa answered politely, "Everything seems to be going fine."

"You've done a good job with tax preparations. I'd like to put you in charge of more audits, but I want to make sure you'll be able to handle some of our male clients."

Lisa sat silently, unsure of what he meant.

"You're a very attractive woman." He winked at her. "I wouldn't want you to be offended if some of our clients flirt with you a bit. Do you know what I mean?"

Was he asking her if she would mind if some of their clients started treating her the way he had when she walked into his office? Did he just imply she was going to have to put up with harassment from clients in order to get ahead?

"I'm not sure what you mean," Lisa answered. Don's hand was still hidden under his desk and his smile was making her stomach turn. She tried to think of a diplomatic response to get her out of this uncomfortable situation. "I would be happy to do more audits if that's what you're asking."

"As I mentioned before, I'm a stickler for good service." Don raised his eyebrows suggestively. "Some of our clients expect to be entertained. If you were to put on a nice short dress and take them for drinks, that sort of thing, it would be good customer service. These guys would really enjoy the attention of a woman such as yourself."

"I'm an accountant, not an escort."

"Keeping clients happy is what business is all about. I'm sure you want to move ahead here at the firm. I can see something special in you, and I want to do everything I can to help."

Lisa had never heard of any of her colleagues having to entertain clients in a short dress. Completely fed up with Don's suggestions, she lost her resolve to avoid confronting him. She stood up. "Are you saying I would have to entertain clients in a short dress if I want to move ahead here? I'm very good at my job and I shouldn't have to be treated any differently than a man."

"Hold on, now. I'm just saying you need to understand how things work around here. I want to be sure you won't get upset if one of our clients is friendlier than you might be expecting in a business situation. Sometimes a man likes to admire a pretty woman and have a little physical contact. I don't want you to overreact and start claiming harassment any time someone touches you. I think if you give it a chance, you might appreciate how this can be mutually beneficial."

There was no winning this argument with him and any further discussion would escalate the situation. Don clearly saw nothing wrong with exploiting her for his own pleasure or for keeping clients happy. This was unbelievable. She knew she needed to get away and collect herself, so she nodded and left.

Walking back to her office, she reflected on the fact she wasn't surprised when Don had touched her this time, but she hadn't expected him to be so blatant about telling her to put up with harassment. There were bound to be times when clients flirted or wanted to get a little too friendly. This was true of many jobs. All of the companies she had worked for in the past were supportive about protecting employees and it was shocking to hear Don come right out and say she should allow herself to be put into a sexual situation with a client.

Was the man who had stormed out of Don's office one of those clients she would be expected to entertain? She wished she knew what they had been discussing. It sounded like they were covering something up that could quite possibly be illegal. She would love to find out what it was that could bring Don down if anyone found out.

She shut down her computer and grabbed her bag, more than ready to get out of there for the day. She needed to talk to someone about this. She knew Rachel was busy with patients and wouldn't be home until later in the evening. Maybe she would stop by the café and get a bite to eat and think it over until she could catch up with Rachel.

Lisa parked on the street in front of the café. She hoped Carrie would be there; she'd had fun meeting her on the road the other day. She had to admit, she wished Carrie had shown a little interest in her. She'd wanted to stare when she saw how good she looked in shorts and a tight T-shirt. She really liked the way she smiled. It was quite extraordinary. She could tell Carrie hadn't wanted to get too close, and Lisa was a little disappointed she hadn't mentioned getting together again. Hopefully they could at least be friends.

There were plenty of empty tables when she walked in. A sign near the counter told customers to seat themselves. She looked behind the counter into the kitchen. Carrie was pulling some trays out of the oven and spotted her. She abandoned the trays and came over to greet Lisa.

"Hi there," Carrie said. "Are you here for an early dinner?"

"I am." She added impulsively, "I wish you could join me."

"I suppose I could for a little while." Carrie looked pleased to be asked. "It's not too busy yet and Angie can handle things in the kitchen. Let's go sit over by the window."

Lisa followed Carrie to a table with a sweeping view of the lake. They sat down, and Lisa reached forward to touch Carrie's arm. "Best table in the house, huh?"

"You bet." Carrie leaned back in her chair. "We have fresh strawberries tonight. We also have some homemade pasta with fresh vegetables you might like."

"I love strawberry season." Lisa pulled back her hand. "Do you ever go pick them?"

"Oh, yeah. Fresh strawberries are the best. I don't have time to pick them myself every day, so I get them delivered for the café, but I try to go at least a couple times while they're in season."

"Take me with you some time, please? I haven't gone in ages."

Carrie nodded without answering, and Lisa began to worry she had made her uncomfortable. Carrie may not want to drag her along if she went strawberry picking.

"So how is Daisy?" Carrie asked.

"She's great." Lisa was glad for the change of topic. "We both had fun running with you the other day. We should do it again sometime."

"That sounds like a good idea."

Ryan walked by their table and Carrie called him over, "Ryan, can you put an order in for us, please?"

"Sure boss. What would you like?"

Carrie ordered the fish tacos and Lisa went with the daily pasta special. They sat in relaxed silence for a minute and Lisa decided to tell her about her encounters with Don. She really wanted to talk to someone about it, and she was drawn to Carrie for some reason. She was having second thoughts about telling Rachel because she'd want her to report Don and she wasn't quite ready to do that. Talking to Carrie might help her decide.

"I've been having some really uncomfortable experiences at work lately," Lisa began.

"What's been going on?"

"I know you're one of our clients, and I don't know if I should even be saying anything." Lisa paused. "I was going to talk to Rachel about it but she's still at work and I feel like I have to tell someone. I guess I want to see if you think it's as awful as I do."

Carrie leaned forward and looked into Lisa's eyes. "If you need someone to talk to, I'd be happy to listen. I won't repeat anything you tell me."

Lisa stared back into Carrie's eyes for a moment. She hadn't noticed what a lovely shade of blue they were. "Uh, thanks." She shook her head to clear her thoughts. "My boss, Don, has touched me in an inappropriate way a couple times. The first time he squeezed my ass and then proceeded to bump into me and claim it was an accident.

"Then I got called into his office this afternoon and he intentionally pushed himself against me when I walked by. He kept trying to press against me. And I think he was touching himself while he was talking to me. It's hard to describe, and he's only done it when there's no one else around, so it would be my word against his if I tried to report him."

"Gross." Carrie made a face. "I thought Don was married, not that it would matter if he was single. Just gross either way."

"Right?" Lisa said. "I know the first time was no accident. His hand was right on my ass and he had plenty of time to stop before he bumped into me."

"I had no idea he was like that. He comes across as very polite and professional."

"There's more. He called me into his office to tell me if I want to move ahead in the company, I would have to entertain male clients and not mind if they wanted a little physical contact, as he put it."

"What does he mean by physical contact?"

"Exactly what I was wondering. I was totally shocked by the whole thing. I don't know if he has some specific client in mind or what he was even talking about."

Carrie sat back and shook her head. "It definitely sounds like sexual harassment to me. What are you going to do?"

"I don't know. There really isn't much I can do about it because there's no way I can prove anything. I think I'll just try to avoid him and hope it doesn't happen again."

"I can see why you wanted to tell someone about it. Have you thought about reporting him to someone at the company?"

"I don't think I should tell anyone at the office because the backlash could be even worse than putting up with Don. It would put me in a really bad light at my new job." Lisa shrugged. "I was completely taken off guard when it first happened, and I really didn't know how to respond. He clearly has no idea I'm not remotely interested in men in the first place."

Ryan interrupted the conversation with their meals. Carrie gave him a nod of thanks and he headed back to the kitchen.

"I understand what you're saying. It could be hard to make people believe he'd do something like that. It would come down to your word against his, and he does have a good reputation, from what I've seen. He's a family man and his company is known for its generosity—they always support the community and donate to several local charities."

"I overheard an argument that he was having with someone today, and I think there's a whole other side to Don. They were talking about a contract and saying if anyone finds out about it, they would all go down."

"Whoah."

"Yeah. I couldn't believe it. But once again, I don't have proof about anything. It was just a conversation. There's nothing in writing or any physical evidence to back me up."

"This is unreal," Carrie said. "I truly believe you, but it's pretty shocking to hear something like this is going on. Everyone sees Don as a successful businessman, but underneath his public persona he's actually a criminal."

Lisa nodded. "I wish I had known what he was really like before I went to work for him."

"Did you know Don is from Winchester?" Carrie asked. "He's at least ten years older than I am, but I went to school with his younger brother, Bruce. He's a big construction contractor in the area."

"That's interesting." Lisa touched Carrie's arm again. "I don't know many people yet, and I'm glad that I've gotten to know you a little better. Thanks for listening. I think I just needed to tell someone."

Carrie looked at her. "I wish there was something I could do to help."

"I'll have to figure it out. I'm afraid Don is just getting started."

CHAPTER FOUR

Lisa tried to concentrate on the figures she was studying, but her mind kept returning to yesterday's conversation with Don. She hadn't seen him today and she hoped she'd be able to avoid him for a while. Yesterday he had said she needed to understand how things worked around here and she had a pretty good idea about what he meant. He expected her to put up with his unwanted advances along with those of her male clients if she wanted to keep her job and move up in the company. She certainly had no intention of putting up with anything from her clients, and she needed to speak up in a way that would get her off the hook without antagonizing him. She really wanted to tell him off, which would surely get her fired. It wasn't easy to find a new job in this area, and she didn't want to move again so soon.

She also couldn't keep her mind off her dinner with Carrie the night before. She had all but thrown herself at her, asking to go running and strawberry picking, and Carrie hadn't responded at all. She'd even mentioned the fact that she wasn't interested in men. Obviously, Carrie just wanted to be friends.

Lisa could take a hint. It would probably save a lot of stress in the long run anyway. She could use a few friends and Carrie was a nice person. Really nice. She just needed to stop thinking about their relationship as anything more than platonic, which wasn't going to be easy because those blue eyes of hers certainly were beautiful.

Looking at one of her accounts, Lisa saw she needed some documentation for the category she was using. She couldn't find a reference in her local files, so she opened up her network directory. She looked on the company's shared drive to see if she could find more information and noticed a file named Lawrence, which was the name she had heard Don mention in the argument she had overheard. It was probably a long shot that this would be the same Lawrence, but the name caught her eye. She looked at the date stamp on the file and saw that it had been touched that day. Curious to find out more, she clicked on the file.

She scanned the information with interest. The filename was apparently in reference to Maine State Senator, William Lawrence. The file contained a memo with Senator Lawrence's name as the subject along with a list of dates and numbers beginning over a year ago and continuing through to the current month. The column of dates was listed chronologically in an eight-digit format and the entries occurred once or twice each month. The adjoining column of numbers was formatted as currency with a dollar symbol in the heading. All of the entries were for even amounts with fairly large numbers. The lowest figure she saw was for $5,000 and the largest was for $80,000. There were no further details, so she couldn't tell what the dates and dollar amounts stood for. The memo was from Don and it was sent to Joe Michaud and Bruce Mills.

Carrie had mentioned she'd gone to school with Bruce, Don's brother. Lisa also recognized Joe Michaud's name, since he was the county sheriff and was often in the news. The town of Winchester was too small to support its own police department, so they relied on the sheriff's department for law enforcement. She hadn't met Michaud personally, but she had seen cars from the sheriff's department around town occasionally. He was a tall, slim man with dark hair and a charming smile.

Lisa's curiosity was definitely piqued. She thought about what the dates and dollar amounts might represent and why Don would have sent them this memo along with the Senator's name. It was possible the numbers were payments from Don, his brother and Joe Michaud as bribes for a contract Senator Lawrence was securing for them. The man in Don's office had said Lawrence was supposed to have a contract in place. If these numbers were payments to the senator, that would explain Don's comment about how they would all go down if anyone found out. She wondered what sort of contract it could be.

She hadn't recognized the man in Don's office, but he could have been Bruce Mills. It would make sense, although she would have to see a picture of him to be sure. She knew the man wasn't Joe Michaud and she had never met Bruce.

There were some holes in her theory. It didn't make a lot of sense that there had been bribes in various amounts once or twice for over a year. It was possible they had varied the amount to avoid suspicion, but it did seem odd.

Also, Lisa wasn't sure how the senator would be able to secure a contract; that was something she would have to try and figure out. She would need to find a way to link this memo to an actual contract if she ever wanted to prove Don's involvement and she was going to have to get a lot more information in order to do so.

She had to admit, the memo could be explained by a more innocent scenario as well. Perhaps the firm was working on some sort of fundraiser for the senator. The entries could be donations which were made toward his latest campaign. She knew Don was friendly with several politicians in Augusta. Many influential people in the area used his firm, which is why it had such a good reputation. A big part of the reason she had accepted this job was based on both Don's and the company's reputations. He certainly was different from the image he presented to the public.

She made a note of the file's location before closing it, and then she went back to looking up information for her client. She wanted to get this task done so she could get home and take Daisy out for a run. She needed to get back on a decent training schedule. It had been embarrassing how winded she had gotten the other day.

Now if she could just stop thinking about Carrie.

CHAPTER FIVE

Customers had begun arriving early for music night on Saturday evening and the café was bustling with activity. Carrie had most of her staff on hand and they were all busy. After making sure Angie had the meal service under control, Carrie went out front to check on the waitstaff. The musician who was performing that night was all set up in the back corner. Her name was Toni and she was going to be singing and playing guitar with another guitarist she'd brought along to accompany her. Toni hadn't played at Harvest before, but she had excellent references, so Carrie was happy to add her to the schedule.

Ryan and the other waiters and waitresses were doing a good job making sure all the diners were seated and had drinks. It looked like everyone was happy for the moment. Carrie walked over to see if Toni was all set.

"How is everything?" Carrie asked.

"Wonderful." Toni leaned her guitar on the wall next to her stool. "I love your place. The art on the walls is great and the view of the lake is awesome."

"Thank you." Carrie gestured at the paintings on the wall behind Toni. "We feature a different local artist every month. We get some really nice pieces."

"Thanks for having me here." Toni gave Carrie a friendly smile. Her silver bracelets caught the light as she adjusted the height of the microphone. "I've heard a lot of good things about Harvest."

"You come highly recommended and I'm glad to have you here." Carrie couldn't help noticing how pretty Toni was. She had a bohemian look going on with her long curly hair and a flowing gypsy skirt. She seemed nice and Carrie was always happy to give musicians a place to play. Her customers loved music night and so did she.

"Let me know if you need anything," Carrie said. "I'll send Ryan by to get your drink orders and we'll be sure to set you up with whatever you want to eat between sets if you like."

"That would be great, thank you."

"Well, I've got to head back to the kitchen. Have a good show."

Carrie was walking back through the dining room when Lisa came through the door. She stopped and waited by the counter to say hello. She wanted to ask her how things were going at work, but there were too many people around. She had been worried about Lisa this week and wondering how she was handling things with her boss.

It had been a nice surprise when Lisa stopped by and asked her to join her for dinner the other night. Not wanting to overstep the bounds of their new friendship, Carrie had been cautious about answering Lisa's requests to get together. She would love to go strawberry picking or running again, but she wanted to be careful about how she answered. Doing either of those things with Lisa would be great, but she needed to remind herself that Lisa wasn't available. She had moved here to join Rachel. Carrie wasn't sure she could be satisfied with keeping things platonic, the emotions that were surfacing were something she had never experienced, and she wanted to proceed cautiously.

Carrie had been too focused on running the restaurant over the years to have time for anything else. She'd had plenty of casual romances but no long-term meaningful relationships since she bought the café. No one had held her interest for long.

It was ironic how she finally met someone who made her want to take a break from working and get to know her only to find she was already in a relationship. Carrie had plenty of chances to meet people. The café was a busy place and she met many nice women, but she hadn't found anyone who stirred the feeling of attraction that was drawing her toward Lisa.

"Hi, Carrie." Lisa's face lit up when she saw her. "Another busy Saturday night for you."

"Hi." Carrie didn't see Lisa's friend Rachel with her, which was interesting. "Are you here all by yourself?"

"Yeah. I thought I'd come see who was playing tonight and get a bite to eat. I hope there's a free table. It looks kind of crowded."

"I'll make sure Ryan finds you a good spot. I've got to get back in the kitchen and help before Angie gets too swamped, but I'll try to catch up with you later."

"Thanks," Lisa said. "I know you're busy. I just wanted to say hi."

Carrie went behind the counter and joined the crew in the kitchen. She spotted Ryan as he walked by and waved him over. "Can you find an open table for my friend? She's standing there by the counter."

"Sure," Ryan said. "There's an empty table near the music corner. I'll take her over to that one."

"Thanks." Carrie turned her attention back to the dinner service. As she immersed herself in creating a risotto dish, her thoughts drifted to Lisa, sitting alone. Perhaps Lisa wasn't as taken as she'd thought.

Lisa followed Ryan to a small table tucked into an alcove near the stage. She hadn't wanted to sit home by herself tonight and she was pleased she'd come, even if she did have to eat alone. She'd figured she would say hello to Carrie and maybe listen to the music for a little while. Carrie would probably be too busy to talk tonight, which was a little disappointing, but she was glad the business was going so well.

The lead singer had her back to the audience and was talking with the guitarist while they tuned their guitars and prepared to get started. She adjusted her microphone one last time and turned around. Lisa's mouth dropped open in surprise as she recognized her old friend Toni.

Toni hadn't noticed her yet and Lisa had a chance to study her for a moment. She hadn't seen or spoken to her in many years. What a strange coincidence to see her right after mentioning her to Rachel the other night. They had all gone to college together in Boston before Toni dropped out and they lost touch. Toni's boyfriend was a star hockey player and it had caused quite a scandal at the time when he was arrested for a hit-and-run accident that had killed another student. Toni hadn't been involved in any way, but the campus rumor mill turned many people against her as they unfairly accused her of being with her boyfriend when the accident took place, a fact Toni had assured Lisa was not true.

Toni looked great, still as beautiful as ever, and she still had the air of a free spirit. The set began and memories of listening to Toni sing at parties in college drifted through Lisa's mind. It had been so long since she'd heard her sing, she'd almost forgotten how good Toni was. Her smooth alto was hitting all the notes with just the right pitch and time had only improved the clarity of her voice. Lisa hadn't forgotten about the crush she'd had on her. She'd spent years thinking about Toni and wondering what would have happened if things had been different.

Lisa had met Toni in their dorm during their freshman year and they'd been good friends from the start. Lisa had been dazzled by everything about Toni, from the way she dressed to the way she seemed to find the best parties. Toni was never boring, and she was always thinking of their next great adventure, which was a fun change for Lisa, the introvert. People were drawn to Toni and she usually got a lot of attention. She had a steady stream of boyfriends, and Lisa tried not to let it bother her.

Lisa had been fighting her attraction to Toni for months and she was swamped with guilt about the way she felt. She didn't know if Toni had any idea, although she had picked up on some vibes a few times when they were alone together. She hadn't known what to do, and it was becoming overwhelming. She didn't want to say anything and ruin their friendship.

When Toni's boyfriend's best friend asked her out, it had been the answer to her problems, or so she thought. John was a genuinely nice guy and she found she really liked him, so she made up her mind to be with him and forget about the overpowering reaction to women that was making her life almost unbearable. She didn't feel any sexual desire toward John, but she was hoping it would grow with time.

Rachel had been a steady friend through all of it. They lived together for all four years of college, and Rachel was like the sister Lisa never had. She never told Rachel or anyone at the time that she might be attracted to women, let alone to Toni. Eventually Toni left school and it got easier for Lisa to hide her feelings. She had made the effort to keep in touch with Toni for a while, but their lives took different paths and she eventually lost track of her phone number. Lisa stayed with John and hoped she could change. It also helped that she never met another woman that flipped her libido like Toni. *Does Carrie do that to me?*

Looking back, she didn't know why she'd tried so hard to fight against herself. She had married John for a brief period until they both realized they were not meant for each other. She would never forget how free and relieved she felt when her marriage ended.

She had come out to her family and friends shortly after she and John split up and she hadn't looked back since. She had drifted apart from some of her friends when they found they no longer had much in common, but Rachel had always been wonderfully supportive. Her parents also always accepted her, and she was proud that she hadn't had to hide who she was from them.

Lisa took a deep breath. She had certainly come a long way since those days. She supposed a lot of people harbored regrets about the way they had done things, and she was no exception.

She didn't want to waste time worrying about the past, though. It was nice to see Toni and she wasn't going to let herself freak out about it.

Toni finished a song and applause filled the room. She nodded appreciatively to the audience and her gaze landed on Lisa. When she saw Toni's look of recognition, Lisa smiled and gave her a wave. Toni's eyes grew wide and she hurriedly spoke into the microphone, "Thanks everyone. We'll be right back after a short break."

Toni set down her guitar and came rushing over to Lisa's table.

"Lisa Owens?" Toni asked. "I can't believe it's you. What are you doing in Maine?"

"I moved to Winchester a little while ago." Lisa stood up to give her a hug. "Remember my roommate Rachel? She lives in Augusta and she talked me into moving up here."

"Of course I remember Rachel." Toni stepped back to look at her. "You look fabulous, as always. You haven't changed a bit."

"That's not quite true, but thanks," Lisa said with a laugh. "It's great to see you. You look pretty fabulous yourself. Can you join me for a few minutes?"

"I'd love to." Toni sat down at the table with Lisa. "I have a little break before we play again."

Ryan came over to the table. "What can I get you ladies? We'll make sure it's ready fast because I know Toni has to get back to the music."

They each ordered the vegetable risotto special with a glass of wine. Ryan left to get the guitarist's order. Toni looked across the table at Lisa and smiled. "It's so amazing to see you here. Tell me how you've been."

"I'm good," Lisa replied. "It's been so long since we've seen each other and so much has happened that I don't know where to start."

"I heard you married John after college."

"Our marriage didn't last very long." Lisa didn't want to get into those details just yet. "How about you, are you married?"

"I was married, but I've been divorced for a while and I live with my daughter on the coast in Camden. It's about an hour from here."

"You have a daughter? That's great."

"How about you?" Toni touched her arm. "Any kids?"

"No, it's just me and my dog here in Winchester."

Toni still had a way of looking at Lisa that made her feel like she was the most important person in the room. Lisa wondered if Toni had thought about her over the years. She wished she had dressed a little better.

Ryan arrived with their drinks and Carrie was right behind him with their meals. She set the two plates down on the table. "Here you go, enjoy."

"Thank you," Toni said. "This looks delicious."

"I really liked your music. You're very good," Carrie said to Toni. She turned to Lisa. "How are you doing?"

"I'm great, thanks Carrie," Lisa said. "I didn't realize Toni was going to be here tonight. We used to go to school together."

"You're kidding." Carrie glanced at the two of them in surprise. "Small world. I'm glad you have someone to eat dinner with."

"Can you join us, or are you too busy tonight?" Lisa asked.

"Sorry, it's a little crazy in the kitchen. In fact, I probably should get back."

"Thank you for bringing dinner out," Toni said. "I appreciate it."

"Carrie's the best cook I've ever met." Lisa looked in Carrie's eyes for a moment.

Carrie smiled. "I'll talk to you later."

Lisa watched her walk back through the crowded dining room. She seemed to have a way of falling for friends who just weren't attracted to her. She turned to Toni and saw she was watching her.

"She's a friend of yours?" Toni asked. "She seems nice, and very attractive too."

Lisa wasn't sure how to respond. Did Toni find Carrie attractive or was she asking about Lisa's relationship with her?

Did Toni even know she dated women? Lisa was confused, which wasn't unusual when she was around Toni.

"I've gotten to know her a little," Lisa said. "She's very nice."

"Are you seeing anyone these days?" Toni asked, taking a bite of her dinner.

"No, I've been getting settled in here and haven't met many people yet. How about you?"

"Oh, you know me. No one serious." Toni touched Lisa's arm and caressed it lightly. "It's so cool to see a familiar face. Especially your lovely face."

The caress made the hair on the back of Lisa's neck stand up. She couldn't help but stare at Toni as her mind raced. Was Toni flirting with her?

Toni ate a few more bites and stood up. "I probably better get back and play some more or people are going to wonder what happened to me. It's great to see you. I've missed you and I really want to spend some more time catching up."

Lisa looked at Toni and felt familiar responses wash over her. She was a much different person now than she had been back in their college days, and she didn't know why Toni was still affecting her like this. She certainly didn't want to fall into the trap again of longing for what she couldn't have.

"It's been really nice." Lisa tried to keep her answer polite and friendly while still keeping her distance. "I'm glad I came by tonight. You sound great and I really loved listening to you."

"I have to leave right after I'm done." Toni paused and stared into Lisa's eyes. "Are you busy tomorrow? Maybe we could get together?"

"Uh, sure." Lisa hesitated, hoping she was doing the right thing and not setting herself up for disappointment. "I live here on the lake. Do you want to come by and maybe go kayaking? I could meet you here at Harvest around noon."

"I would love to." Toni smiled and touched Lisa's arm again as she bent down and spoke softly into her ear, "I always regretted that I never gave us a chance."

CHAPTER SIX

Carrie looked up from the sandwich she was making and saw Lisa walk in through the café's big wooden front door. The morning hadn't been too busy, which gave her a chance to get caught up from the busy night before. The lunch crowd would arrive in a little while, but it was quiet enough now for her to take a few minutes to talk to Lisa.

"Hi there," Carrie said as Lisa walked to the counter. "Back so soon?"

"Hi," Lisa said. "I guess I can't get enough of this place."

"That works for me. How was your dinner last night? We were so busy that I didn't have much of a chance to talk with you."

"Dinner was exquisite, as usual. Now I'm planning to order a couple sandwiches to go for lunch. I know yours will be so much better than anything I'd make."

"Oh, I guess you've got plans for this afternoon. That's too bad, I was hoping to see if you and Daisy wanted to go running again."

"Shoot, that would have been great. Do you want to go for a run tomorrow after I get out of work? You're closed on Mondays, right?"

"Yes, we're closed tomorrow so that would be good," Carrie said. "I could use a running partner. It will help keep me motivated."

"It looked like you were in great shape. I was the one gasping for breath." Lisa took her phone out of her pocket. "What's your number? I'll call when I get home from work tomorrow."

After giving her number to Lisa, Carrie took the sandwich order to Angie in the kitchen and came back out to join Lisa at one of the tables near the counter.

"Angie will have those ready in a few minutes," Carrie said. "So, what are your plans for today?"

"It's the craziest thing." Lisa hesitated for a moment. "Remember I told you that I had gone to school with Toni?"

"Yes. Did you go to college with her or did you know her back in high school?"

"We went to college together for a couple years, and I haven't seen her since." Lisa glanced away from Carrie and looked out the window. "It's actually kind of embarrassing. I had the biggest crush on her. It was awful, really, but I didn't think she ever knew."

"I can understand that. She's very pretty and she has a lot of personality."

"Right." Lisa looked back at Carrie with a little smile. "I didn't know what to do with myself at the time, and I ended up getting married to a man for a while. I was always attracted to women, not men, but I was just trying to deny and conform, you know?"

"Well, at least you were able to figure things out. We all take different paths in life."

"That's true. I think my struggles made me truly appreciate where I am now," Lisa said. "What about you? Did you ever have any confusion about yourself?"

"Not really. I've always known I was attracted to women and it's never been anything I've wanted to hide from my family or anyone else."

"I admire your confidence."

"Was it hard seeing Toni again?"

"That's the crazy thing." Lisa raised her shoulders in a shrug. "She's the one who wanted to get together today, and she told me last night she regrets that she didn't give us a chance."

"Oh." Carrie leaned back in her chair. She hadn't expected that. She was surprised to hear Lisa was meeting Toni when she was involved with someone else. "What about Rachel?"

"What do you mean?" Lisa looked at her quizzically. "Rachel knew her too, but they weren't very close."

"Rachel went to school with you, too?" Carrie was startled to hear Toni and Rachel knew each other. It must have been an interesting place to go to school.

"Sure, that's where I met both of them."

"Rachel doesn't mind if you get together with Toni?" Carrie knew she was missing something.

"No, why would she mind? She's probably busy with her family today."

"Her family?" Carrie asked. This was confusing. Did Rachel have someone else and was Lisa having some sort of affair with her?

"Rachel and her husband have two kids and they're always busy. I was lucky to get her to come out here last weekend. I try to get together with her every week or so now that I live up here, but sometimes it's hard to catch up with her."

"I thought you moved up here to be near her."

"I did. She's like a sister to me. My mother died a couple years ago, and I don't have any brothers or sisters. I needed a change from things in Massachusetts, so I came here."

"She's like a sister," Carrie repeated. She had completely misread the situation. This whole time she'd been so careful around Lisa, thinking she was unavailable. Unfortunately, now when she found out she was wrong, Lisa was on her way to meet up with her fantasy woman.

Angie carried a bag over to the counter and put it down. "Your order's ready."

"Just in time. There's Toni now." Lisa stood up and looked out the window. "Thanks for keeping me company while I waited."

"Have fun today." Carrie tried to put enthusiasm into her words. She was actually hoping things didn't go too well with Toni, but she couldn't say that out loud.

"I'll be sure give you a call about running tomorrow, and I'll fill you in on everything when I see you."

"Okay." Carrie tried to give a carefree wave as she watched Lisa go out the door. Her heart sank as she saw Toni greet Lisa on the street with a big hug before they got in their cars and drove away.

Lisa drove into her driveway and Toni pulled in behind her. She was glad Toni had suggested they meet today because if she'd had to wait and worry about this for a whole week, she would have lost her mind. As it was, she'd tossed and turned for half the night, analyzing the situation and trying to figure out what she should do. She knew she was overthinking it and she was trying not to get too nervous. She would just wait and see how Toni behaved and maybe that would give her a clue.

Toni looked around at the woods and the path leading down to the lake. "What a great spot. It's so peaceful out here."

"Come on inside." Lisa held up the bag from the café. "I picked up some lunch for us from Harvest. We can sit out on the deck and have a bite to eat before we go out in the kayaks."

They walked across the gravel driveway and Lisa held the door open for Toni. The entrance opened into a hallway with a stairway that led to an upstairs living room. Daisy came running down the stairs to greet them and Lisa knelt to pet her.

"This is Daisy. She's very friendly and I apologize in advance if you get dog hair on that nice white shirt you're wearing."

"Hi, Daisy." Toni rubbed Daisy's long, floppy ears as Daisy sniffed her, excited to meet a new person. "I don't mind a little dog hair."

"The bedrooms are downstairs, and the living room and kitchen are up here." Lisa led Toni up the stairs. "It was built this way to take better advantage of the view of the lake. The deck is up here, off the living room."

They reached the top of the stairs and Toni looked around. The second floor had an open kitchen and living room with a bathroom tucked into the corner. The exposed beams framed the cathedral ceiling and a wall of windows overlooked the lake.

"The view is amazing. You must love it here."

"I really do. I moved here last fall. It looks a lot different in the winter. It's still gorgeous, but much more quiet and isolated. Believe me, driving to work on snowy days can be a challenge. I think it's worth it, though. Winchester is a beautiful area and I love being right on the lake. How about you? Do you like living in Camden?"

"I've lived there for the past ten years and it's been great. I like living on the coast and my daughter is flourishing there. She has some good friends and she loves her school."

"What's her name?" Lisa asked. "I should have told you to bring her. She might have enjoyed going for a swim."

"Her name is Amelia and she stays with her father on the weekends. We share custody, which works out pretty well because I usually have shows on Saturday nights."

Lisa got some glasses and plates out of the cupboard and set them on the counter next to the bag of sandwiches. She grabbed a pitcher of water out of the refrigerator. "Let's go out on the deck. I hope you like the sandwich I got for you."

"Let me help." Toni picked up the plates and held the door to the deck open for Lisa. Daisy followed closely behind, hoping to share their lunch.

They set everything on the table outside and took their seats under the shade of the umbrella. A light breeze came off the lake and blew Toni's curly hair softly around her face. Daisy settled patiently under Lisa's chair while she poured their drinks and they started eating.

"So, what do you do during the week?" Lisa asked. She wanted to hear about what Toni had been doing since college, but she didn't want to be too nosy.

"I'm an art teacher and I love my job. I work at my daughter's school, which is really convenient."

"I bet you're good at it. You were always very creative."

"Thank you for saying that. I went back to school a few years after I left and finished my degree. I love my music, but it doesn't pay the bills."

Lisa nodded as she took another bite of her sandwich. She had always liked listening to Toni talk. It was strange to think she was sitting here with Toni at her house after all these years.

"I always felt bad that we fell out of touch," Toni said. "The first couple years after I left school were crazy. I bounced around to different addresses and was just trying to figure out what I wanted to do. I meant to call you lots of times, but I got sidetracked by one thing or another."

"I'm sure that was a hard time for you. You were treated so unfairly at school after the accident. I know you didn't have anything to do with it, of course."

"Yeah, it was a painful period of my life, but thankfully it was a long time ago and it's all good now. So, what about you? What did you end up doing when you grew up?"

"I'm an accountant. Not too exciting, I'm afraid, but I like what I do."

"That's what matters, right?" Toni leaned back and looked at Lisa. "These sandwiches are good. Did your friend at Harvest make them?"

"No, one of the other cooks did." Lisa's thoughts shifted to Carrie and she wondered if she was still at work or what she might be doing right now. She was starting to feel self-conscious with Toni watching her so closely. She couldn't think of anything to say and began tapping her foot under the table.

Daisy sighed in annoyance and squirmed beside her feet. Lisa resisted the temptation to slip her a bite of sandwich as that would only encourage her to beg.

"Are you nervous around me?" Toni leaned toward Lisa and put her hand on Lisa's bare arm. "I hope not. I really want us to get to know each other again. Even though we lost touch, I never forgot what a good friend you were."

"I'm not nervous." Lisa jumped up, trying to cover up her anxiety. "But we should probably get going before it gets too late to go kayaking."

"All right. We have plenty of time, though, so don't worry. I don't have to pick Amelia up until later this evening." Toni smiled up at her. "Do you remember some of the great times we had together?"

A memory from a night they had spent together in Toni's dorm room came flooding back to Lisa. They had come back from a party at Toni's latest boyfriend's frat house where they had been drinking Long Island iced teas, which packed a much more powerful punch than either of them was used to. Somehow, they made it back to Toni's room and crashed on her bed. Lisa's memory was hazy, but she had a clear recollection of waking up with her face buried in Toni's neck and Toni's arms wrapped around her. It was a heavenly feeling and she remembered lying there quietly, trying not to wake her and have it come to an end.

That was a long time ago. Did Toni remember that night?

CHAPTER SEVEN

Lisa followed Toni and Daisy downstairs and outside into the bright sunshine. They walked down the rocky pathway through the trees to the dock where the kayaks were pulled up on the shore. Lisa handed a lifejacket to Toni and tossed one for herself into the closest kayak.

Toni put the lifejacket on over her tank top and turned to Lisa. "Can you check the straps on this for me?"

Lisa moved closer to Toni and tugged on the lower strap that went around her waist, making sure it was tight. Her gaze lingered on the smooth skin of Toni's cleavage as she cinched the strap that went around her chest. Toni looked good. She had put on a little weight over the years but she still had a great body. Lisa knew her own body hadn't stood the test of time as well as Toni's. She hadn't put on much weight, but she had certainly changed.

Toni looked into her eyes. "Do you need any help with yours?"

"No thanks, I'm all set." Lisa stepped back to give herself some space. "I get too hot when I wear a lifejacket, so I'm going to keep mine behind my seat."

They carried each kayak over the rocky shore to the dock. Lisa passed a paddle to Toni and helped her slide one of the kayaks into the lake and get into it. She boarded hers, rocking gently as she shifted to get comfortable.

"Stay here, Daisy," Lisa called. Daisy barked excitedly from the dock for a minute and then went to find a spot in the shade.

They glided along near the shore, enjoying the warm summer day. A soft breeze cooled them as they made their way around the cove. The lake was peaceful and quiet. There were a few fishermen in the distance and another boat was pulling a water skier across the lake, but they weren't close enough to bother them.

"We should have put on some sunscreen," Lisa said. "I totally forgot."

"I probably won't last too long out here anyway. I've always avoided exercise whenever possible."

Lisa laughed. "I'd forgotten that about you."

"You were the active one. I preferred to sit on the sidelines with a drink and entertain people."

That was true. Lisa was more comfortable if she kept moving while Toni enjoyed socializing with everyone. After reaching the other end of the cove, Lisa swung back toward her house. "Let's go hang out on the dock. Did you bring your bathing suit?"

"I have it on underneath."

Lisa immediately wished she hadn't said anything about bathing suits. She didn't want to wear hers in front of Toni. If she did put her suit on, she would have to be careful to cover up when she wasn't in the water. They headed back to the dock and Daisy spotted them. Jumping up from her shady spot under a tree, she barked enthusiastically at them as they approached.

Lisa pulled up to the dock first and waved Toni over. She held her steady while Toni grabbed the ladder and climbed out on wobbling feet. Together they carried the kayaks over to the shore and sat down in the chairs next to the dock.

"I'm surprised I managed that without falling in," Toni said.

An image of Toni, dripping wet, flashed through Lisa's mind. Maybe she shouldn't have been so helpful when they got to the dock.

"This is nice." Toni rested her hand on Lisa's. "I'm really glad I'm here with you."

"Would you like to go for a swim?" Lisa asked. Although she didn't really want to go swimming, being alone with Toni like this was making her nervous. She needed to make sure they stayed busy and avoided any awkward silences. She stood up and gestured toward the house. "I'll just run in and get my suit on and grab a couple towels."

"Take your time. I'll relax and wait right here."

Lisa went into the house and pulled a bathing suit out of her bureau. She stripped off her shorts and T-shirt and looked at herself critically in the mirror. She looked fine from the waist down because she made sure she kept in shape. When she looked in the mirror she could see her bathing suit didn't hide the scars she had from treatment she'd completed the previous year for breast cancer.

She had a large scar on her right upper chest from the port, which had been put in for her chemotherapy. She also had a long scar under her arm from the surgery she had undergone to remove some of her lymph nodes. The most noticeable thing was the fact that her left breast was less than half the size of her right one and a scar extended over to her side from the lumpectomy. There was a pattern of small black dots from the radiation treatments as well, but those weren't very obvious.

She shrugged and put on a white linen shirt and left it unbuttoned. She certainly wasn't ashamed of her body. She just didn't feel like going into detail about her treatment right now. Here was her chance to spend time with Toni, who had basically been her dream girl back in college. She didn't want Toni to feel sorry for her or be put off by the scars; that could end up being quite embarrassing for both of them.

Lisa squared her shoulders and took a deep breath. Toni might not even notice, and if she did, Lisa would tell her about it.

Lisa found Daisy next to Toni, who was sitting on the dock in her bathing suit with her feet in the water. Kicking off her sandals, Lisa sat down next to her and passed her one of the bottles of beer she had grabbed out of the fridge. A pair of dragonflies buzzed around them.

Lisa winced as she dipped her feet in up past her ankles. "The water's freezing cold."

"It's not bad once you get used to it and it's a lot warmer than the ocean." Toni took a sip from her bottle and put her hand on Lisa's again. "You're not going to run off again, are you?"

Lisa tried not to jump from Toni's touch. She wasn't sure exactly where Toni was going with this and she didn't want to misinterpret anything. She didn't even really know Toni anymore, and she wasn't going to open herself up to heartache again.

Lisa looked out across the water. "I need to say something. I'm not sure if you realize how I used to feel about you back in school."

Toni leaned against her. "I knew how you felt. I was just pretending that I didn't because I was scared."

Lisa looked at her in astonishment. "What?"

"Remember all those nights you gave me backrubs? I would always tell you that my back was hurting, but it never actually was. I just wanted you to touch me."

Lisa remembered those backrubs very clearly. She thought about the night in Toni's room again. "Do you remember the night we came back from the frat party and we slept in your bed together?"

"Of course I do. We'd both had too much to drink and I remember hoping that finally we would be able to let go and lose our inhibitions. I had my arms around you and it felt so good."

Lisa looked at her in amazement. "When I woke up the next morning, I was afraid you were going to be really upset."

"I desperately wanted you to do something, but you never did, and I never dared to say anything either," Toni said. "After that you started dating John and I started partying way too much. Then the accident happened, and I left, but I remember I always wished you would've said something."

"I had no idea. I thought you'd hate me if I said anything. I didn't want to ruin our friendship."

Toni reached up to touch Lisa's cheek and leaned in to kiss her. Lisa's heart was pounding so hard she was afraid Toni would notice. She was actually kissing Toni after all these years. She put her arm around Toni's waist and pulled her closer, opening her lips as their tongues explored each other's mouths.

Lisa's brain was in a fog. She had wanted this so much all those years ago. She felt Toni moan as their lips ground together. She tried to catch her breath and slow down as Toni reached over to press her back against the dock. The next thing she knew, they were lying in the sun and Toni's body was on top of hers. She felt a wave of arousal as Toni pressed their hips together. She slid her hand along the smooth tight fabric of Toni's suit. It was glorious and she didn't want to stop, but she didn't know if she was ready to move quite this fast.

Lisa opened her eyes and pressed Toni's lips with a gentle kiss. Toni opened her eyes and looked back at her, breathing heavily.

"Wow," Lisa said. "I can't believe I actually kissed you."

"You're beautiful." Toni pressed her lips to Lisa's. She ran her tongue along Lisa's ear and whispered softly, "We don't need to stop."

"You know how special you are to me." Lisa tried to explain. "I've wanted this for so long, I don't want to rush it."

Toni slid off her with a sigh. "You could also say we've waited so long we shouldn't wait any longer."

Lisa ran her hand along Toni's side and caressed her shoulder, touching her soft skin. "I have to get my mind around the fact you want to be with me."

"I do want to be with you." Toni kissed her softly. "It's all I've been thinking about since I saw you last night."

Toni reached over and slipped her hand inside Lisa's shirt and started to caress her breast through her bathing suit. Lisa pulled back and sat up quickly.

Toni looked at her, startled. "What's wrong?"

"Nothing, sorry." Lisa felt foolish about her reaction. "I'm a little self-conscious."

"Why?" Toni rose up and sat next to her. "I think you look beautiful."

"Thank you. And I think you're stunning. It's just that I haven't mentioned to you I had breast cancer and I have some scars that aren't very attractive."

"Oh, you poor thing." Toni looked at Lisa with concern in her eyes. "I feel so bad for you. Are you all right now?"

"I'm perfectly fine. I just thought I should mention it." Lisa really hated it when anyone called her a poor thing. It was time to change the subject. "I want us to get to know each other again."

"Me too."

"Are you attracted to women?" Lisa asked. "I mean, have you ever dated a woman before?"

"Yes." Toni laughed. "I thought that was kind of obvious."

"When did you start?"

"Quite a while ago." Toni smiled at Lisa. "I don't think I ever got you out of my mind."

"You're such a smooth talker." Lisa smiled back at her. She checked her shirt, making sure the buttons were closed and her chest was covered. "You could always talk me into anything with your charming ways."

"Anything?" Toni winked at her suggestively and slipped her hand around Lisa's waist.

CHAPTER EIGHT

Carrie stood on her porch and debated whether she should wait for Lisa to call before going for a run. She wasn't sure Lisa would remember, and she didn't know what time she got home from work. She decided to change into her running clothes and was headed into the house when her phone rang. She didn't recognize the number and answered, hoping it was Lisa.

"Hello."

"Hi Carrie, it's Lisa. Still want to go for a run with me and Daisy?"

"Sure," Carrie answered. "Where should I meet you?"

"I'm not sure where you live, so how about if you come over to my house and we leave from here?"

"Sounds good. I'll be there in a few minutes."

The drive was only around three miles, so she pulled her Jeep into Lisa's driveway a short time later. Carrie had just opened the door to step out when Daisy bounded over to greet her.

"That was speedy," Lisa called from the doorway. "Are you ready to go?"

"I'm ready whenever you are." Carrie bent down to pet Daisy. "What route do you want to take?"

"Can we go past your house? I want to see where you live."

"That will take us on a six-mile run," Carrie advised. "Are you sure you want to go that far?"

"It sounds good at the moment, but if I collapse, you'll have to come back and get me after you finish."

They made their way out to the main road and headed toward Carrie's house. Daisy trotted along happily in front of them.

"So how was your day yesterday?" Carrie asked. She wasn't sure she really wanted to know about Lisa's visit with Toni, but she'd been thinking about her since she'd seen her at the café.

"It was amazing, actually," Lisa replied. "All that time I spent pining away over Toni, thinking she had no idea how I felt. It turns out she did know and just didn't say anything."

That sounded messed up to Carrie. "Why didn't she say anything?"

"I guess she was scared." Lisa gave a shrug as she ran. "Anyway, she definitely wants to be with me now. She made that very clear. I'm going to go see her sing again this weekend at a place in Camden, which is where she lives."

Carrie felt a stab of disappointment. She wished she had asked Lisa out when she had the chance. Now it might be too late. Toni was back in Lisa's life, and Lisa was obviously happy about it. She didn't want to compete with someone Lisa had been dreaming about for years. Carrie had hoped she could be content to keep their relationship platonic, but when she found out yesterday Rachel was just a friend, she'd realized she wanted a chance with Lisa. She would wait and see if Lisa followed through with Toni this weekend. If Lisa wanted to be with Toni, then Carrie would have to give up on anything but friendship. That was definitely going to be hard.

"How are things at work?" Carrie asked. "I hope your boss didn't do anything else."

"I've managed to avoid him for the most part. I ran into him today and a few times last week, but there were other people around. I feel like he's always staring at me, but that could be my imagination."

"I doubt it's your imagination. Not after the way he acted before. What are you going to do if he tries anything else?"

"I don't know." Lisa slowed as they came to a big hill. "I really want to report him or tell him off, but I don't have anything I could actually prove. I'm sure he would say that he bumped into me accidentally, and he'd deny the whole conversation about pleasing clients or he'd say that I misinterpreted his comments."

"I wonder if he's tried anything with other women at your office?"

"I don't really know any of them that well. I suppose I could try to ask them discreetly, which might be tricky."

"If there's anything I can do, just ask. You know I'd be happy to help."

Carrie jogged ahead as Lisa struggled up the hill. She glanced back and saw Lisa staring at her. Their eyes met, and Lisa looked away quickly. Carrie smiled. Maybe Lisa wasn't too hung up on Toni after all.

Lisa reached the top of the hill with a gasp and the run leveled off for a little while. They were getting close to the turnoff for Carrie's road when Lisa spoke again. "I saw an interesting file the other day. I think it might have something to do with that argument I overheard."

"The one about a contract?"

"Yeah. The man Don was arguing with said something about a contract from Lawrence. I was on the network and I came across a file named Lawrence and it caught my eye. It was a memo from Don with Senator Lawrence's name and a bunch of dates and dollar amounts. It was sent to Bruce Mills and Joe Michaud. I know it wasn't Michaud that I saw arguing with Don, so it must have been Bruce Mills, although I'm not positive."

"Do you think Senator Lawrence is involved in getting contracts for Bruce Mills's company?"

"That's exactly what I think. It's too much of a coincidence that they were arguing about a contract with Lawrence and then I find this memo with the senator's name on it. They must be sending him bribes or something, I'm not sure."

"It's possible that the numbers are legitimate," Carrie pointed out. "It does sound suspicious, but we have to be careful not to jump to conclusions."

"That's true. I couldn't tell what the numbers were, but it got me thinking that maybe I should look around some more. There might be some other files or information that I could use if I ever decide to report him."

"That's actually a good idea," Carrie said. "It would definitely bolster your credibility if people saw that Don was involved in other illegal activity besides sexual harassment. Just make sure you don't get in trouble for snooping. You wouldn't want Don to find out and fire you."

"I don't think anyone would be able to tell if I look around on the network, as long as I don't change any files. I'll start there."

They reached a house set back in the woods along the lake and Carrie stopped. "This is my house."

"This is beautiful, Carrie. I love how your house fits the setting perfectly. I want to come back and see the inside some time. May I please?"

"I'm glad you like it. I'll have you over for dinner some evening." Carrie had worked hard on her house and she was proud of it, so it was nice to know when someone appreciated it.

"That would be awesome." Lisa turned to follow Carrie back down the road. "A dinner with my favorite chef."

CHAPTER NINE

Lisa greeted the receptionist the next morning and headed to her desk. She was hoping to quickly review the reports that were due, so she would have time to look around on the network. She also wanted to talk to some of her female colleagues. This wasn't the type of workplace where people congregated in a common area, so she would have to go to their individual offices and track them down without being too obvious.

One of her coworkers walked by. Lisa waited a minute before getting up and walking out her door and over to the woman's office. She paused in the doorway. "Good morning, Mary."

"Hello." Mary was an attractive, full-figured brunette. Lisa envied her creamy white complexion. She ran her fingers through her own short, blond hair.

"How was your weekend?" Lisa asked.

"It was good. How was yours?"

"Too short, as usual." Lisa knew Mary must have been wondering why she was there. "I wanted to ask you about the company picnic that's coming up."

"Sure, what did you want to know?"

"I was just wondering if it was something everyone in the office went to. At the last firm where I worked, no one bothered to go to the company outings, so I thought I'd ask. I didn't want to show up and be the only one there."

"I would say that most of us go to the picnic every year. You're expected to attend, whether you really want to or not. Don wouldn't be too happy if you skipped it."

"We wouldn't want that." Lisa forced a chuckle.

Mary nodded. "Exactly."

"How long have you worked here, Mary?"

"I've been here for twelve years."

"That's a long time. I'm impressed. You must really like your job to have stayed here that long."

"I do like the paycheck, and I have some clients that have become good friends."

"Has Don been a pretty good boss?" Lisa tried to keep her tone casual.

"I like the paycheck," Mary repeated.

"Don't take this the wrong way, but has he ever made you uncomfortable?"

Mary looked at her intently. "Not in any way that I would ever be able to document or want to share."

"Yes, I understand. It happened to me and I wasn't sure if I was the only one."

Lisa could see from Mary's demeanor that she wasn't going to say much more. She gave her a wave and backed out of the doorway. "Well, thanks for your time. I'll talk to you later."

There were some other women she wanted to talk to, but she decided that it would be more discreet to take her time rather than go door to door all at once. Apparently, Mary had experienced some problems with Don too. It would have been helpful if she had wanted to talk about it a little more, but Lisa certainly understood her reluctance. She wondered if Don harassed all the female employees or if he were more selective.

She returned to her desk and began looking around the shared files. She checked the network file system for the

Lawrence document she had come across the other day. It wasn't in the location where she thought it had been, which was strange. She searched through all the directories for it, but the file was nowhere to be found. Giving up with a sigh, she turned her attention to scanning though the shared files for anything connected with Don that struck her as unusual.

She didn't think he would keep confidential files in an unrestricted area on the shared network, but it didn't hurt to look. He may have put something there unintentionally or he may have assumed no one would notice it. The names in the missing Lawrence memo might show up in another file also, so she looked for references to Bruce Mills and Joe Michaud along with William Lawrence.

After searching for a while with no results, she decided to try and look more closely at Don's home directory and see if there was anything there that might be of interest. Each employee in the company had a home directory that was created for them to store corporate documentation in. This was not an area for storage of personal information, but he may have been careless.

She saw a directory named Fundraisers and opened it. There were several files and directories inside, including a directory named WL. She looked inside WL and saw a file named Michaud-Payments. Finally, something intriguing.

Clicking open the file, she scanned through the contents. As the filename implied, it appeared to be a list of payments. There was a spreadsheet containing entries with dates, names, and currency amounts under a heading reading "Payments from Bruce Mills." The payments were being made to Joe Michaud and Don Mills, and they occurred once each month beginning the previous fall.

This had to be another piece of the puzzle. Taken alone, the spreadsheet could be perfectly innocent, but now that she had seen the memo with the other monetary amounts and heard Don arguing with the man in her office, she knew they were somehow tied together.

She needed to find out what these payments were for. Why would a contractor be paying an accountant and a sheriff and why would this file be saved under the directory WL? The only

WL she could think of was William Lawrence, and although she had her theory, she still didn't know what the memo she had seen earlier with the dates and amounts was for. She wished she'd saved it or printed it out, but now it was gone.

It was time to get back to work, so she emailed a copy of the file to her personal account where she would be able to keep a private copy away from the company network. She hadn't altered the file, so there was really no way anyone would notice it had been sent. Carrie might be able to tell her more about the Mills brothers since she knew everyone in town. Lisa would have to talk to her about all of this after work tomorrow. It was too bad she couldn't catch up with her tonight, but she was planning to meet Rachel for dinner.

The thought of Carrie brought a smile to her face. The more she got to know her, the more she liked being around her. She was so easy to talk to, which was a nice change from all the conflict she felt when she was around Toni. Of course, she was really happy Toni was back in her life and that Toni wanted them to be together. It was just that Toni had a very intense presence. Lisa knew she could easily get swept away by her and end up getting hurt if Toni changed her mind. Lisa wanted to be careful, but all those old feelings had flooded back when she was with her. She was going to have to guard her heart until she was more certain.

Her feelings for Carrie were different. Carrie only wanted to be friends, and although that was not what Lisa would have chosen, she'd resigned herself to a platonic relationship. She told herself it was going to work out for the best, because now it looked like she might be starting a relationship with Toni. One thing she remembered about Toni was how hard it was to tell where you stood with her. Carrie, on the other hand, was clearly the kind of person you could count on to be there if you needed her, not to mention that Carrie had looked really good while they were running yesterday.

Lisa was a little embarrassed that Carrie had caught her checking her out. They were just friends, after all. But it had been hard not to notice when she was right in front of her looking so hot. It had certainly made the run bearable.

CHAPTER TEN

Rachel rushed to the table. "Sorry I'm late."

"It's fine." Lisa tucked her phone away in her bag. "I was catching up on my email."

Rachel had called Lisa that morning and told her she wanted to get out of the house for the evening, so they were meeting at a chain restaurant in Augusta. Since it was an early weeknight, the place was quiet. A waitress came over and took Rachel's order for a glass of wine.

"How's your week going?" Lisa asked.

"It's been hectic. We leave for our vacation at the cape in a couple weeks and I can't wait."

"Your face looks thinner. Have you lost weight?" Lisa couldn't really tell, because Rachel's weight always looked fine to her, but she knew her friend was probably stressing about it.

"I've been sticking to my diet most of the time, which is why I'm starving right now."

"Well I've got some news that should take your mind off your hunger."

Rachel looked at her with eager curiosity. "That sounds interesting. What kind of news?"

"You'll never guess who I saw at the Harvest café last weekend."

"I have no idea." Rachel raised her shoulders in a shrug. "Who?"

"Toni. She was there singing for music night."

"You're kidding me. We were just talking about her. You haven't spoken with her since college, have you?"

"Not really. I kept in touch for a little while, but it's been ages since we've talked. I couldn't believe it was her at first. We got a chance to chat for a little while that night and then she came over to visit me on Sunday."

"Hold on. What did you say? Toni came over to your house?"

"Yeah. It's the strangest thing seeing her after all this time. She lives in Maine, too, in Camden. She's divorced and has a daughter."

The waitress came back to their table with Rachel's wine. They both put in their orders and picked up the conversation again after she left.

Rachel looked at Lisa intently. "Are you doing all right with this, seeing her again?"

"What do you mean?"

"Well, I know you were really close, and I could tell you cared about her a lot. I remember you'd started dating John, but it was still hard for you when she left."

"Not just me. She had lots of friends who missed her."

"Lisa, I'm your best friend, remember? I know how you felt about her. It was pretty obvious."

"Seriously? I didn't think anyone had a clue. Now I find out you and Toni both knew. I was agonizing over it all that time and I didn't dare say anything."

"You followed her around like a puppy." Rachel held up a hand to stop Lisa's protest. "I'm sorry, but it's true. She was a lot of fun and I liked her, but I have to say I never liked how she treated you."

"What do you mean? We were good friends and she didn't treat me badly. I thought she was great."

"I always thought she liked having you worship her. I didn't like seeing you get hurt while you watched her with other people. I know I'm being hard on her, but it was tough to watch you pining away."

"I wish I had talked to you about it. I was afraid you wouldn't want to room together if you knew."

"As if." Rachel took a sip of her wine. "It's all in the past now. It was ages ago and we both survived. So, tell me, how was your visit?"

"It was interesting." Lisa took a sip of her drink and watched Rachel's reaction out of the corner of her eye as she set down her glass. "Toni wants to be more than friends."

Rachel started coughing. Lisa watched as she put her hand on her chest and took some deep breaths. She finally spoke, "You and Toni?"

"I was pretty surprised myself. She was very assertive about it actually."

"I bet she was. Did you sleep with her?"

"No," Lisa exclaimed. She smiled at Rachel. "I was tempted, though."

"Oh my God. You and Toni?"

"I know." Lisa shook her head. "I'm still in shock."

"Just be careful." Rachel put her hand on Lisa's arm. "I'm thrilled for you if she makes you happy, but I don't want you to get hurt."

"I'm definitely trying to be careful. I don't even know her very well anymore."

"I'm sure she's changed over the years, like we all have. I just remember she was never one to settle down for long with anyone."

"That was a long time ago and we were just kids." Lisa found herself coming to Toni's defense. "Like I said, she has a daughter and she's also a teacher. She seems very settled and she was really nice."

The waitress arrived with their meals, setting a salad down in front of each of them. Rachel watched her walk away and turned to Lisa. "Does she know about your breast cancer?"

"Yes. I didn't want to scare her away with bad news, but I was afraid she'd notice so I told her."

"There's nothing scary about it. You're all done with treatment."

"I know, but the scars and the fact I had it might be a turnoff. I think she felt sorry for me, which didn't exactly make me feel very attractive."

Rachel was quiet for a minute. "The main thing is you're healthy. You look great, you know. If someone was turned off by something about you, would you really want to be with her in the first place?"

"That sounds reasonable, but things are never that simple." Lisa wanted to change the subject. "Enough about me. What's going on with the kids?"

* * *

Lisa powered down her laptop and picked up her bag. It had been an unremarkable day. She had tried to strike up a casual conversation with the two women who worked in the reception area. It had been tricky because they worked together in the same section of the office and she hadn't been able to catch either of them alone. They both had been with the company for years and neither of them gave any indication they'd ever noticed any problems working with Don. Maybe he never caught them alone or maybe he just selected a few women to harass and Lisa happened to be one of the unlucky ones.

She walked out of her office and down the hall. It was getting late and most people had left for the day. As she turned the corner to head for the front door, she heard a voice behind her.

"Lisa," Don called. "Hold on for a minute."

Lisa put a polite smile on her face as she turned around. "Hello, Don."

Don walked over and stood in front of her while she backed up to keep a little more distance between them. She started to worry that he had heard she was asking questions about him, although she had been very careful to ask discreet questions disguised as small talk.

"How are those reports coming along for the lumber company financials?"

She breathed a quick sigh of relief. "The reports will be ready by the end of the week like you asked. I'm almost done with them."

"Good." He stepped a little closer. "Have you given any more thought to the increased auditing responsibilities that I mentioned the other day?"

"I would certainly be interested in doing more audits. I'm sure I can handle myself appropriately in any situation."

"That's good to know." He looked back over his shoulder to make sure no one was nearby before reaching out to squeeze her shoulder. "I wouldn't want you to overreact or misinterpret what we discussed. There are a lot of things I can teach you."

Lisa took another step away from him as she tried to think of a reply that would shut him down without getting her fired. She was saved from responding by the approach of another accountant. Don stepped back to let the other man pass in the narrow hallway. He glanced at his watch as the man turned the corner and disappeared.

"I have a meeting. We can continue this discussion later." He turned and walked away.

Lisa knew she needed to find a way to handle this situation. He still hadn't done anything that she could necessarily prove, but she didn't want to put up with this environment any longer. She headed for the door and tried to think of what she should do. Maybe Carrie would have some ideas. She wanted to tell her about the latest file she found too. Hopefully Carrie was at work. She'd go by the café and try to catch up with her.

* * *

Carrie looked up from the grill and saw Lisa come through the door. She had been thinking about her a lot since the past weekend, but she was surprised at the rush of happiness she felt when she saw her. Carrie knew the smart thing to do would be to find a summer visitor and have some fun like she usually did, but she wasn't interested in that this year. She wanted to get to know Lisa better. Meanwhile, she was going to stick to her plan to wait and see how things turned out and hope Lisa didn't fall for Toni.

The café wasn't too busy at the moment, so she left Angie in charge of the kitchen and walked over to the counter to say hello.

"Hi there," Carrie said.

"Hi, Carrie." Lisa smiled as she greeted her. "How are you?"

"I'm doing well, thanks. Are you here for dinner?"

"Sure, but I mostly wanted to see you."

"I'm glad you came in." Carrie leaned on the counter with a smile. "What's up?"

"I found another interesting file at work that I wanted to tell you about. I don't want to bug you if you're busy, but it's really helpful to talk things over with you."

Carrie was delighted to hear that Lisa liked talking with her. "I'd be happy to help if I can. It's quiet for the moment. Why don't I get us something to eat and we can sit over by the window?"

"That would be great. I'll meet you at our favorite table."

"What would you like?"

"I like everything you make, remember? Surprise me."

Carrie headed back to the kitchen before Lisa could notice her reaction. She'd certainly like to surprise her, but Lisa was talking about dinner. She served up two plates with the nightly vegetarian special and brought them out to the table by the window.

"That looks really good," Lisa exclaimed. "Is it quiche with broccoli and mushrooms?"

"Yes, and everything is fresh. I get all our dairy products from one of the farms here in town and most of our vegetables also come from farms in the area."

Lisa took a bite. "Mmm, delicious. You are the best cook I've ever met."

"Thanks." Carrie tried not to watch Lisa's lips too closely. She took a bite and reminded herself to relax. She didn't know why she was getting worked up. It wasn't as though Lisa realized she was interested in her. Maybe she should tell Lisa how she felt, but it didn't seem like a good idea when Lisa had just connected with Toni. This was way too complicated for Carrie; usually she kept her relationships casual and undemanding. She would be much better off if she just chilled out about this whole situation.

"So, tell me about what's going on at work," Carrie said, trying to keep her mind focused on something other than her feelings for Lisa.

"I took your advice from the other day and talked to some of the women in the office. One of them sounded like she had issues with Don, but it was nothing she wanted to talk about. I think she's just decided to put up with him."

Carrie nodded. "Has he done anything else?"

"Nothing tangible. He's just a creep, you know? I need to do something about it; either find a new job or speak up. Probably I should find a new job, regardless."

"That's too bad, but I wouldn't want to stay there either."

"Yeah, I do like my job. I just don't like my boss." Lisa sighed. "Meanwhile, I was looking through the files on our network to see if I could find any references that Don might have made about any of the women in the office. I didn't see anything, but I came across another file that looked interesting."

"What was it?"

"First I decided to take another look at that file I told you about the other day, the one with Senator Lawrence's name on it? I couldn't find it. It was gone. I looked around some more and found a directory named WL with a file in it which had a list of payments from Bruce Mills to Don Mills and Joe Michaud, the sheriff."

"It certainly sounds suspicious when you think about the contract argument," Carrie mused. "It wouldn't seem so out of place if it were just Bruce making payments to his brother, but I wonder why he'd be paying Don and Joe for anything that had to do with William Lawrence."

"That's what I wondered too. I suppose it's possible Joe and Don loaned Bruce money for something, but why would Lawrence have anything to do with it?"

"It could be some sort of payoff." Carrie took another bite of quiche while she thought about possible scenarios. "That sounds kind of far-fetched, but the fact that it involves a politician makes you wonder."

"Maybe I'm being overly suspicious now that I know what Don's really like. Do you think he'd be involved with something illegal?"

"Like I said, he was a lot older, so I never knew him very well. I grew up with Bruce and Joe, and they were always best friends back in school. I think they still are."

"Were you in the same class at school with Bruce and Joe?"

"Yes. It was a small school, so everyone knew each other. Bruce and Joe were never my favorite people. I remember they were both obnoxious back then, although they're polite enough these days."

"How were they obnoxious?"

"They were both jocks and they picked on kids who weren't as popular." Carrie paused. "I remember them constantly making fun of this one poor girl who had a major crush on Bruce. She was kind of homely, and they would pretend to flirt with her all the time and then laugh at her with their friends. It was really cruel."

"That's awful. Did anyone try to stop them?"

"Yeah, but it didn't do any good. Anyone who said anything against them became their next target. I wasn't one of the popular girls, but I was good at sports, so they left me alone. And my big brother would have beaten them up if they tried anything."

"I'm glad about that, at least. I guess Don isn't the only Mills brother who's a creep."

"I don't think he lives in Winchester anymore," Carrie said. "I think he lives in Augusta now."

"Do Bruce and Joe both live here?"

"Yes. They live near each other in big houses on Lakeshore Drive. They come in to the café every now and then with their wives."

The door opened, and Carrie looked over. A group of people entered and headed for the counter. She didn't want to leave Lisa sitting by herself, but she knew Angie was going to need some help in a few minutes.

Carrie stood up and picked up her plate. "I'd better get back to the kitchen."

"Thank you for listening to me." Lisa touched Carrie's arm. "I'm really glad we've become friends. It's such a relief to have someone to talk to about all this."

Carrie felt a rush of heat where Lisa touched her. She wanted to spend more time with her, so she tried to think of something they could do together. Lisa's request from dinner the other night came to mind and Carrie tried to keep it casual. "Do you want to come strawberry picking with me later this week? You mentioned it the other day and I might be going anyway."

"I'd love to." Lisa grinned at her. "I was hoping you'd take me, but I didn't want to keep asking. When are you going?"

"How about Saturday morning? I can have someone cover here as long as I'm back in the afternoon to get ready for dinner."

"That sounds great. I'll talk to you before then, I'm sure, and you can tell me what time to be ready."

"Okay."

Carrie walked back to the kitchen, wondering what was wrong with her lately. She had never had this problem before. She'd always been very confident about asking women out. She wanted to ask Lisa on an actual date, but Lisa obviously saw her as just a friend. Her strawberry picking suggestion had sounded so dull it was embarrassing, but it was the first thing that popped into her head. Maybe she needed to rethink her strategy of waiting to see what happened with Lisa and Toni. This was getting ridiculous. She should just stick to work, where at least she knew what she was doing.

* * *

Lisa thought about Joe Michaud and Bruce Mills while she drove home. Don had some influential people in his corner if he was friendly with the sheriff and with Senator Lawrence, so she would have to be careful if she ever tried to accuse him of anything. It was a good thing she had someone like Carrie to talk to about everything going on, or she would surely be going out of her mind.

She pulled into her driveway and went in the house. Daisy came running down the stairs to greet her. It was a beautiful evening, still warm and sunny with a nice breeze. It was a good night to go sit down by the water after she fed Daisy.

"Hello, little girl. Let's go get you some dinner." Lisa bent down to pet Daisy and gave her a quick hug. They walked back up the stairs into the kitchen and Lisa filled Daisy's bowl. She watched Daisy eat her dinner and decided to give Toni a call. She hadn't talked to her since she left on Sunday, and over the past few days she had found herself thinking about the kisses they had shared. She wondered if Toni had thought about her at all. She'd been hoping to hear from her, but Toni had never been predictable about getting in touch.

Lisa grabbed her phone and went outside with Daisy. She walked down by the dock and sat in one of the chairs while she watched Daisy chase a squirrel. She dialed Toni's number.

"Hello, beautiful," Toni answered.

"Hi there, you smooth talker. How was your day?"

"Better now that I'm talking to you. Are we still on for Saturday?"

"Yes, I'm looking forward to it."

"Are you going to spend the night?" Toni asked in a soft voice. "It's a long drive back to Winchester and I'd love to have you stay."

The thought had crossed Lisa's mind, and she'd had a feeling Toni would want her to stay. She wanted to stay with her, but it was a big step and it made her nervous. "It depends on if I can find someone to keep an eye on Daisy."

"Daisy is welcome to stay too. She's a good dog. I'm sure she'd be fine."

There went that excuse. What was she worrying so much for anyway? Spending the night with Toni would be fantastic. "Okay, as long as you don't mind having both of us."

"It's going to be my pleasure. Yours too, hopefully."

Lisa took a deep breath. Toni was never one to hold back. "I'm sure it will be."

"Listen, I have to get going," Toni said. "I need to go pick up Amelia. I'll send you my address and we can meet here on Saturday evening, okay?"

Lisa hung up the phone with a shiver of anticipation. She would have liked to talk a little longer, but that was all right. They would have plenty of time this weekend, although she and Toni might have some plans that didn't involve a lot of talking.

CHAPTER ELEVEN

Lisa couldn't keep her mind focused on the account she was working on. She had too many things going through her head. She couldn't stop thinking about the upcoming weekend with Toni. It sounded like it was going to be everything she had dreamed about when she was younger, but was that what she wanted now? Toni had always been able to make life more exciting when she was around. She was like a burst of energy that could engulf you if you got caught up in it and knock you down when it was over. Lisa wasn't sure if Toni was still as intense about her relationships as she had been back in college, but she certainly seemed to be. Lisa just hoped she was ready for it. The longing she had felt for Toni on the night they had spent together all those years ago had taken her a long time to get over.

Since meeting her again the other night, Toni had come on so strongly it made her slightly nervous. She wasn't sure how much she really meant to Toni, and she worried it could be a mistake to jump into something with her. Maybe she was thinking about it too much, and she should just enjoy herself while she had the chance.

She certainly was due for some fun and it didn't mean there had to be a commitment. She hadn't dated anyone since well before her mother died. She'd been too busy caring for her and then too grief stricken to be social. Her breast cancer diagnosis had come just a few months later. It had been a year since she finished treatment, and she was finally starting to feel like herself again.

Thoughts of her conversation with Carrie had also been on her mind all morning. She had to find a way to expose Don. If she could uncover more details about the bribery scandal she was convinced he was involved in, then people would see the type of person he was and would believe her when she reported the harassment that was taking place at his company. After talking with Mary, she no longer thought she was the only one he had targeted. He had to be stopped.

If she was going to prove any of their theories, the key would be gathering more facts. She planned to keep looking on the network, but the best way to find information would be to access Don's email somehow. She was going to have to think of a way to do that. It would also be good if she could look through his desk and see if he had anything tucked away. That would be a lot riskier, but she was going to look for an opportunity. She could try to get into his office while he was away at a meeting or at one of his long lunches. Many people left their office doors unlocked during the day, maybe he did too.

She looked around again on the network file system. There were several directory listings with client names. Lisa didn't recognize most of them; she was only familiar with the names of the clients she had worked for. There were also some folders with general headings. She noticed a folder titled "Contracts" and opened it. After opening several of the files in the directory, she didn't see anything of interest. She continued looking and came to a sub-directory named "MBC." Since she wasn't sure what that might stand for, it caught her attention and she opened it.

There were a handful of files inside the directory. She opened the first one and saw it was a contract between the State of Maine and Mills Building Construction for the large state office complex project near Augusta that had begun construction last fall. She looked through the other files and saw they contained further details about the same project. One of the files listed the members on the state procurement committee that had approved the contract. The head of the committee was Senator Lawrence.

This could be connected with the other files she had seen. The first file she found had listed dates and dollar amounts, with no references for what the amounts stood for. The second file had also listed dates and dollar amounts, but that one had identified the amounts as payments from Bruce Mills that began approximately the same time as this office park project had begun—last fall. All of the files were linked to Senator Lawrence in some way. Did they all come back to this contract?

She had even more questions now. She still wanted to know why Bruce had been making payments to Don and Joe. It was possible they had helped him with the contract somehow. It was worth a huge sum of money. What if Senator Lawrence's committee had awarded the contract to Mills Building Construction and not the lowest bidder? From what she now knew about the Mills brothers, she'd be willing to bet they had either paid off Senator Lawrence or held some sort of influence over him.

There was also the question of the contract that Don had been arguing about with the man in his office, presumably his brother. The man was angry because a contract wasn't in place yet, which meant that the payoffs with Senator Lawrence were an ongoing arrangement with multiple contracts and even more money involved.

Lisa closed the files and sat back in her chair. Pushing back her hair with one hand, she tapped her fingers on the desk and tried to think of how she could dig deeper into this. She was going to start looking for job openings and sending out her résumé too. She wasn't planning to continue working for a man like Don Mills. She didn't want to put other people's jobs at risk by stirring up controversy, but there was no way she could let him continue his harassment and possible illegal activities if she could help it. Meanwhile she would see if she could find out more about the contract that Senator Lawrence had given to Mills Building Construction for the state office complex.

She looked out her doorway into the quiet hallway. No one was around, so she decided to see if Don was in his office. She picked up a folder to carry with her so she looked busy and strolled down the hall past the reception area over toward his corner. His door was shut, but she wasn't sure if he was in or not. She didn't want to talk to him if she didn't have to, so she hesitated before knocking on his door.

"Are you looking for Don?" a voice behind her asked.

Lisa turned around and saw Mary. "Hi, Mary. I need to catch up with him and I was just wondering if he was in."

"I believe he had a meeting this afternoon."

"Okay, I guess I'll try him back later. Thanks."

Lisa breathed a sigh of relief as she headed back to her office. She had planned to check the door and slip in if no one answered. That would have been a big mistake. Maybe she could stay late one day and see if she could get in after everyone left. That would probably be the safer approach.

The only thing that would have been worse than Mary seeing her try to open Don's door would have been to open the door and find him sitting at his desk.

CHAPTER TWELVE

Saturday morning finally arrived. The café had been busy last night, and Carrie had gotten home late. She would have slept in a little later, but she wanted to be sure to have plenty of time to pick strawberries with Lisa before the day got too hot. Carrie got out of bed and looked at the lake outside her window while she dialed Lisa's number.

"Hi Carrie," Lisa answered. "Are we still on for this morning?"

"You bet. I just need to take a quick shower and I'll be ready."

"I'll meet you at your house in a half hour."

Carrie grabbed some clean shorts and a T-shirt and went to take a shower. A half hour wasn't much time to get ready, so it was a good thing she wasn't too high maintenance. She hurried to get dressed and dry her hair. She took a look around and made sure everything was picked up before going downstairs.

The kitchen and living room looked fairly tidy. She wasn't one to leave things lying around. The morning light was streaming in through the banks of windows in the kitchen that faced the driveway. The living room wall faced the lake with large French doors opening to a deck. When she built the house she made sure to include a large deck and screened porch so she could enjoy being outside as much as possible.

She poured some granola in a bowl along with some yogurt and was just finishing her breakfast when she heard a car approaching. Looking out one of the kitchen windows, she saw Lisa's car pull into her driveway and headed out onto the porch.

"Hi, you're right on time."

"I hate being late." Lisa got out of her car and walked to the porch steps. "I hope I didn't rush you, though."

"I'm just about ready. Come in for a second."

"Your screened porch is nice. Sometimes the bugs are so bad around here it's hard to sit out on the deck at my house without getting eaten alive."

Carrie laughed. "I know, especially in the evening."

"So where are we going picking?"

Carrie couldn't help but notice how pretty Lisa looked in the morning sunshine. She looked away for a minute as they walked into the house and tried to focus on Lisa's question. "There's a nice farm a couple towns over. It'll be good to go early because it's supposed to get hot later."

Lisa stood in the kitchen and looked around. "I love your house. The kitchen cabinets and countertops are beautiful. The greenish gray color you used on the cabinets is perfect. In fact, all of the colors go really well together."

"Thank you, I'm glad you like it. My father made the cabinets and I painted them. He helped me do a lot of the finish work here."

"That's why it looks so special. I can see the custom touches everywhere, like the trim around the windows and all the built-in shelves in your living room."

"Yeah, my father and I had a good time doing all this. It took quite a while, but I ended up having things done the way that I wanted them without spending a fortune."

Carrie grabbed a couple bottles of water from the refrigerator and put them in a small cooler along with some fruit bars she had made at the café the day before.

Lisa spotted the bowl on the table. "I interrupted your breakfast. Go ahead and finish. There's no need to rush. I've tasted the granola you make at the café, and it's too good to waste."

"Thanks, but I was pretty much all done." Carrie picked up the bowl and put it in the sink. "Let's get going."

They got into Carrie's Jeep and headed down the road. Carrie pointed out her parents' house to Lisa as they drove by. "That's where I grew up. My parents have lived there since they got married."

"It must be really nice to have your parents so close."

"It is. I try to stop by as often as I can, but sometimes I get so busy I don't see them for a week or so." Carrie glanced over at Lisa. "I remember you said both of your parents have passed away. I'm sorry. It must have been hard to lose them."

"Yeah. It's been about two years since my mom died and I miss her a lot. It's hard to lose the one person that loves you unconditionally, you know? No matter how obnoxious I was, she loved me. I would be at my worst and she would still always support me."

Carrie thought about her mother and nodded. "I never thought about it like that but you're right. My mom is always there for me."

"It's nice to have someone to talk to who understands." Lisa smiled at her. "I'm glad I moved here. It's been a good change, even if my boss is a detestable human being."

CHAPTER THIRTEEN

They arrived at the fields and picked up several empty flats of containers at the check-in booth. Lisa hung on while Carrie drove her Jeep along the bumpy path across the open strawberry fields to where the berries were ripe and ready for picking. They parked and got out with their boxes and found a spot with some empty aisles. The sun was creeping up in the cloudless sky and the heat of the day was beginning to build as they walked along the row to find a good starting point.

"Wow, it's hotter than I thought out here." Lisa pushed her hair back from her sweaty forehead. She looked across the long rows of strawberry plants growing in straight green columns with brown dirt paths in between. Two children and their mother were busy picking a few feet away. The little girl was eating more strawberries than she picked while her mother and brother worked steadily.

"I love hot days." Carrie knelt down and started plucking berries and putting them in the box she had placed on the ground next to her. "I'd like to live down south in the winter if I could."

"That would be ideal, wouldn't it?" Lisa crouched down on the other side of the aisle, facing Carrie. "Where would you go?"

"I'm not sure. I usually take a month off in the winter and I've visited a lot of different areas. There are a few places that I really like. I don't know if I can pick a favorite yet. I'll need to do more research."

The sweltering heat was making Lisa lethargic. She was falling into a trance as she picked berries and listened to Carrie's mesmerizing voice. She glanced up occasionally to watch Carrie's powerful arms and legs flex as she moved around, reaching through the leafy plants to pick the plumpest berries. Lisa listened with fascination as she talked about some of her trips to Florida and Louisiana.

She knew Carrie only thought of her platonically, but being with her right now made Lisa wish it could be more. It was incredibly nice to relax and enjoy being with her. She was so easy to talk to and one of the sexiest women she had ever known. Lisa could sit here all day, just watching her and dreaming about trips they could take together to some of the places she was talking about.

"Hey there." Carrie was looking at Lisa with concern. "Are you all right?"

Lisa's eyes widened, and her stomach gave a little flutter as she glanced into Carrie's eyes, which were bright blue in the sunshine. She shouldn't be looking at her friend like that. It must have been the heat that was making her heart race.

"I'm good." Lisa quickly started picking some berries. She changed the subject. "So, are you going to deliver all these berries to the café or are you going to keep some at home?"

"I'll probably take some to my mom and some to the cafe. I also want to keep a few at home for fresh strawberry drinks. You're welcome to come over for dinner and I'll make you one some night this week."

"That sounds heavenly." Lisa looked over at Carrie who was still focused on picking berries. She would love to go to Carrie's place and have dinner and spend more time with her. It must have been the heat of the sultry summer day that was making her feel this incredible attraction to Carrie.

She was going to be meeting Toni this evening, so she needed to stop thinking about how good Carrie looked. Their date was sure to be very special and she had been looking forward to it all week. Toni was a beautiful woman and Lisa couldn't wait to see what tonight would bring. The thought of kissing her again and having her soft and waiting under her fingertips sounded spectacular.

How was it possible that she had these feelings for Carrie when just the thought of Toni was enough to arouse her? She had never married again after she split up with her husband, but she had had a few relationships and she was always faithful. She had always been in monogamous relationships and had no desire for anything else, so why was she having feelings for both of these women?

It was a moot point anyway because Carrie didn't look at her that way.

"Whew, I need to stand up for a minute." Carrie pressed her hands into her lower back and shifted back and forth, stretching. "So, anything new at the office?"

"I've been meaning to fill you in." Lisa was relieved to settle into a new topic. "I found some more information. I was looking through more files on the network and I found a contract that was approved by Senator Lawrence for Bruce Mills's construction company. It's a big project for an office building complex in Augusta and the dates tie in with the spreadsheet that I told you about with the payments from Bruce."

"I know where that office park is. You think the payments from Bruce were linked somehow with the office project?"

"I think it's pretty suspicious, don't you? I mean, the spreadsheet and the other file I saw both were under Lawrence's name. What we don't know is why Bruce would be making payments to Don and Joe and why would the dates line up like they do?"

"One possibility is that Don and Joe may have loaned money to Bruce to pay off Senator Lawrence for the contract.

Or maybe they simply loaned him money to finance the project and it's all innocent."

"I suppose, but I can't see a sheriff loaning large amounts of money to a builder. I think maybe they have something on Lawrence and that's how Bruce got the contract. I need to find out if they're up to something and I want to expose them if they are. I don't have any proof that Don harasses women, but maybe I can find some proof about this."

"Lisa, you need to be careful around Joe Michaud. I've heard some things about him that are seriously scary. You don't want to get on his bad side. There are a lot of rumors about things that happened to people who crossed him, and I don't want anything to happen to you."

"I'll be careful." Lisa was touched that Carrie was worried about her. "And I wouldn't do anything until I had some proof."

Once their flats were overflowing with ripe strawberries, they carried the containers back to the Jeep. Carrie opened her cooler and passed a cold bottle to Lisa before pouring a long stream of water into her mouth and splashing handfuls over her face.

Lisa took a deep drink while she watched Carrie. Her mouth was parched, and the cold water tasted wonderful. "God, that tastes so good."

She poured some water on a handful of strawberries to wash them off. She popped a couple in her mouth and held out her hand to Carrie. "They taste warm and delicious. Try them."

Carrie took a couple of the berries from Lisa's hand and put them in her mouth. "Mmm, they taste like summer."

Lisa was flooded with arousal. She couldn't stop staring at the way the water dripped off Carrie's face. She licked strawberry juice from her lips and thought about how good it would taste to kiss Carrie's lips. The strawberries in her hand dropped on the ground, startling her back to reality.

Feeling a rush of guilt, Lisa quickly opened the door to get into the Jeep. She left it open to let out some heat while Carrie got in. Carrie glanced at her for a moment while she started the car, and then they headed to the parking lot to weigh their containers.

Lisa didn't know what had just happened, and she hoped Carrie wasn't upset with her. She didn't mean to look at her like that. Sometimes when she was with Carrie, she couldn't control her body's responses even though she knew Carrie wasn't interested. She would have to try harder to restrain herself. It wasn't fair to Carrie to keep pressuring her with unwanted advances, and it wasn't fair to Toni, who she was on her way to see tonight. What was wrong with her lately?

Carrie pulled up to the booth at the entrance and brought the berries over to the teenagers running the scales. Once that was done, she placed the flats back into the Jeep and took a deep breath. Carrie was melting from the heat and watching Lisa. She needed to step back for a second and cool down. Lisa didn't realize how tempting she was. Carrie was seriously turned on right now and she wasn't quite sure what to do.

Climbing back in the Jeep to head home, she gripped the steering wheel with her pink-stained hands and tried to keep her gaze straight ahead. She couldn't look at Lisa at the moment; all she wanted to do was eat more strawberries out of Lisa's hand.

She needed to think about revising her plan to wait and see what happened with Lisa and Toni because she wasn't sure she'd be able to hold out much longer without touching her. There was a lot to think about. Carrie drove silently for a few minutes, listening to Lisa while she hummed along with the radio.

"So, are you going to see Toni perform tonight?" Carrie knew that topic would certainly cool her down.

"Yes. She's singing at a place in Camden."

"That should be fun." Carrie wished that Lisa had never met up with Toni. It was her own fault for booking Toni at the café.

"It should be," Lisa answered softly.

"Do you want to come over for dinner on Sunday night? I think you'll like my strawberry drinks."

"Yes, I'd like that and I'm sure I'll love your drinks. You've never let me down yet."

"You're right. I won't let you down." Carrie glanced over and caught Lisa looking at her. They stared at each other for a moment before Carrie brought her attention back to the road.

"After working at the café all day, you'll be tired of cooking by Sunday night," Lisa said. "I can help you."

"I thought you didn't like cooking?"

"That's true, but I want to help out so you don't do all the work."

"All right, sounds good. I'll be looking forward to it."

They reached Carrie's house and got out of the Jeep. Carrie opened the back and pulled out a small container of strawberries. She passed them to Lisa. "Are you sure that's all you want to take home?"

"Yes. I can always get some more, and that's plenty for now. Thank you for taking me, Carrie. I had a great time."

"Thanks for coming with me." Carrie looked in Lisa's eyes. She wished Lisa wasn't going to Camden.

"I'll see you tomorrow night." Lisa got into her car and drove off with a wave.

Carrie watched her go and decided she didn't feel like being alone. Her parents were probably home, and this would be a good time to deliver some berries. She got back in the Jeep and headed down the road for the quick drive to their house. Her father's truck wasn't there, but hopefully her mother was home. She parked near the steps and took out one of the large flats of strawberries. The door opened as she approached, and her mother, Susan, stepped out onto the porch.

"Hi, sweetie. What a nice surprise. Did you just pick those?"

"Yes." Carrie headed to the kitchen and put the box down on the counter near the sink. "I hope to be repaid with a jar of jam at some point. It's way too hot for making jam today, though."

"Are you thirsty? Let me get you a drink."

"I'm dying for a drink, but I can get it." Carrie poured herself a cold drink of water from the pitcher in the refrigerator. She sat down next to her mother at the old wooden kitchen table. "What are your plans today?"

"I'm meeting Aunt Ruth later and taking her grocery shopping. I hope you get some rest before you have to go to the café."

"I will." Carrie's mind was still on Lisa. She found herself wishing again that Lisa wasn't spending the evening with someone else. She didn't even want to think about Lisa spending the night there.

"How have you been? Did you have a good week at the café?"

"I'm fine. We were pretty busy, which is good."

"I don't like how much you work in the summer, but I know that's when you make your money."

"It's all right, Mom. I like to be there when it's busy."

"Just make sure you take time to have some fun. I worry that you're lonely sometimes."

"I'm not lonely," Carrie reassured her mother.

Susan studied her daughter. "Is there something bothering you?"

Somehow, her mother always noticed when Carrie was feeling out of sorts. "I met a new friend, and I think you'd like her."

"Is that right?" Susan raised her eyebrow, questioningly. "Tell me about her."

"She's just a friend, unfortunately." Carrie shrugged. "That's the problem. She's involved with someone else."

"Does she know how you feel?"

"No. When I was with her this morning, I could tell she was attracted to me, but I haven't said or done anything to let her know how I feel. I'd like to, though."

"Oh sweetie, that must be hard. I've never heard you talk like this about anyone. Usually you keep your relationships casual. I never even get to meet the ladies that you go out with."

"I know." Carrie traced a finger through the condensation on her glass. "This time it feels different. When I'm with her I feel comfortable and really happy just to be around her. I think about her all the time. It's not just a physical attraction. But it's complicated because there's someone else involved."

"Maybe you should tell her how you feel?"

Carrie shook her head. "I don't know. I want to see what happens with the other person and not get tangled up in some complicated situation."

"Maybe if she knew you were interested, it might change things for her."

"I just don't know." Carrie took another sip of water and stood to leave. "This is why I like to keep things casual. I never had to worry about anything like this before I met Lisa."

Susan rose and gave Carrie a hug, walking her to the door. "Sometimes it's worth it to put yourself out there. If she's as special as she sounds, then she's going to see how wonderful you are and how lucky she'd be to have you in her life."

"Thanks Mom. It's nice to have you in my corner."

CHAPTER FOURTEEN

Lisa fought the urge to think about Carrie all the way to Camden. She wanted to focus on how happy she was to be spending the night with Toni, who was gorgeous and talented. After all, Lisa had spent years longing for her. At the moment, though, all Lisa could think about was how much she wished she was spending the night with Carrie, who didn't seem to care one bit that she was seeing another woman.

Her friendship with Carrie was growing more important to her and she didn't want to lose it by throwing herself at her and driving Carrie away. She needed to keep her mind on Toni. It was going to be great to hear her sing again. Her voice had sounded really good at the café and it brought back memories of the times she had listened to her sing back when they were in school.

A painfully slow car ahead of her on the meandering road forced her to go at a snail's pace for the forty-mile drive down Route 17. Daisy loved car rides, and a breeze was blowing loudly through car because she especially loved to have her head out the window. Lisa sighed as she noted the drool, which now covered the passenger door. Daisy wagged her tail, happy and excited to be on a road trip.

She breathed a sigh of relief when she finally turned onto the route heading into town. It was a postcard-perfect day and she could smell the salty air. Boats filled the harbor and the downtown was packed with tourists. The shops and sidewalks bustled with people, as she found the road Toni had listed in her directions. A short time later she pulled into the driveway of a small home about a mile from the harbor.

She parked next to Toni's car and grabbed Daisy's leash before getting out and looking around. Daisy pulled her along, wanting to run off and explore. Lisa tried to keep a firm grip on her nerves as well as the leash as they walked to the door. It was a small, white-shingled cottage with purple and green shutters. Flowerbeds surrounded the house and several lawn sculptures were displayed among the plants. There was a wooden bear in the side yard, and a spinning metal piece that looked like a windmill stood in the front among the lilies.

Lisa knocked on the door just as Toni opened it. Daisy leaped across the doorway to greet Toni. She laughed and knelt down to pet the enthusiastic dog. "Hello, Daisy. Nice to see you."

Toni stood and looked at Lisa with a smile. "It's nice to see you, too. Come on in."

Lisa walked into Toni's colorful kitchen and let go of Daisy, who immediately began to sniff around. Toni leaned toward her and gave her a quick kiss. Lisa put her arms around her and drew her in for a deeper one, savoring the taste of her lips for a moment before releasing her and pulling back with a smile.

"Hi," Lisa said. "I need to grab a couple things out of my car, and then I'll be right back."

Leaving the dog in the house, Lisa went back to her car and got her overnight bag and a backpack full of Daisy's many accessories. Setting her bags on the floor by the door, Lisa passed a bouquet of flowers and a bottle of wine to Toni. "These are for you. I think this is what you were drinking at Harvest last weekend."

"Thank you, these are lovely," Toni exclaimed. She put the wine and flowers on the counter and wrapped her arms around Lisa. "We're going to have so much fun tonight."

"Is it all right if I put Daisy out front on her tie out?" Lisa asked. "She doesn't dig, and she'd be happy to sit in the yard and watch people go by."

"Of course. Here, let me get her some water. Can I get you something to drink, too? Maybe a glass of wine?"

Lisa didn't want a repeat of their previous night together all those years ago when they had too much to drink and fell asleep. She was planning to take it easy on the alcohol tonight. "No thanks. I'm all set."

They got Daisy situated in a shady area in the front yard and came back into the house. Taking a seat at the kitchen table, Toni gestured to the chair next to her. "Come sit down and relax with me."

Lisa sat down and looked around the kitchen, which opened to an adjoining living room. The walls in both rooms were covered with a colorful array of artwork. "I love your place. It's very funky, just like you."

"Thank you." Toni leaned toward her with a laugh. "I didn't know you thought I was funky."

"Oh yes." Lisa looked appreciatively at the stylish patterned blouse and silk pants that Toni wore. "You have your own special style that I've always admired."

"I always liked your style too."

"I don't think anyone has ever said that to me before." Lisa shook her head. "I'm not one of the most fashionable people. I find something I like and stick with it."

"It's not always what you're wearing. It's how you wear it." Toni smiled at Lisa. "Believe me, you're wearing those jeans well."

Lisa was glad she had taken the time to dress nicely in spite of the hot day. "So, what's the schedule for tonight? What time do you have to be there?"

"I need to meet the guys at a place called the High Tide in an hour or two. I thought we could head over there soon and get there a little early. That will give us a chance to have dinner beforehand and hang out for a little while. Their food is pretty good, although it's not quite as good as Harvest."

At the mention of Harvest, Lisa's mind drifted to Carrie again and she wondered if she was having a busy evening at the café tonight. She looked at the beautiful woman next to her and brought her focus back to their evening.

"I'm sure the food at High Tide will be good, but mostly I can't wait to hear you sing again."

"Aw, thanks. I'm really glad you came to see me. I've been thinking about you a lot this week. I can't believe it's been almost twenty years since college."

"I wish I had known that you were sharing some of the same feelings that I had for you back then. I was so attracted to you and I was terrified that you'd find out and not want to have anything to do with me." Lisa put her hand on Toni's.

"I wish I hadn't been too scared to let you know." Toni wrapped her fingers around Lisa's. "There are a lot of things we could have done differently, but who knows where we'd be now? You can't change the past. And I'm very glad to be here with you now."

Lisa could feel herself falling under Toni's spell as they talked. She always knew just the right thing to say to make Lisa feel like she was special. It was an intoxicating feeling to be here with this lovely, talented woman.

Toni turned to look at the clock on the wall. "We probably should get going soon."

"That sounds good. Let me just bring Daisy inside and get her settled."

Lisa opened the door and called to Daisy, who was lying in the yard watching people and cars as they passed by the cottage. She brought her in and got her settled, making sure she had plenty of food, water, and toys.

"Be a good girl." Lisa gave her a final pet and stood up.

"Apparently it's more of a process than I realized to bring your dog with you." Toni said.

"She should be all set, and I think I'm finally ready."

"I hope so. I know I'm ready." Toni reached for Lisa's waist and pulled her closer. She pressed her lips to Lisa's, kissing her softly.

Lisa closed her eyes as she ran her fingers through Toni's long curly hair. An image of Carrie passed through her mind. She opened her eyes and stepped back. "We should probably get going. I wouldn't want you to be late."

Toni looked in her eyes. "I guess you're right."

Lisa couldn't understand what had just happened. Here she was with this amazing woman she had always wanted, and she was thinking of someone else who wasn't even interested in her. Maybe it was just nerves because it had been so long since she had dated anyone. She must be more nervous about tonight than she had realized. That was the only explanation, because she was certainly attracted to Toni. Hopefully she hadn't noticed anything.

They got in Toni's car and drove toward the waterfront where they found a parking spot near the High Tide restaurant. The dining room was crowded when they entered, but the host recognized Toni and waved her over.

"Hi Sean," Toni said. "This place is busy tonight. Do you have a table for me and my friend?"

"Hi there, Toni," Sean said. "I heard you were playing tonight. We're pretty packed, but I always have a spot for you."

He led them through the dining room, and Toni set her guitar on the small stage in the back corner. Sean took them outside to a table for two on the deck overlooking the harbor.

"This is great, Sean," Toni said. "Thanks."

Sean gave her a flirtatious grin. "Sing a song for me tonight."

"Absolutely."

"I see you've still got it," Lisa said with a smile as they sat down. She remembered how men would fall at Toni's feet when they were younger. For all Lisa knew, there were women doing the same thing now. Toni had a way of attracting attention without even trying.

"I'm very happy to be here with you." Toni looked into her eyes. "Let's enjoy ourselves on this beautiful night and not worry about anyone else."

That sounded good to Lisa. She leaned back in her chair and relaxed. It wasn't like she had any reason to be stressed, and it would be foolish to keep thinking about Carrie.

The waiter approached their table and they each ordered a glass of beer. They sat back and gazed out at the sailboats and yachts docked in the harbor. The cool sea breeze kept the temperature comfortable on the sunny deck.

"Do you perform every weekend?" Lisa asked.

"Usually I do. I love being able to sing on the weekends. I have a couple guys that I play with, depending on where we're going."

"I'm so glad I caught you at Harvest last week. You were really good and I'm not just saying that because you're letting me sleep over."

"Thanks, I'm glad you caught me too." Toni laughed. "I always hoped I'd see you again and here we are."

Lisa was interrupted from answering as their waiter brought over their drinks. He took their dinner orders and walked away.

"Here's to catching up with old friends." Lisa raised her glass to Toni's.

Toni leaned close to Lisa's ear. "You know what I want?"

"I'm not sure." Lisa raised an eyebrow. "But I have an idea."

"I want a backrub later." Toni reached over and put her hand on Lisa's. "It's been a long time, and I think you might be a little better at it these days."

Lisa swallowed as she felt a rush of heat. She took a sip of her beer, trying not to get flustered before looking at Toni. "Yeah, it has been a long time and I would say I'm much better at it now."

Toni smiled at her reaction.

"So, what songs are you playing tonight?"

Toni listed the songs she planned to sing and described why she picked them. Just like Lisa remembered from their college days, Toni could turn a discussion on just about anything into a fascinating exchange and they never ran into any awkward lulls while they talked. The conversation continued to flow after the waiter brought their meals and they began eating.

Before she knew it, their plates were being cleared.

Toni checked her phone. "Time to head inside. The guys should be here any minute."

A small table near the stage provided Lisa with the perfect spot to watch Toni and her band. They had a strong local following and the dinner crowd had been replaced by a full house of people that were there to hear the band. Toni's voice sounded even better than the week before, and Lisa was enthralled as she listened to them.

"This next song is for Sean," Toni announced, gesturing toward the host.

Sean stood up from his seat at the bar and bowed to his friends as they all clapped. Toni began singing and the crowd loved it. There was a mix of people of all ages, and Lisa didn't feel out of place even though she was sitting alone. She was captivated by Toni's voice. She loved seeing how well Toni was doing here and how happy everyone was to hear her sing.

It was a rush for her to realize how flattering it was to have this desirable woman choose to be with her. Toni could probably have her pick of whoever she wanted. Many of the men and women in the crowd couldn't take their eyes off her. That might have caused her to feel insecure, but Toni had been so attentive she knew there was nothing to worry about.

The next few songs were fast and loud. Some people danced, and everyone enjoyed the energy in room. Toni finished a song and spoke into the microphone. "I've got one more song and then we're going to take a short break. I want to dedicate this one to someone special who's here with me tonight."

Toni looked at Lisa and began to sing a cover of Neil Young's "Helpless." She played softly on her guitar and watched Lisa while she sang the words. The crowd grew quiet and listened attentively as Toni's soaring voice carried through the room. Lisa felt the intensity of Toni's passion directed at her as she returned her gaze. Her heart was racing as she thought about the night ahead and how much she wanted Toni. The song ended, and Toni flashed a grin while the crowd cheered loudly.

Toni set her guitar down and gave the crowd a wave as she sat down next to Lisa, breathing hard. Lisa wanted to give her a hug, but she settled for pouring her a glass of water from the pitcher on the table. Toni took a long sip and sat back, looking at Lisa closely.

"Whew, so what did you think?" Toni asked.

"All I can say is that entire set was sensational, Toni. You're a rock star here in Camden, and you have the crowd eating out of your hand, including me."

"Yeah, well it's a small pond, but I'm glad you liked it."

"I loved it. I wanted to throw myself on the stage along with everyone else here. Or at least throw you my phone number."

Toni laughed and put her hand on Lisa's leg under the table. "I wanted to sing something special for you."

Lisa put her hand on Toni's and squeezed it. "I've never had anyone sing a song for me like that. It was beautiful."

Toni caressed Lisa's leg. "I thought you'd like something with a little imagination."

"I love that song and this night has been amazing." Lisa couldn't help but be enchanted. "You still know just how to put people under your spell, especially me."

Toni bent forward to reply when two men and a woman approached the table. One of the men, a good-looking blond, was carrying a glass of wine, which he placed on the table in front of Toni. "Hi, I'm Mark and my friends and I really enjoyed your music tonight. We thought you might be thirsty, and the bartender said this was what you were drinking."

"Thank you very much." Toni leaned back and turned in her chair to face the group. She smiled and nodded at them.

The woman, a pretty redhead in her thirties, spoke up next. "Hi, my name's Sherry and this is Justin." She gestured to the heavyset man standing beside her. "Your first set was great. We loved it."

"We've heard you play before, and we try to catch you whenever we get a chance," Justin said. "Sherry and I live nearby in Rockland."

"That's very nice of you to say. I live right here in Camden myself." Toni reached over and touched Lisa's shoulder. "This is my friend, Lisa."

The group nodded a greeting to Lisa and turned back to Toni. They began asking questions about her music and how long she'd been playing. A lengthy conversation ensued. Lisa waited patiently until they finished their questions and left.

"Sorry about that. I didn't mean to ignore you," Toni said. "Sometimes people like to talk about my music and it's hard not to get into a discussion. Plus, it's nice to get to know everyone."

"Don't be sorry. I think it's fantastic that your music is so popular," Lisa replied. "I can see why you like it here in Camden. It's such a beautiful area and you're obviously a local favorite."

"Yes, I really do like it here. It's great to be able to work at my daughter's school and be able to live close enough to my ex-husband that our daughter can share time with both of us."

Toni reached into the bag hanging on the back of her chair and pulled out her phone. She checked the screen and looked up at Lisa. "Speaking of my ex, I thought I heard my phone earlier and it looks like he tried to call me. I'd better call back and make sure Amelia is all right. I'm going to step out on the deck where it's quieter. I'll be right back, okay?"

"Of course," Lisa said.

Toni reappeared a few minutes later. "Lisa, I'm so sorry, but I'm going to have to leave."

"What's wrong?" Lisa asked, seeing the worried look on Toni's face.

"Amelia's sick. Josh, my ex-husband, thinks it's just the stomach flu, but she's feeling pretty lousy and really wants her mom."

"I'm sure she does. The poor kid. We'd better get going so you can get home to her."

"I'll go tell the band. Listen, I feel really bad leaving like this."

"Toni, it's out of your control. I completely understand. I'll wait here while you tell the guys."

Toni rushed over to tell the other musicians what was going on. Lisa's heart sank as she thought about how close she had come to finally sleeping with Toni. She had overcome her doubts and was ready to drop her inhibitions and have a night of passion. The fates seemed to be against them.

Toni returned to the table. "John is going to fill in for me on the second set."

"Let's go." Lisa picked up her bag. "If you drop me at your house, I can get Daisy and take off before you get back with your daughter."

"I feel terrible you're not going to stay over," Toni said as they hurried to the door. "But I'm sure you wouldn't want to be around a sick kid."

"I think she'll need to have you all to herself." They walked over to Toni's car. "We have plenty of time and we can do this again soon."

"You're the best." Toni kissed Lisa before she started the car. "I guess we've waited this long. What's a few more days?"

She knew Toni was right, waiting a few more days wasn't a big deal. But Toni didn't realize how hard it had been to put aside the conflicting emotions in her head and allow herself to let go tonight. Between battling her insecurities about her surgical scars and fighting her feelings for Carrie, it had been a real struggle for Lisa to get to the point where she was ready to give Toni a chance. Not to mention it had been years since she'd had sex.

They pulled up to the house and Lisa turned to Toni. "I know you need to get going. I hope your daughter feels better soon."

"Do you know how much I wanted you tonight?" Toni leaned over to Lisa and gave her a lingering kiss.

Lisa felt her body responding and she reached out to pull her closer. The seat divider blocked their progress as the intensity of their kiss grew. Lisa was longing to feel Toni's skin and she opened the top buttons on her shirt, sliding one hand into her bra and caressing her breast. Toni groaned as she pressed against her hand and reached for the button on Lisa's jeans.

Just as Toni's hand began to slide into Lisa's panties, a pair of headlights appeared on the darkened street and approached the house. They quickly pulled away from each other as the vehicle drove into the driveway. Toni hastily buttoned her shirt while Lisa fastened her pants and tried to catch her breath.

"I'm sorry. That's my ex," Toni said. She let out a deep sigh as they watched a man and a young girl get out of the car. "I told him I'd pick Amelia up, but he must have gotten impatient. Dammit."

"Don't worry. I had a wonderful evening. Life with you is always an adventure."

CHAPTER FIFTEEN

Lisa woke on Sunday morning to the sun shining through her bedroom windows. It was going to be a beautiful day. She couldn't help but wonder what it would have been like to spend the night with Toni and wake up in her bed. Hopefully her daughter was all better. She would call and check on her later; she didn't want to wake them up this early. She went to the window to look out at the lake.

It had been quite an evening in Camden. She had loved listening to Toni sing. It was a major turn-on for her, and it had been impressive to see how popular she was with the crowd at the restaurant. She had looked beautiful and had gone out of her way to make Lisa feel special last night. It was easy to get caught up in the excitement of the moment whenever she spent time with her.

Lisa had thought she was sure she wanted to stay overnight at Toni's, and those last moments in her car had been incredibly arousing, but maybe it wasn't so bad that she'd ended up coming home. It had been so long since she had dated anyone, she wasn't sure she was ready to sleep with Toni quite yet. It seemed like there was always something in their way. She was very apprehensive about how Toni was going to react when she saw the scars from her breast cancer. She knew she'd get irritated if Toni started pitying her again. It was infuriating to be referred to as a poor thing.

It was time to get moving and get some things done around the house. She opened up the door for Daisy who was waiting patiently to go out. She wanted to drive in to Augusta and do some errands before she went over to Carrie's for dinner later.

It was exasperating how she couldn't seem to get Carrie out of her mind. Now she finally had a chance with Toni, and she kept sabotaging herself by thinking of Carrie, which was foolish. She was lucky to have made a good friend in town, that was all. She needed to stop obsessing over it. She was going to call Rachel and get her opinion on the situation. She was one person Lisa could talk to about anything.

What she should be thinking about was how to find out what was going on with Don, his brother, and the sheriff. Maybe she and Carrie could think of some other ways to get more information about the details behind Bruce Mills's state contract. This week she needed to try and find an evening to stay late at work when no one else was there. She really wanted to look around Don's office and see if she could find anything about Senator Lawrence. She decided to send Carrie a text asking her to call.

Lisa called for Daisy to come in just as her phone started to ring. Daisy gave her a playful bark and walked in the other direction while Lisa answered. "Hi, Carrie."

"Hi there," Carrie said. "What's up?"

"Not much at the moment. Just trying to get my dog to listen to me," Lisa answered. "I've got a few errands to run this morning and then I'm free. What time should I come over tonight and what can I bring?"

"You don't need to bring a thing. I've got all the ingredients. Do you want to go for a run this afternoon? We can go for a swim after and then have dinner."

"That sounds great. I just hope it's not too hot this afternoon."

"You'll be fine. Don't worry."

"All right, drill sergeant. You'll have to carry me and Daisy home if we collapse."

"No problem. Why don't you meet me over here at around three and we can take a different route than last time? That way you'll have your car."

"Okay, I'll see you at three."

* * *

Carrie heard a car pull into the driveway and looked up from the sink where she was washing her hands. Lisa was here, right on time. Carrie dried her hands and went outside to welcome her. Lisa carried a gym bag and a plastic shopping bag.

"Hi there." Lisa set the bags on the porch next to the stairs.

"Hi," Carrie said. "You ready to run?"

"You have to admit it's pretty hot." Lisa peered through her sunglasses at Carrie. "I had no idea you were so demanding. Hold on a minute."

Lisa went back to the car and let Daisy out. Daisy ran over to greet Carrie, wagging her tail and wriggling with excitement.

Carrie knelt and gave some attention to Daisy. "Well, hello girl. It's nice to see you. You're not going to be a wimp about the heat today, are you Daisy?"

"Oh, now you're asking for it." Lisa walked back to the porch and picked up the plastic bag and handed it to Carrie. "We got you a present."

"You did?" Carrie was startled by the unexpected gift. "Why'd you do that?"

"Because it's very nice of you to have me over for dinner and I appreciate it. You do a lot of nice things for me and I wanted to do something for you."

Carrie looked in the bag and pulled out a lightweight red T-shirt and a pair of running shorts. "Hey, these are great. I love them, thanks."

"I thought you might like them. The fabric stays nice and cool. I hope I got the right size?"

"The size is perfect." Carrie hadn't expected Lisa to know what sizes she wore. She smiled with pleasure at her thoughtfulness. "Thank you, Lisa. It was really sweet of you to get these for me."

"You're very welcome. Now let's get going and we'll see who's a wimp."

They jogged out to the gravel road and turned toward Carrie's parents' house. The afternoon sun was beating down, providing little shade along the the tree-lined road. Carrie kept a slow pace so Daisy wouldn't get overheated.

"We could start training, you know," Carrie said.

"Training for something in particular?"

"The summer lake festival is in a few weeks. Every year the festival starts off in the morning with a 5K race and it's usually pretty fun. Do you think you might want to sign up for it with me?"

"I take it you've done it before?"

"Yes, I try to run in it every year. The route goes right past the café. There are usually people of all ability levels, so you don't have to be too fast."

"You don't think I'm fast?" Lisa teased.

"I didn't mean it like that." Carrie hoped she hadn't hurt Lisa's feelings. "I think you're in great shape. I mean, you'd do fine."

"All right, let's sign up. I do have one condition; you have to help me make sure I don't embarrass myself. I want to have a respectable time."

They passed a farmhouse with white clapboards and a large front porch. The front yard was blooming with flowers and perennials.

"There's my parents' house," Carrie said. "It looks like they're home."

"Do you want to stop and say hello?" Lisa huffed. "Maybe take a water break?"

"No way. We're just getting started."

Daisy had run ahead to take a drink from the stream across the street from the house. She waited for them to catch up and jogged alongside Lisa. They ran in silence for a while before turning around and circling back toward Sawyer Road. Carrie's thoughts drifted as she wondered whether she should keep waiting for Lisa to be free, or if she should take her mother's advice and put herself out there. She looked over at Lisa to see how she was holding up. She seemed to be moving along pretty well, but her face was flaming red.

"How're you doing?" Carrie asked.

"Other than the fact my legs feel like they're weighted down with sandbags and I'm drenched with sweat, I'm fine."

"We'll be going back by my parents' in a minute." Carrie thought Lisa probably should get some water. "Do you want to stop and get a drink for Daisy?"

"Yes, Daisy should get some water and I'm happy to use her as an excuse."

They reached the house and Daisy ran back to the stream she had found earlier and started drinking and splashing around happily.

"I guess she's okay," Lisa said. "We didn't need to stop after all."

"I wanted to stop for a minute anyway." Carrie knew Lisa could use a break. She could see her mother through the kitchen window and most likely she had spotted them by now. Sure enough, her parents came out the kitchen door a moment later.

"Hello," Carrie called out.

"Hi sweetie," Susan said. "Isn't it too hot to be running?"

"We're fine, Mom. This is my friend, Lisa," Carrie said. "Lisa, this is my father, David, and this is my mother, Susan."

"Hello." Lisa bent over to lean on her knees. "Sorry, I just need to catch my breath for a second."

"Hi, Lisa," David Sawyer said. "Let me get you some water. You look awfully red."

"Water sounds wonderful, thank you."

"Hello, Lisa," Susan said. "It's very nice to meet you. Carrie has told me so many nice things about you."

"She did?" Lisa straightened up.

"Of course I did." Carrie smiled.

"It's nice to meet you, too," Lisa said to Susan. "You have a lovely home."

"Thank you," Susan said. "I hope Carrie hasn't been running you too hard. She's used to being in a hot kitchen and she never stops working."

"I'm starting to notice that," Lisa said.

David returned with two glasses of water and passed them to Carrie and Lisa.

"Thank you so much." Lisa gulped down her water. "You're an angel."

"Do you want to come sit down?" Susan asked. "Maybe you should cool off."

"We're going to go for a swim when we get back," Carrie replied. "We're training for the 5K at the festival."

"If I survive that long," Lisa commented. She turned to David. "Carrie showed me the work you did at her house. It's beautiful."

"Thank you." David smiled proudly at his daughter. "We worked hard on it. Carrie was very particular, and she came up with some great ideas."

"I'm very proud of both of them." Susan caught her daughter's eye and raised an eyebrow at Lisa.

Carrie gave her mother a small shrug and smiled. "We should probably get going. Are you ready to head back to my place and go for a swim, Lisa?"

"I can't wait to jump in the water." Lisa passed her empty glass back to David. "Thank you very much for the drink. I hope I see you both again soon."

"So do I," Susan said with a smile. "Have a nice afternoon."

"Feel better?" Carrie asked as they started back down the road with Daisy trailing happily behind them.

"I feel fine," Lisa said. "I wouldn't have needed to stop if it hadn't been for Daisy."

"Glad to hear it." Carrie chuckled.

Carrie's house came into view as they turned the corner. Lisa got a burst of energy and sprinted to the driveway before stopping and putting her hands on her knees, gasping for breath. Daisy trotted up beside her and kept going toward the shore where she waded into the lake with her tail wagging.

"As soon as I can move, I'm going to run to the dock and jump in," Lisa said. "I brought my suit, but I don't care, I'm going in just like this. I'm too hot to be embarrassed."

"That sounds like a good idea." Carrie walked past Lisa toward the path to the shoreline. She reached the dock and slipped off her shoes and socks and set them next to one of the chairs sitting on the shore. Taking a deep breath, she ran the length of the dock and dove in to the lake. The cold water shocked her overheated body and she burst back up to the surface with a gasp.

"It feels great," Carrie swam back toward the dock and called to Lisa. "Come on in."

She watched Lisa take off her shoes and jog out to join her. After reaching down to test the water, she dove in with a splash.

"Oh my God, this feels so good." Lisa floated on her back next to Carrie. "I'm just going to relax and stay here in this nice cool water for the rest of the day."

Daisy ran up onto the dock and barked at them.

"Come on in, girl," Carrie called to the dog. She reached for the ladder on the dock and climbed out. Taking a couple steps back, she sprinted to the end of the dock and dove in again, splashing Lisa. Daisy stayed on the dock and barked a few more times before lying down and watching them.

"This water is so invigorating." Lisa swam over to Carrie. "Do you swim much?"

"I usually go for a swim if I'm home in the afternoon," Carrie replied. "I don't go very far."

"Want to have a race?"

"Are you serious?" Carrie looked at her. "I thought you were tired from our run and wanted to relax for a while."

Lisa smiled. "You're not scared, are you?"

"Oh, here we go. You're on now." Carrie pointed to a birch tree that had bent over into the water a short distance down the shore. "Let's swim over to that tree and back to the dock."

"We need a prize," Lisa said. "What does the winner get?"

Carrie looked closely at Lisa, treading water next to her. She knew what she'd like to have, but she certainly wasn't going to tell Lisa what it was. "How about the loser does the dishes after dinner?"

"Deal." Lisa splashed Carrie as she turned and took off toward the tree.

"Hey," Carrie protested. She quickly started swimming after Lisa, who was surprisingly fast in the water. Carrie had the advantage with her long arms and legs, but she couldn't catch her, and Lisa reached the tree well before Carrie. Lisa turned smoothly and headed back to the dock as Carrie lagged behind. By the time Carrie reached the dock, Lisa had climbed out and was sitting on it, looking at her with a smile.

"You tricked me." Carrie pulled herself up the ladder and climbed out. She slicked her wet hair back with her hands, pushing it away from her face. Her arms and legs were burning as she flopped down next to Lisa. "I didn't know you were such a good swimmer."

"I like to swim." Lisa shook her short blond hair. "Did you assume I'd be slow?"

"I promise not to assume anything about you again." Carrie's gaze traveled down Lisa's body. Her wet shirt was plastered to her skin and Carrie tried to not to stare. All she could think about was how much she wanted to touch her. It was getting almost unbearable.

Carrie looked up and saw Lisa watching her. Carrie quickly turned away in embarrassment.

"Did you notice I'm a little uneven?" Lisa asked.

Carrie was confused. Was Lisa upset because Carrie had been checking her out? "I'm not sure what you mean."

"I had breast cancer a couple years ago. The surgery left me with one side much smaller than the other, and I thought you might have noticed and been wondering."

"Oh." Carrie looked into Lisa's eyes. "I would never have known. Are you healthy now?"

"Yes, I'm fine. I guess I'm self-conscious about it and I thought you might have noticed I look a little odd."

"No, I would never think that." Carrie wanted to tell her she looked beautiful. "I'm glad you're all right. It must have been really hard for you. Is that part of the reason you moved to Maine?"

"I was ready for a change. After my mother died and I went through treatment, I just needed to get away and get back to being myself, if that makes any sense. It's taken a while, but I finally feel like I'm me again." Lisa paused. "It's hard to explain."

"I couldn't possibly understand how you feel, but I'm here if you ever want to talk about anything." Carrie put her arm around Lisa. "The most important thing is that you're okay now."

"I'm fine." Lisa leaned against Carrie's shoulder. "I haven't talked about this with many people. I'm glad you didn't call me a poor thing, or I would have had to hurt you."

"It hasn't slowed you down and you're certainly not a poor thing. You did cheat a little in our race, though."

"I did not." Lisa straightened up to look at Carrie. "I just got a faster start than you."

"I want a rematch one of these days."

This was the first time Carrie had ever touched Lisa and she wanted to pull her closer. The feel of her arm around Lisa's waist was making her skin tingle. It felt so right to be touching her, but she needed to know that Lisa wasn't interested in anyone else but her. She licked her lips, thinking about how much she wanted to kiss her.

Lisa smiled at Carrie. "I'm ready for one of those strawberry drinks. How about you?"

CHAPTER SIXTEEN

Lisa watched from the other end of the counter as Carrie blended fresh strawberries into the rum and ice for their drinks. She added a few other ingredients and then they were ready for tasting. She brought a glass over to Lisa.

"Try this and tell me what you think," Carrie said.

Lisa set down the peas she was shelling and took a sip. "Oh my God. This is the best drink I've ever had."

"I appreciate how you're always enthusiastic about my food." Carrie laughed as she took a seat at the kitchen table. "I think you're my biggest fan."

"How did you end up running your own restaurant?"

"I always loved to cook. I was only planning to work at the café temporarily after college, but the owner was diagnosed with cancer and I tried to help out as much as I could. I learned how to manage the staff and the kitchen, and I realized I loved the restaurant business. When the owner offered me the opportunity to buy him out, I jumped at the chance. Thanks to my parents backing, I was able to do it and I've been building the business up ever since."

"That's very impressive. It must have been a ton of work."

"Sometimes it feels nonstop, but it's been worth it."

"This really is delicious. I don't think I could drink too many without getting full."

"That's true. They're very filling. Since you have to go to work in the morning, it's probably not a good idea to drink too much anyway."

"Speaking of me going to work, we need to think of some way to find out more about what Don is up to."

"I've been meaning to tell you that I spoke with Bruce Mills's wife, Leanne." Carrie reached under the table to pet Daisy. "She came by the café in a panic yesterday afternoon."

"Why was she in a panic?"

"They're having a big dinner party next weekend and she wants me to cater it for them. It's the sort of thing that takes a lot longer than a week to plan."

"It will be good for your business, right? How come she didn't ask you sooner?"

"I guess they decided to have it at the last minute. Yes, it's good for business, but I wish they had planned ahead because it's going to be a lot of work in a very short time and I'm already busy. Get this. Leanne said there are going to be a lot of local politicians attending."

"Do you think Senator Lawrence will be there?"

"I wouldn't be surprised if Don, Bruce, Joe, and Senator Lawrence are all there."

"There could be some really interesting conversations if the Senator still hasn't delivered on the contract Don was talking about in his office."

"There are going to be a lot of people there." Carrie sipped her drink. "I'll be too busy in the kitchen to pay any attention."

"Have you been hired for parties like this before?"

"I usually cater a few events during the summer. It'll be tough to pull it all together by next weekend. I'm trying not to get too stressed out about it."

"What can I do to help?"

"I need to get all the food and drinks ready, not to mention line up servers and bartenders. I've been talking to people and it should work out fine, but it's going to be crazy busy this week, so you'll have to excuse me if I get a little tense."

"I could be a server." Lisa started thinking of the possibilities. "I'd love to help out and it would also be a great way to get a look at the senator if he's there. It could be our chance to see if there's anything going on with the Mills brothers and the sheriff."

"I think I'll be too busy to see anything but the food we'll be cooking and serving. I'd love to have your help. I have to warn you, it's hard work to be a server."

"I waited tables back in college, and I remember it wasn't easy. I have to admit I wasn't too good at it. It can be very hard to keep people happy when their meals are involved. Some people get really hostile if they have to wait, which I could never handle."

"You've got that right. Some people are hard to please. On the other hand, it's also very rewarding to create a meal that people love. I get a lot of satisfaction when I can make people happy with the food I serve them."

"That's what makes you special," Lisa said. Although Carrie didn't bring attention to herself, Lisa had seen how hard she worked at the café. "I'm not just being polite when I tell you how great you are. The food at Harvest is as good as anywhere I've ever been."

"Thanks, it means a lot to hear you say that." Carrie smiled as she finished the last swallow of her strawberry drink. "So how are things going with Don at the office?"

"I've been trying to avoid him. He hasn't done much lately, but I can't stand to be around him. I know it's a matter of time before he tries to touch me again. I started sending my résumé around."

"I hope you find another job you like."

"Me, too." Lisa finished her drink and set down her glass. "I'm sure I'll find something. It's important we get more information before I leave so Don's criminal behavior can be exposed. The man is a sexual predator and he's also ripping off taxpayers with his illegal contracts."

"Just be careful, please." Carrie stood up. "It's getting late. I'm going to go start the grill and get dinner ready."

"What can I do to help?"

Carrie went outside to light the grill and returned moments later. Together they set the table and brought all the food to the cooking area. Lisa sat in one of the deck chairs while Carrie prepared an array of vegetables.

"How was Camden last night?" Carrie asked.

"Toni sang at a restaurant in the harbor." Lisa wasn't sure if she should go into many details. "She was really good, and it was a fun night."

"I'm glad you had a good time." Carrie turned her attention back to the grill.

Lisa watched Carrie and tried to hide her dejection. She knew it shouldn't bother her that Carrie didn't care one way or the other if she was dating someone. It was time to let go of the hope that Carrie would show any interest in her. There had been a few times where she could have sworn Carrie was looking at her with mutual attraction, but maybe it was wishful thinking.

Lisa knew she had to stop staring at her all the time or she was going to get on Carrie's nerves. She didn't want to do anything to risk their friendship.

Both women were silent as Carrie continued cooking. The sound of loons calling across the water filled the peaceful night air. Lisa watched Carrie scoop up the corn and other vegetables onto serving platters.

"Everything's ready," Carrie said. "Can you please help me take one of these plates inside?"

Lisa jumped up to help. "I can practice my serving skills for the dinner party."

Carrie smiled and passed her the plate. "Here you go."

Seeing Carrie smile made Lisa's heart ache. No matter how much she wished Carrie felt something other than friendship, it wasn't going to happen. It was wrong for her to be wishing for Carrie, anyway. She had been ready to spend the night with Toni last night and here she was thinking about another woman.

What was the matter with her? She needed to figure out what she really wanted and stop acting this way. Lisa tried to smile back as she took the plate from Carrie's hands and brought it into the house.

"This all looks delicious," Lisa said as they sat down together at the table. "Thanks again for having me over. I might even help with the dishes."

"You can't beat fresh food on the grill in the summer." Carrie took some potatoes and zucchini from one of the serving plates and passed it to Lisa. "I lost the bet, so I'll do the dishes, but you won't be so lucky next time. We'll have another contest and it'll be your turn to pay the price."

"I don't think so." Lisa smiled, happy to hear Carrie mention they might do this again. "Luck had nothing to do with it."

They settled into a relaxed silence while they enjoyed their meal. After seeing how easily Carrie had grilled their dinner, Lisa was curious to find out how she made everything taste so good.

"How do you take simple ingredients and give them such great flavor?" Lisa asked. "I grill vegetables at home and they don't taste like this at all."

"It's all about the spices. I've learned some techniques over the years that I'd be happy to show you."

Lisa's mind went in a different direction at the thought of Carrie showing her some techniques she'd learned.

"Does it bother you to talk about your breast cancer?" Carrie asked. "I'd like to know more about your treatment, but maybe you'd rather not discuss it. I don't want to ignore the whole topic if you do feel like talking about it."

"I don't mind talking about it." Lisa shrugged. "I don't know. I usually don't like telling people about it because I don't want them to feel sorry for me or make a big deal about it. I was lucky I had a very treatable form of cancer and I'm fine now."

"Did you have chemotherapy?"

"Yes, I used to have long hair, but now I kind of like it short."

"I love your hair. I think it suits you perfectly."

"Thanks." Lisa tried not to show how much Carrie's compliment meant to her, but she was going to remember those words. "I also had surgery and radiation. The chemotherapy was hard, but the radiation really wasn't bad."

"You seem to be doing great now."

"I really am. There were a lot of people I met while I was getting treatment who were so much worse off than me. It made me grateful for what I had."

Carrie nodded. "That's the case with a lot of things in life, isn't it?"

"For sure. I also had an amazing doctor at Mass General Hospital. She was one of those people you can tell are gifted and special when they walk in the room. She was brilliant, and I was really lucky to find her."

"Luck is all how you look at it, don't you think?"

"I'm definitely lucky in a lot of ways," Lisa agreed. "I was diagnosed right after my mother died. Compared to losing her, having cancer didn't seem to matter as much. It wasn't easy, but like I said, I feel like I'm back on track now."

"I don't even want to think about losing my mother." Carrie shook her head. "It must have been really tough. I'm glad you're doing so well."

"I try to stay in shape and watch what I eat so I'll stay healthy. I don't know if it makes much of a difference, but I figure it can't hurt."

"Your positive attitude must have helped you make it through some tough times during treatment." Carrie looked into Lisa's eyes. "I admire that you don't waste time feeling sorry for yourself."

Lisa tried to break her gaze away from Carrie's blue eyes. All she wanted to do was kiss Carrie's lips, but she knew she shouldn't be thinking about her friend like this.

Daisy yipped at the door, startling them both back to reality.

"I'd better let her out." Lisa stood up quickly. "It's getting kind of late. I should probably get going soon."

"Of course." Carrie pushed back her chair and stood up. "I didn't mean to keep you so long."

"You didn't keep me. This has been really nice, and I'd like to stay longer, but I do have to get up early tomorrow." Lisa carried her plate over to the sink. "Let me help you clear off these empty dishes."

Carrie met her at the sink with a stack of plates. "Don't worry. I've got this."

Lisa stepped back. "Thank you for dinner. It was wonderful."

"You're welcome. We'll have to do it again soon." Carrie walked Lisa to the door. "I'll check in with you about the dinner party and we can also figure out when to go running again."

Lisa's heart ached as she drove home with Daisy. She couldn't take much more of this feeling of being torn between longing for something she couldn't have with Carrie and worrying about whether she was opening herself up for heartbreak with Toni. She was going to have to figure out what to do.

CHAPTER SEVENTEEN

Lisa heard a knock and looked up from her computer. Mary was standing in her doorway holding a manila folder.

"Hello, Mary." Lisa was surprised to see her. Mary had never stopped by her office before.

"Hi, Lisa. Do you have a minute? Don wanted me to go over some information with you."

"Sure, come on in." Lisa was relieved Don had sent Mary rather than stopping by himself.

Mary walked in and took a seat in the chair across from her desk, smoothing the wrinkles from her skirt as she sat. She placed the folder she was carrying on Lisa's desk. "Here's the contact information for Poulin Lumber, which is one of the accounts I'm currently overseeing. Don wants you to take this one over since I have more accounts than I can handle at the moment. I'd be glad to have the help."

"That sounds interesting." Lisa knew the account could be affected by her job search. She wanted to think this over before she agreed to anything. It wouldn't be right to leave anyone in a bind if she took another job. She opened the folder and scanned through the listing of the client's information.

"Can you tell me a little more about this account?" Lisa asked. "Don mentioned I need to entertain clients and keep them happy if they get a little flirtatious, as he put it. Is that how you've had to handle Poulin Lumber?"

Mary blew out her breath through clenched teeth. "This is so exasperating. Our clients aren't like that. Don's the one you have to look out for."

"You don't have to deal with clients hitting on you?" It would be a major relief to know that wasn't something she would have to worry about.

"No, not at all." Mary leaned forward. "It sounds like you got the same talk from Don that I had, warning me about how I needed to keep our male clients happy and not be offended if they flirt. It was ridiculous."

"Then why would he say those things?"

"I think he wanted to see how you'd respond," said Mary. She looked over her shoulder into the hallway and lowered her voice. "He enjoys holding his power over people. He knows we want to move ahead, and I think he wants to see what we'll put up with."

"I know you told me there wasn't anything he'd done that you could document or repeat, but don't you want to stop him somehow?"

"He's always been basically harmless," Mary whispered. "When you asked me before if he ever made me uncomfortable, I didn't want to say too much because I wouldn't want to lose my job. I guess I'm used to putting up with his groping and disgusting comments. The thing is, even though he's a sleazy guy to work for, he's got such a good reputation I don't think anyone would believe me if I told them, and it isn't worth risking my job."

Lisa tried to contain her mounting anger. She didn't blame Mary for being too scared to do anything, but Don shouldn't be allowed to continue treating people this way, and she was going to do something about it. "Have you heard if he's done this to anyone else here?"

"A few women have mentioned problems with Don, but it isn't something we've ever discussed openly. I was right out of college when I started, and I've been here a while. This has never been the sort of place where people talk about their personal matters publicly."

"I'm just surprised no one has ever tried to report him to someone in the Portland office."

"I know one or two women who didn't put up with his harassment. He found ways to let them go. The Portland office is either clueless or they choose to ignore how he operates as long as the company is successful."

Lisa didn't want to go along with it. There wasn't much she could do at the moment to prove Don's harassment. She was going to have to work on finding a way. Meanwhile, she was more determined than ever to figure out what he was involved in with his brother and the sheriff.

* * *

Carrie hung up the phone and updated the list in her notebook. The details for the Mills' dinner party this coming weekend were coming together. She had lined up a couple of her friends to bartend, and she had contacted her supplier for the extra linens and dishes she would need. The menu was set and all the ingredients were ordered. She had been too busy organizing everything today to take a break and it was starting to get dark. Mondays were her day off, but she had spent most of the day getting things ready for the upcoming week.

The evening had gotten away from her. She had meant to check and see if Lisa wanted to go for a run, but it was getting too dark now. They would have to find time to run more often over the next few weeks to prepare for the 5K.

Carrie's mind drifted back to the day before. The more time they spent together, the more Carrie realized how many things she liked about Lisa that went beyond simple attraction. She knew there could be something special between them, and she had seen from the way Lisa looked at her, that sometimes she felt it too. The problem was, every time Carrie thought about pursuing more than friendship with her, she was reminded of how Lisa was involved with someone else. Maybe it was wishful thinking on her part, but she wanted Lisa to be all hers. She didn't want to pursue her if Lisa wasn't completely sure of her feelings. Carrie knew she wouldn't be able to share her with someone else.

She rose from the couch and stretched. This was usually a good time of day to go down to the lake and take a couple casts to see if the fish were biting. Her phone chimed, and she checked the screen.

"Hi Lisa," Carrie answered. "What's up?"

"Are you home?" Lisa asked in a panicked voice.

"Is everything all right?" Carrie was immediately concerned.

"Daisy got into it with a porcupine and I need some help."

"Hang on, I'll be right there."

Porcupines were common in the area and Carrie remembered their dogs tangling with them when she was growing up. It was still an ongoing problem for her brother. He and his wife had a Labrador who never learned his lesson and had to get quills removed at least once or twice each summer.

Carrie jumped in her Jeep and dialed her brother's number as she drove to Lisa's house. Hopefully Mike was home.

"Hello, sis," Mike answered.

"Mike, can you help me with a friend whose dog got quilled by a porcupine?"

"Sure. I'll bring my pliers and be right there."

Carrie gave him the address and pulled into Lisa's driveway. She didn't see anyone outside, so she knocked on the door. Lisa called for her to come in and she stepped into the entryway. "Lisa?"

"We're up here."

Carrie found Lisa sitting on the floor with Daisy next to the glass doors that opened to the deck. Carrie could see Daisy's black snout was bristling with white quills.

"Poor baby. How's she doing?"

"She won't let me touch her face. She was outside, and I

heard her start yelping and crying. I went running out and there she was. I never saw the porcupine."

Carrie patted Daisy gently and tried to take a look at her face. Daisy whined and rubbed at her nose with her paw, turning away from Carrie.

"My brother is on his way," Carrie said. "His dog isn't bright enough to learn his lesson and he's always going after porcupines. Mike's an expert at taking out quills."

"Thank you for coming and for calling your brother. I tried calling the vet, but the office is closed. The emergency vet clinic is open, but I'd need some help bringing her there. She keeps rubbing at her nose and crying."

"If my brother can't take care of it, I'd be happy to go with you." Carrie continued to pet Daisy calmly while they spoke. "We'll fix you, Daisy."

"Thank you so much. I owe you one."

A knock sounded on the door.

"There's Mike. I'll go let him in. I love your house, by the way."

Carrie returned a few minutes later with the male version of herself and she saw Lisa do a double take at their similarity. He was a little heavier than Carrie, but they were both tall and muscular with short, dark hair.

"This is my brother, Mike." Carrie knelt down next to Daisy and patted her. "These are my friends Lisa and Daisy."

"Hello, Mike," Lisa said. "I really appreciate you coming over like this."

"I don't mind at all," Mike said. "Let's see what we can do."

Mike had Lisa and Carrie hold Daisy down while he used the pliers to pluck out the quills, which were all over her snout and inside her lips. Daisy thrashed around miserably until finally they were done. They all sat back, hot and sweating, while Daisy ran over to her water dish to get a drink.

"That was horrible," Lisa said. "I don't know what I would have done without you guys. Let me get you a cold drink. Beer or water?"

"I'll take a beer, thanks," Mike said.

"Water for me, please." Carrie stood up. "I think I'll wash my hands too, if you don't mind."

"Of course, come on over."

Carrie and Mike washed up while Lisa got the drinks. Then they went out to the deck to cool off. The summer air was warm and comfortable. The only sound was the loons making their nightly calls out on the lake.

"God, I hope she never does that again," Lisa said with a sigh.

"Some dogs learn to stay away and some don't," Mike said. "My dog's too dumb. He sees a porcupine and chases it down every time. The problem is porcupines are really slow and it's easy for a dog to run right up to one."

"I'm so lucky that you came over," Lisa said.

"I heard Carrie had a new friend who lived near us." Mike grinned at his sister. "It's nice to meet you. We usually don't get introduced to her friends."

Carrie kicked him discreetly to make him be quiet.

"Yes, I met your parents yesterday when Carrie and I went running." Lisa smiled. "It's great to be meeting people around town. I really like it here in Winchester."

"Most of the people in town are friendly enough, once you get to know them," Mike said.

"I work for Don Mills. You must have known him and his brother in school."

"Yeah." Mike grimaced. "I never thought too much of those guys. They seemed a little disagreeable when we were growing up and they still are, if you ask me."

"That sounds like what Carrie told me," Lisa said. "So far, I've only met Don, and you're certainly right about him."

"I have to admit, the Mills brothers are good customers," Mike said. "I do appreciate their business, so I shouldn't say anything too bad about them."

"They come to you because you do good work and have fair prices," Carrie interjected. She explained to Lisa, "Mike has a service garage in Augusta."

"That's good to know if I ever need to have my car repaired."

"We'll take care of you," Mike said. "I'd be happy to work on your car any time. I bet you're a lot nicer to work for than Don and Bruce."

"You should just tell them you're busy," Carrie said.

"I can't complain," Mike said. "Don and Bruce have referred quite a few people to me over the years, including some big shots who don't mind spending money. They sent Senator Lawrence to my shop a while back and he's been a good customer ever since."

Lisa widened her eyes at Carrie before turning to Mike. "The Mills brothers had you work on Senator Lawrence's car?"

Mike nodded. "Bruce called me up and had me fit him in. I guess he hit a deer and dented the front bumper. He needed it fixed quickly. It was about a year ago."

"It's certainly an interesting coincidence," Carrie said to Lisa.

"What is?" Mike asked.

"We've just been wondering about Bruce Mills's connection to Senator Lawrence," Carrie said. "Bruce got a nice state contract for an office complex he's building in Augusta thanks to Senator Lawrence."

"If Bruce is friendly enough with Senator Lawrence that he'd help him get his car repaired, don't you think it's suspicious that Senator Lawrence awarded a big contract to Mills Building Construction?" Lisa asked.

"Exactly," Carrie replied. She didn't want to mention the payments in front of Mike, but she wondered if the car repairs were somehow tied in as well.

"You be careful," Mike said sternly. "I don't think the contract sounds suspicious, and I don't want you to get on his bad side by stirring things up. Bruce and his buddies could make things hard for you. I've seen him and Joe Michaud go after people who have crossed them. They're merciless."

"We're just curious, and we aren't going to say anything to anyone else." Carrie didn't want her brother to be worried, so she changed the subject. "Anyway, I'm glad you were home and you weren't working late when I called tonight."

"Speaking of which, I'd better get going. Thank you for the beer." Mike stood up. "Melissa is going to get ugly if I'm out too late."

"I'd better head home too," Carrie said. "We've all got to get up early tomorrow."

An exhausted Daisy stayed fast asleep in her bed while Lisa walked them downstairs and out to the driveway. Mike and Carrie stood next to their cars while they say goodbye.

"Thank you both so much for helping me." Lisa pulled Mike into a big hug. "I'm really grateful and I don't know what I would have done without you."

"I was happy to help," said Mike. "It's nice to finally meet a friend of Carrie's."

"You mentioned Carrie doesn't usually introduce you to her friends but I'm certainly glad that she introduced you to me." Lisa turned to Carrie. "How did I get so lucky? I guess we have Daisy to thank."

"Mike is just trying to stir things up. Ignore him." Carrie pushed Mike toward his truck before he embarrassed her any further. By the sound of it, her mother had probably told Mike how Carrie felt about Lisa, and Carrie didn't trust him to keep his mouth shut. Mike laughed and offered a wave before he drove away.

Carrie turned to Lisa. "Well, I guess I'll talk to you later."

Before Carrie could say anything else, Lisa pulled her close. She felt her heart pounding hard in her chest and hoped Lisa wouldn't notice. Carrie reached to put her arms around her and pressed against her for just a moment. Once she was in her arms, Carrie didn't want to let her go. She thought back to her earlier resolve of not pursuing things with Lisa if she had to share her with someone else. She wanted so much more with Lisa.

"Thank you," Lisa whispered in her ear.

Carrie pulled back and looked into Lisa's eyes. "You're welcome. Goodnight."

Lisa nodded wordlessly and stepped back toward the house.

Carrie left with a wave and walked to her Jeep, not trusting herself to speak.

CHAPTER EIGHTEEN

Lisa needed to check in with Rachel. Her situation was becoming clearer to her and she wanted to talk to her friend and get some advice. She needed to make some choices about whether she wanted to see how things would turn out with Toni, because if she did, then she needed to set better boundaries for herself with Carrie. It was getting too hard to have these feelings for both of them, and it wasn't fair to anyone.

She glanced at her phone screen and saw she'd missed a text. She opened up the message and saw it was from Toni, asking her if she wanted to get together this upcoming weekend. She decided to call Toni back and speak with her in person rather than via text. They hadn't found any time to talk since Lisa had visited on Saturday, and she wanted to make sure Toni's daughter was all right, among other things. She dialed Toni's number, hoping to catch her in between classes.

"Hello there," Toni answered.

"Hi. I got your message and I was wondering how you and Amelia are doing?"

"We're both good, thanks. She was feeling fine after I texted you on Sunday. Apparently, she just had a little flu bug."

"That's good to hear. I'm glad you didn't catch it too." Lisa wanted to have a talk with Toni about their relationship, and she didn't want to do it over the phone. "Listen, I know you're busy at school and can't talk right now, but I was calling to find out if we could get together on Friday night."

"That would be perfect. I want to make up for lost time. I'm singing at a place in Rockland, so maybe we can meet there?"

"Sure, I'd love to hear you sing again." Lisa had been hoping they would be able to talk privately, but there probably wouldn't be time before Toni's show. It would be fun to go hear her sing and they would have a chance to talk afterward.

"Can you stay over? You can drop off Daisy at the house if you want."

"Sorry, but I can't. I promised a friend I'd help her with a catering job on Saturday and I need to be there early in the morning."

"Helping your lovely friend Carrie, by any chance?"

"Yes."

"My plans to get you alone keep getting thwarted. Should I be jealous that you'd rather work with Carrie than stay up late with me?"

"It's not that I don't want to stay, but I'd already said that I would help and it's going to be a long day." Lisa felt a stab of guilt, which was exactly why her feelings toward Carrie weren't fair to Toni. "Maybe you can come over on Sunday and we could go kayaking?"

"That sounds good. I have to get going now, but I'll send you the address of the place for Friday night, okay?"

"Okay. I'll talk to you later."

Lisa dialed Rachel's number next.

"Hi Lisa," Rachel answered. "Sorry I didn't call you back yesterday."

"No big deal," Lisa said. "I just wanted to see if we could get together some night for dinner."

"I'd love to. I'm busy tomorrow, but how about the next night?"

"Sounds great, I'll see you then."

Lisa decided to check and see if anyone was around. She had some work she needed to get done, but Don had an offsite meeting scheduled and the office was quiet today. She took a quick walk down the empty corridor and noticed there were only a few people at their desks. Everyone would be going home soon, so this could be a good time to stay late and see if she could do a little exploring in Don's office. She heard voices approaching and looked around the corner of the reception area. She was dismayed to see him walking toward his office with another man. He had returned earlier than expected. She was hoping he wouldn't come back to the office after his meeting. Now she would have to try to find another opportunity.

* * *

The lunch crowd was long gone, and it was still a little early for people to come in for dinner, so the café was quiet. Angie and Ryan were outside taking a well-deserved break while Carrie worked on one of her ingredient lists.

Even though the money was good, and it would be good for business, she was almost wishing she hadn't agreed to take the catering job. She hadn't had a spare minute all week, and Leanne Mills treated her like an indentured servant every time she talked to her. She would need to overlook Leanne's attitude and just get through the weekend.

Ryan and Angie came back into the kitchen and Carrie turned to greet them. "Hey guys. Are you able to keep an eye on things here during dinnertime on Saturday while I'm working over at the Mills's house?"

"We will definitely be able to handle things here," Angie said. "We were just talking about how we're glad we don't have be at the party."

"Bruce Mills and his buddy Joe Michaud are two of the biggest jerks in town," Ryan said. "I can't stand either of them."

"Me either," Angie said. "I don't want to have to wait on them at the party."

"No way," Ryan agreed. "It's different here at the café, not like being in someone's house."

"Why the hostility?" Carrie asked.

"Michaud's given both of us a hard time before," Ryan said. "He's the kind of guy who gets off on showing you he's in charge. He likes to do things like pull people over for no reason and bust them."

"I've never been pulled over by him," Carrie said. "Maybe he hasn't noticed me."

"Whatever the reason, you're lucky he hasn't stopped you," Angie said. "He pulled our friend Rich over, and he didn't like the way Rich spoke back to him, so he busted him for drug possession even though Rich didn't have anything on him."

"Yeah," Ryan chimed in. "Michaud planted some pills in his car and it was his word against Rich's."

"I have heard some rumors like that about Michaud," Carrie said. "I guess I'd better be careful around him. I hope they like the food this weekend or I could be in trouble."

"Seriously," Ryan said. "You have to watch yourself around those guys."

The front door opened, and Lisa appeared.

"Hi there."

Lisa greeted her with a smile. "Hi."

Lisa's hug from the night before had been on Carrie's mind all day. It would be nice if they start hugging each other more often, just to be friendly.

"I wanted to stop by and thank you again for helping me with Daisy last night. I just checked on her before I came here and she's doing fine today. You can't even tell the quills were there."

"I'm glad she's all right. Mike can be pretty handy to have around at times."

"Mike is awesome and he's gorgeous, too. He looks just like you."

"Well, thank you." Carrie smiled. She was flattered by Lisa's indirect compliment and she wasn't sure how to respond. "I'm not going to tell him you said that. He's already got a big enough ego."

Carrie watched with surprise as Lisa gave an embarrassed laugh and blushed.

"So, how's the dinner party coming along?"

"We're in decent shape." Carrie was happy to change the subject and ease Lisa's obvious discomfort. "I've got a lot of things to do this week to get ready, but I think it should be fine."

"I'm planning to come here Saturday morning and help out. You still want me to serve that night, right?"

"As long as you don't mind, I'd love an extra pair of hands. Thank you."

"I'm glad I can be useful. I hope you don't change your mind about my helpfulness when you see my waitressing skills."

"I'm sure you'll be great at it. If you're not, I'll just have you wash dishes."

"Uh, okay, I guess. That will be a good motivator to make sure I don't mess up."

"I'm sure you won't mess anything up." Carrie leaned on the counter. "Are you hungry? I can make you something."

"Only if you sit with me and have something too. I bet you haven't taken a break all day."

"There's so much to do that I should probably keep working." Carrie looked around at the empty tables. "But I guess it's slow right now, so a break wouldn't hurt."

"Good, you can keep me company and relax for a few minutes."

"Why don't you go find our table and I'll make us some dinner?"

Carrie brought two veggie wraps out to the dining room a few minutes later and found Lisa waiting at the table near the window. Carrie set the plates down and took a seat next to her.

"I thought these would be good on a hot night."

"A perfect choice." Lisa picked hers up and took a bite. "Very tasty, thank you."

"What do you eat when you don't come here?"

"I'm extremely lazy," Lisa answered. "I usually have a salad or a sandwich. I try eat healthy, but I don't do a lot of cooking."

"That sounds kind of pathetic. You should come here more often."

"You're right, I should. You know, when I met you I thought you were kind of intimidating. Now I know you're actually very sweet."

"Why did you think I was intimidating?" Carrie was surprised. She liked meeting people and tried to be friendly with all of her customers.

"I don't know, exactly. I guess because you're tall and quiet. At least I thought you seemed quiet when I first met you. You're also very intense when you're working."

"I can be intense." Carrie laughed. "But I'm not quiet."

"No, you're not, but you certainly aren't a loudmouth, either. What did you think of me when we first met?"

Carrie looked into Lisa's eyes. "I thought you were very pretty and I was impressed by how knowledgeable you were when you helped me with my taxes."

"Thank you," Lisa said softly, returning Carrie's gaze.

Ryan walked by their table. "Are you all set over here?"

"Yes, thanks, Ryan." Carrie took another bite of her sandwich and looked out the window at a boat going by. "Ryan and Angie were telling me about a friend of theirs who had a run-in with Sheriff Michaud. They said he planted some drugs on the kid and arrested him."

"You've got to be kidding. How would he get away with something like that?"

"I'm sure it would have been hard for the kid to prove it wasn't his. It's an important reminder for us. We need to be really careful when we look for information about the contracts."

"It also shows these guys need to be stopped. They shouldn't be able to get away with whatever they want. I was talking to one of the ladies in the office about Don yesterday."

"What did she say?"

"From what she told me, Don has been harassing some of the women who work for him for years. She said she puts up with it because other women who complained have lost their jobs."

Carrie shook her head in disgust. "I really can't stand that man. I'm glad you're applying for a new job and I'll do whatever I can to help you stop him."

"I would love to stop him, but we have to find some solid proof. I was hoping to look around his office this evening, but he was still there when I left."

"Please be careful. I don't even want to think about what would happen if Don caught you snooping in his office. He'd have Joe arrest you in a heartbeat and plant whatever evidence they wanted."

"I'm being extremely careful. I'm only going to look around if I'm certain it's safe." Lisa touched Carrie's hand. "I'm hoping we get a chance to look around at Bruce Mills's house this weekend. He probably has a home office and maybe I can take a peek."

"Take a peek? Did you hear what I said about Joe Michaud? If he caught you sneaking into Bruce's office, we'd both be in big trouble because you'd be there working for me."

"Don't worry. I'm not going to sneak around. I'll just take a quick look if the chance arises. I'll be very careful not to do anything if anyone is around. I would never want to get you in trouble."

"That sounds like a very sketchy plan. I don't think it's a good idea."

"Well, then I'll try to think of a better plan. This could be our best chance to find out what's going on."

"Okay." Carrie relented for the moment with a sigh. The restaurant was starting to fill up with diners, so she stood up. "I'd better get back to work."

"Thank you for the delicious dinner. Since Daisy was fine when I checked on her, there's no rush to get home. I might hang out here for a little while."

"Okay, I'll see you later." Carrie picked up their empty plates and carried them back to the kitchen. Life was getting more and more complicated. Not only was she stressed about preparing the meal for the upcoming dinner party, but now she was going to have to make sure she kept an eye on Lisa so she didn't put herself in danger.

Lisa sat back quietly and observed the other diners for a few moments. It was nice to recognize some familiar faces from around town and not feel like such a stranger. She looked out over the lake and tried to think of a good plan for searching Bruce Mills's office this weekend. It would probably make sense to come up with a better plan for searching Don's office too. Waiting for everyone to leave at night didn't seem to be working. Maybe she should go into the office early before everyone got there.

She supposed it was time to head home. She was embarrassed about blurting out to Carrie that she thought she was gorgeous. Carrie's beauty wasn't the first thing she had noticed about her, but now that they were friends, Lisa thought Carrie was absolutely beautiful—inside and out.

She stopped at the counter to say goodbye. Carrie was putting a dessert tray into the bakery case and the entryway was empty for the moment.

"Thanks again for dinner. It was wonderful as always."

Carrie turned around and saw her. "Thanks for coming by."

Last night's hug had gone well, so Lisa thought she'd try it again. Hopefully she wasn't being annoying. Leaning forward, she put her arms around Carrie and gave her a quick squeeze. She felt Carrie's strong arms pull her closer. Lisa tried not to gasp as she felt Carrie press against her for a brief moment of contact.

Carrie dropped her arms and stepped back. "Goodnight."

"Goodnight." Lisa walked out the door in a daze, wondering if there was any way she could get Carrie to be interested in her. There was also the question of what she should do about her attraction to Toni and whether she should pursue a relationship with her.

She really needed some advice from Rachel.

CHAPTER NINETEEN

A shrill alarm woke Lisa from a deep sleep early the next morning. Forcing herself to get up, she pulled back the covers and slid out of bed. Daisy opened one eye to check things out and promptly went back to sleep.

She was planning to get to the office well before her colleagues arrived. If anyone questioned why she was there, she would say she had a lot of work to do and couldn't sleep so she came in early.

Awake and alert after showering and having a bowl of cereal, she headed to her office in Augusta, formulating a plan of attack while she drove. The lights were off in the building and there were no other cars in the lot, so she was alone. She wasn't often the first to arrive. Usually the door would be unlocked, and the alarm would be off. There had been a couple times during tax season when she'd had to use her key to get in, so thankfully she was familiar with the process of disarming the alarm. Glancing up at the security camera in the entryway, she opened the door and turned on the lights as she walked into the office.

Carefully covering her tracks in case someone else came in early, she went to her office first and powered up her computer. She took out some files she had been working on and made sure it looked like she was busy. Double-checking her phone was in her pocket, she walked down the hallway and past the reception area to Don's office. His door was shut, but she breathed a sigh of relief when she tried the knob and it wasn't locked.

She swung the door open and turned on the lights. She had debated putting on gloves like a detective in a crime show, but she'd decided that would be a little over the top. If it came down to checking for fingerprints, hers were already all over the office anyway. Her heart was pounding as she cautiously looked around the room.

The desk was in the back with shelves mounted on the wall behind it. Large windows took up the wall to the right of the desk and the wall to the left was lined with bookcases. The most likely place to find anything of interest would probably be the desk, so she checked there first.

Don had a large picture of his wife on one of the shelves behind the desk along with an assortment of photos of his children and other family members. She looked at his wife's photo with sympathy. It would certainly be miserable to be married to someone like him. The thought of it made her cringe.

She took a seat in his overstuffed leather chair while she scanned the top of the desk. His laptop was sitting there, but since she didn't know his password, there wasn't much point in trying to get into it. She paged through the papers in a tray he had on the side of the blotter and didn't see anything other than routine office communications. She lifted up his blotter and spotted a few sticky notes tucked underneath. Carefully lifting the large pad out of the way, she took out her phone and took some close-up photos of the notes, making sure she caught everything.

He had written down a few different passwords on the notes and placed them there for safekeeping. She was surprised the head of the company would leave his passwords lying around unsecured. He was supposed to be using password manager software, but it was good news for her that he hadn't bothered to be more careful.

She checked the time on her phone. She wasn't sure when people might start arriving, so she needed to hurry if she was going to be able to search everywhere. She would have to see if there was time later to try any of the passwords on the laptop.

The top drawer of the desk contained an assortment of miscellaneous pens and office supplies, nothing she cared about. One of the side drawers revealed a wooden box when she slid it open. She lifted up the cover and saw a shiny Smith and Wesson revolver. That was interesting, but not what she was looking for. The drawer below it contained a bottle of scotch. Definitely not what she was looking for.

The large file drawer on the other side of the desk was locked. She scanned the room, wondering where he might have put the key. He wasn't very cautious about his passwords, so maybe he left the key laying around in one of the other drawers. She opened the top drawer and looked more thoroughly, but she didn't find it there or in the other drawers.

Turning around to examine the shelves behind her, she looked behind some of the photos and books and still couldn't find the key. *Where could it be?* Running out of ideas, she glanced around and tried to think where she would hide a key. As she settled back into the plush seat, she had an idea. She knelt down to take a look underneath the chair.

"Yes," she whispered as she spotted a key sticking out of a slot under one of the arms. Slipping the key out of its hiding place, she tried opening the locked drawer. The key slid into the lock and turned easily. She pulled open the drawer to reveal a row of files, which were organized into large hanging folders.

There wasn't going to be time to look at all the files, so she took several pictures and tried to capture any files with labels. A folder titled "Employees" caught her attention, and she pulled the files out to look at them.

Each of the files was labeled with a different female employee's name. She spotted the one with her name and opened it first. It contained her employment application along with notes Don had taken. The first page of notes included a detailed description of the encounter she'd had with him when they discussed possible interaction with male clients. His notes were carefully worded to avoid anything incriminating. This documentation of their conversations was clearly in place to protect him from any accusations she might make about his inappropriate behavior.

The second page of notes was much more disturbing. He had written up a profile of her physical description including her height, weight, and his guess at her bra size. His guesses were surprisingly close. The description was followed by comments he'd made of their conversations. The day he'd talked to her about entertaining clients he'd written, "*She walked in front of me and I grabbed her ass and slid my fingers in. I know she liked it. Will try again soon.*"

Lisa felt a wave of revulsion as she read the next comment, "*Discussed entertainment and I was hard as a rock. I got off right in front of her while she sat there talking. Next time I might let her see.*"

Don's words were so disgusting she didn't even want to touch the paper. Using her phone, she captured images of the notes in her file and then paged through the other files as quickly as she could, taking as many photos as possible. She didn't recognize many of the names other than Mary's, and she didn't have time to read the comments that were contained in each of them, but they appeared to follow a similar format to the ones in her own file.

She opened the last file and was shocked to see several pages of photographs of women from the office, including herself.

The photos were captured in different areas of the office. Some appeared to have come from the security cameras located at the entrance and in the hallways near the reception area. There were also many photos from the women's bathroom along with other photos, which must have been taken by a hidden camera in his office. He had managed to isolate and enlarge various shots of each of the women.

The women from the security cameras were all clothed, so the photos were not particularly revealing, although it was disturbing to see herself in a few of them. The women were completely unaware and vulnerable in the shots that showed their faces along with their cleavage and crotches. She recognized a favorite pair of pants that showed up in one of the close-up crotch shots.

More concerning where the photos from the women's bathroom. He hadn't taken pictures from inside the bathroom stalls, thankfully, but he had managed to hide a camera in the main area by the sinks. These were an appalling invasion of privacy. The camera had captured shots of women adjusting and changing their clothing. While none of the women were nude, there were some photos of women in their bras. The women that were fully clothed were unknowingly being photographed while they touched up their hair and makeup and did other personal grooming that Don had no right to observe.

The camera in his office had captured much more intimate photos. It had been set up to take photos at a direct angle from the base of the desk where the visitor's chair sat, up toward the seat of the chair. Lisa imaged that when a female employee sat down across from him, he adjusted the camera from his computer under the guise that he was reading something on his screen.

These pictures enabled him to see up the legs of any woman that sat or stood at his desk wearing a dress or skirt. Lisa glanced through the revealing photos of unsuspecting women wearing various types of underwear from thongs to lace panties. Thankfully, the women's faces weren't visible in the photos. Lisa breathed a sigh of relief that she had always worn pants to work.

Lisa captured shots of the photos with her phone before putting everything carefully back in the drawer. She began flipping through the rest of the folders and she felt her adrenaline surge as she spotted one labeled "Lawrence" near the back of the drawer. Pulling the folder out of the drawer excitedly, she looked at the files inside. The first was a file with a repair bill for work done at Michael Sawyer's garage. She paged through the papers in the rest of the files, snapping pictures with her phone as quickly as she could. She wouldn't be able to read through everything now, but she should be able to see it all clearly from the pictures. It was time for her to wrap things up and get out, so she closed the files and put them back in the drawer.

Checking to make sure all the folders were neatly in place, she closed the drawer and locked it. She was kneeling down to slide the key back into place when she heard the sound of the door slamming shut in the silent office. She stood up and looked around frantically. As far as she could tell, everything was exactly where she had found it. She hustled over to the door and stepped out into the hall. Just as she eased the door shut and stepped away from his office, she heard someone coming down the hall toward her.

"Lisa, you're here early," a voice said behind her.

She turned and saw one of the receptionists. "Good morning, Denise. I couldn't get back to sleep so I figured I'd come in and get caught up on some work."

"What are you doing down here? Are you looking for something?"

"I thought I heard someone come in a little while ago and I came to see who it was. It turns out I must have been hearing things because I don't think anyone else is actually here."

Hoping her explanation didn't sound too ridiculous, she smiled at Denise and tried to think of something to say. "You're an early bird yourself, I see."

"Yes," Denise said, straightening her shoulders proudly. "I'm usually the first one here."

"Well I'm glad because I didn't like being alone in the office. It made me kind of nervous. That's probably why I thought I heard something."

"Sometimes the air-conditioning makes funny noises. Maybe that's what you heard."

Relieved that Denise didn't seem suspicious, she nodded. "That must have been it."

She walked back to her office and collapsed into her chair. The stress of her morning search had been worth it. The information she had found in Don's files should provide strong evidence when she was ready to expose his harassment.

She couldn't wait to tell Carrie about her adventure and show her the photos from the Lawrence files.

CHAPTER TWENTY

Carrie took a pan of muffins from the oven just as her phone rang. "Good morning."

"Hi Carrie," Lisa said. "You won't believe where I've been this morning."

"Hmm, let's see. Did it involve Don Mills?"

"How'd you guess?" Lisa lowered her voice. "I finally got a chance to look around in his office this morning. I came in early before anyone was here."

"I guessed because I know how determined you are to get him. That sounds like an awfully risky thing to do. What if you had gotten caught?"

"I was careful, and I had some excuses prepared. Anyway, I want to show you the pictures of the files I took. Do you have any time to get together this afternoon or before dinner? I'm going to be home by three."

"I'm pretty busy, but I do want to see what you found." Carrie thought about her schedule for a moment. "Why don't I meet you for a run at three and you can show me the pictures after?"

"That sounds good and I suppose a run isn't a bad idea, either. I'll meet you at your place."

Carrie hung up and got back to work, but thoughts of Lisa kept interfering. She remembered the way it had felt to pull her close for a moment last night. It was getting harder to hold back from telling Lisa how she felt. She kept coming back to her previous conclusion: if Lisa were truly interested in her, then she wouldn't be dating someone else. It was that simple. Carrie knew Lisa cared about her, and lately the feeling had been getting stronger, so why was she still seeing Toni?

* * *

Lisa was sitting on Carrie's porch steps waiting when the Jeep pulled in and parked next to Lisa's car. Daisy went running over to greet her.

"Hi there," Lisa called.

"Thanks for meeting at my house," Carrie said. "Looks like you're all ready to go. Come on in while I get changed and I'll be right with you."

"I'll wait out here with Daisy. She was playing in the lake and she's all wet."

Carrie came back out a few minutes later wearing the shirt and shorts Lisa had given her.

"Wow, you look great." Lisa stood up from the porch steps to take a closer look. "Those shorts fit perfectly."

"Thanks. They're very comfortable and this shirt is nice and light."

Lisa hadn't realized how form-fitting the shorts and shirt were going to be. She didn't want to make Carrie self-conscious by gawking at her, but she looked so good it was hard not to stare. She leaned down and reached for her toes, stretching out her legs and getting ready for their run.

From her upside-down viewpoint, she watched as Carrie flexed her arms and began to reach her palms down to the ground, loosening up her calves and hamstrings. They ran through a few different stretches together, warming up their legs in preparation for the run.

Carrie straightened up. "I guess we'd better get going."

"Right." Lisa gave her quads one last stretch before releasing her grip on her ankle and falling into place beside Carrie.

They headed toward Lisa's house with Daisy trotting along beside them in the shady ditch along the side of the road. The day was overcast, so the temperature was slightly cooler than the last time they'd gone running together. The light breeze blowing off the lake felt good as they ran along.

"So, tell me about this morning," Carrie said.

"I'll try to talk and run at the same time. If I hyperventilate, it's your fault."

"It must have been pretty nerve-racking to sneak into Don's office."

"You've got that right."

She told Carrie about finding the key to the locked drawer and gave her all the details about the contents of the files she had found and the pictures she had taken.

"Taking pictures with your phone was a good idea."

"Yes, I think it worked well. I haven't had a chance to look at them very carefully yet, but I think I got some good ones. I'm going to see if I can get into Don's email account with one of the passwords I found. I wouldn't expect he kept anything too revealing in his work email, but I still want to check it. He may also have a personal account on Gmail or another site, but it could be hard to find without knowing the email address."

"I'm sure it would be great to find something on Don, but are you sure you want to hack into his email account?"

"Carrie, you should see some of the things he says in his notes." Lisa slowed down for a minute. "We need to take this guy down."

"I'm just worried he'll take you down if you get caught."

They continued down the road and came to one of the more challenging hills. Lisa couldn't talk and run up the steep incline at the same time, so she waited until they reached the top and caught her breath.

"I was petrified this morning, but I was very cautious. It's worth the risk because we know there's something illegal going on, and we've got to find more evidence."

Lisa's road came into view. They reached her house and turned around to start heading back the way they came. Lisa was surprised how quickly they had made it to the halfway point. She didn't feel like she was going to collapse at any moment like she'd felt the last time they'd run. It was empowering to feel how she was improving.

"The Lawrence folder could be just what we're looking for," Carrie said as they ran along the gravel road. "Was there anything good in it?"

"I haven't checked the pictures yet because I wanted us to look at it together. If you want to, that is."

"Of course I want to. You know I'll help you any way I can."

Lisa did know. Carrie was the kind of friend she could count on, which was why she needed to be careful not to keep throwing herself at her and risk losing their friendship.

They made their way back to Carrie's house and Lisa stopped in the driveway, gasping for breath. Daisy ran happily to the water and waded in.

Carrie walked over to the porch. "I'll go get us a couple drinks of water."

Lisa flopped onto the steps to wait for her.

Carrie came back and passed her a glass. "Are you going to jump in the lake?"

"I wasn't sure if we had time." Lisa took a long drink from her glass. "When do you have to get back to work?"

"There's definitely time for a quick dip." Carrie took off her shoes and headed for the shoreline. She jogged out onto the dock and dove in.

Lisa quickly took off her sneakers and socks and followed Carrie's lead. She dove into the cool, refreshing water and swam up to the surface near Carrie.

"This feels fantastic," Lisa said. "Too bad we don't have time for any contests today."

"I don't know about that. How about I race you back to the porch? The winner gets to pick something the loser has to do."

"Like what?"

Carrie started swimming toward the dock. "Better hurry up."

"Wait a minute." Lisa started swimming after her. "You didn't say to go."

She had almost caught up with Carrie by the time she reached the dock, but Carrie was faster getting out of the water and easily beat her running up the dock to the porch.

"You tricked me." Lisa leaned against the railing to catch her breath.

"Did not." Carrie stood in the doorway with a smile. "Now I'm going to have to think of something good I want you to do."

Lisa looked up at Carrie and their eyes met. Lisa was struck by how blue Carrie's eyes were with her wet hair slicked back away from her face. Her skin tingled as she thought about what she wanted Carrie to have her do. Carrie's gaze stayed locked on Lisa's for another moment before she looked away.

"I'll have to give it a little more thought." Carrie turned to go inside. "I'd better take a quick shower before we look at the pictures. Make yourself at home and I'll be back in a couple minutes."

Lisa checked on Daisy, grabbed her bag from her car and went inside to change. Seated at the table a short time later, Lisa plugged in her laptop so she could get the pictures ready to show Carrie. Her phone was synced with Google Photos, so they would be able to go online and look at them. Carrie came downstairs a few minutes later, dressed in khaki shorts and a light summer shirt.

"Are you all set?" Lisa asked. "I've got the pictures ready."

"I have to be back at the café in about half an hour." Carrie sat down at the table next to Lisa. "Let's see what you've got."

They started looking through the images on the screen. The first few shots showed the sticky notes under the blotter with random phrases scribbled on them.

"I really want to see if I can get into Don's email," Lisa said. "I don't think anyone would ever find out it was me."

"I just don't want you to get in trouble. If you found something incriminating, what would you do? If you turned him in, wouldn't you be in trouble for getting into his email?"

"I guess it would depend on what I found. We'd have to think of a way to get the information to the police, not the sheriff's department, of course. Maybe I'd send it anonymously to the state police. His reputation would be shot even if I didn't come forward to press charges."

"I'm not surprised he's got a gun in his desk," Carrie commented when she saw the photo of the revolver in the drawer.

Lisa came to the photos from the Employees folder. She showed Carrie the pictures she had taken of the file with her information and watched as Carrie read Don's comments.

"Oh my God," Carrie murmured, staring at the picture. "You told me what happened but reading his disgusting notes about it makes me sick. The man is a perverted pig and I'm so sorry he went anywhere near you."

"I think he made the first page of notes to cover himself in case anyone reports him," Lisa said. "The second page of notes must be for his personal enjoyment."

Lisa showed Carrie the photos she had taken of the other women's files. They glanced through them silently.

"Don't you think this would be enough to expose Don?" Carrie asked.

"Probably. But now we know about the bribes and contract with Senator Lawrence, I think we should try to uncover what's going on, so they don't get away with it."

"I wouldn't want them to get away with it, but I don't want Don to keep doing this to you or to anyone else in your office."

"It won't be hard to hold him off while we keep looking for a little while. I can put up with him for now."

"I told you before I'd help you any way I can," Carrie said. "He needs to be stopped."

"Wait, there's more." Lisa showed Carrie the photos of all the women Don had saved in the file.

"The guy's a sicko, and he's also a peeping Tom. The pictures in the hallway are creepy, but not as bad as the ones in the ladies' room. The pictures that he took up women's skirts of their crotches are awful. How mortifying."

Lisa pointed out the pictures she was in. "Those are the only ones of me. Thankfully, I have never worn a dress or skirt to the office and I never changed my clothes in the bathroom."

"I'm glad he didn't get any of you in his office, but I still don't like him looking at you—at all."

"I know. It's weird and disturbing. Even though everyone is fully dressed, it feels so intrusive."

"It's really cool you're brave enough to try and do something to stop him. I just don't want anything to happen to you. The more we find out about Don, the worse it gets."

"Let's keep looking. Here are the pictures from the Lawrence file."

Carrie pointed to the image of the receipt from her brother's garage. "We should try to find out why Don and Bruce would have taken care of car repairs for Lawrence."

"Maybe something happened around that date." Lisa enlarged the photo so she could look at it more closely. "It looks like Mike did the work in June of last year. I can do some online research and see if I find anything."

"Good idea." Carrie clicked through the other pictures.

"These look like the files I already found with dates and payment amounts." Lisa pointed to images of spreadsheets as they came up on the laptop screen. "I'm not sure what these other files are referencing, but they look like payment schedules too."

"Here's a memo about another contract Bruce Mills's company is trying to get." Carrie stopped to examine one of the photos. "They're discussing the contract with Lawrence and he says here he's going to assist them. It's for a new school in Augusta."

"That can't be legal, right? Still, this doesn't seem like enough proof of any specific wrongdoing."

"Hmm, here are some dollar amounts listed with the names of several construction companies, including Mills Building Construction." Carrie pointed to a picture of another spreadsheet. "This could be a list of the bids for the job and you can see Mills is nowhere near the lowest bid."

"Wow, this could be great information. I'm going to go back over this again later and take a closer look at everything. Maybe I'll be able to figure out what some of the accounts are on the payment schedules. I also think Mike's invoice is important."

"I think so, too. Mike might get upset if I ask him about it again because he doesn't want us to antagonize Joe Michaud or the Mills brothers, but you could be on to something with the date." Carrie sat back from the table. "You did a great job getting all this information."

"I don't know how we'd be able to get it to the police without revealing the fact I broke into Don's locked desk drawer."

"We have a lot of things to think about."

"You probably should get going." Lisa shut down the laptop and closed the cover. "I didn't mean to keep you so long."

They stood up and went to the door. Carrie held it open for Lisa and followed her out to the driveway. Lisa called to Daisy and she came running over to Carrie.

"We probably won't get another chance to go running this week," Lisa said. "You're busy at the café and I'll be busy the next couple nights too."

"What are your plans?" Carrie asked, reaching down to pet Daisy.

"I'm meeting Rachel for dinner tomorrow night." Lisa hesitated before continuing. "Then I'm going to see Toni sing in Rockland on Friday night."

"That sounds fun." Carrie walked briskly to her car. "I guess I'll see you on Saturday, if you still want to help."

"Yes, of course I still want to help. I'll be there Saturday morning."

"See you then." Carrie gave a quick wave as she drove off.

Lisa watched her go and wondered once again if there was any chance Carrie would ever want to be more than friends. She didn't seem to show any reaction when Lisa mentioned she'd be meeting Toni on Friday. Even though Carrie didn't seem to care, Lisa knew she couldn't go on spending time with Carrie and seeing Toni.

Back in college she had thought Toni would be the perfect match for her. She had a lot of special memories of those days and it was amazing how they had finally gotten together. Toni had so much going for her. She was beautiful, talented, and charismatic. The problem was, the closer she got to Carrie, the more she didn't feel right about continuing her relationship with Toni. Lisa was definitely attracted to her and spending time with Toni was intoxicating. On the other hand, she wasn't sure she would ever be able to depend on her. She had the nagging doubt in her mind that Toni's interest was fickle, and she was going to move on to the next person who caught her attention.

Lisa wasn't the same person she was back in college, and her idea of the perfect match had changed. She needed more than just physical attraction. She wanted someone she could trust and depend on. Someone like Carrie, but that brought her back to the same fact she'd been trying to face for weeks: Carrie did not want her.

She knew she was falling for Carrie, even if it meant she'd end up alone.

CHAPTER TWENTY-ONE

Carrie leaned against the counter and waved as one of her regulars left with their coffee and muffin in hand. The café was empty, and she was caught up for the moment. The morning rush had kept her too busy to think about Lisa and the pictures from Don's office.

Last night when she was trying to get to sleep, Carrie hadn't been able to stop her mind from dwelling on her feelings for Lisa. She didn't want to think about it anymore. She was tired of the whole thing. If Lisa wanted to date Toni, then Carrie was going to take a step back. She didn't want to be a second choice for anyone and Lisa seemed to have chosen Toni first.

The files from Don's office had also been on Carrie's mind. She had told Lisa she would help her, and she meant it. Lisa didn't realize how dangerous it could be if the Mills brothers or Joe Michaud found out they were investigating the three of them. Carrie and Lisa needed to be very careful, especially Saturday night at the dinner party. It was sure to be a busy night, but Carrie was going to try and keep an eye on Lisa. Even if they weren't together, Carrie was still going to watch out for her since Carrie didn't believe Lisa was being cautious enough.

Ryan came in through the back door. "Good morning."

"Hi Ryan. It looks like things have slowed down for now. I think I'm going to head home for a bit and come back around lunchtime. I need to make some calls and check on things for this weekend. Are you and Angie going to be all set here?"

"You bet," Ryan answered. "Anything you need me to do while it's quiet?"

"I've got a punch list of all the things we need to work on over there on the counter. If you have time, you can pick something."

"Okay," Ryan said.

Carrie took off her apron and hung it on the rack out back. "Thanks, see you later."

The sky was blue and cloudless, and the birds were chirping as she walked to her Jeep. She ought to be feeling happy on such a nice day, but instead she was feeling lonely and depressed. She started driving toward her house and decided to stop in and say hello to her mother on the way.

Carrie pulled into her parents' driveway and parked next to her mother's car. When she walked into the kitchen, she found her mother sitting at the table drinking a cup of coffee.

"Good morning," Susan greeted her. "How are you, sweetheart?"

Carrie sat down next to her. "I'm headed home to make a few calls and I thought I'd stop and see what was going on."

"Your father just left. He'll be sorry he missed you. Are you all ready for the dinner party Saturday night?"

"It should be fine." Carrie sat quietly for a moment, wanting to tell her mother what was going on with Lisa but not sure how to bring the subject up.

"How is your friend, Lisa? She seemed very nice the other day when you stopped by."

"Yes, she is nice. We get along great and I really care about her, but I don't think she's the one for me because she's still seeing someone else."

"Remember what we talked about before?" Susan asked. "Did you ever let her know how you feel?"

"Not exactly. I can't help thinking if she cared about me she wouldn't want to be with anyone else. I was waiting to see what happened and I've gotten sick and tired of it."

"That's too bad, sweetie. You know, sometimes you hide your feelings too much. It makes things hard for you and it makes it hard on the other person as well. Like we talked about before, I think if Lisa knew you were interested, it might change things for her."

"I'm just feeling kind of lonely all of a sudden and I don't know why. I've got a full life with a great family and lots of good friends."

"You've been working too hard lately," her mother said. "I hope you can slow down after this party and enjoy yourself a little more."

"I like working hard, but maybe after this party, I'll find something fun to do." Carrie stood up to go. "I'd better get moving."

"Please don't forget what we've been talking about. It might be worth it to put yourself out there so Lisa knows how you feel. I hate to see you so upset."

"I'm not sure how she feels, and I can't let myself go until I know. She's going on a date tomorrow night, in fact."

"I'm sorry, sweetie. I hope it works out for you. It certainly looked like Lisa cared about you the other day."

"We'll see. I'll talk to you later, Mom."

* * *

Lisa checked her phone. Rachel wasn't too late—yet. They were meeting at their usual spot in Augusta. It was a busy night and the tables around her were full. She started thinking about the dates on the files she had seen in Don's desk. She had searched online for accidents on the date Mike had done the car repairs for Senator Lawrence, but she hadn't found any interesting results. Maybe he really had hit a deer or maybe the accident hadn't been in Augusta. It was hard to tell.

Rachel rushed over to the table and sat across from her. "Sorry I'm late."

"You're not really late, don't worry."

"I swear there's a construction project on every road in town and I always get held up."

"Before I forget to ask, why don't you come out to the lake on Sunday? It's supposed to be hot this weekend."

"That sounds like fun," Rachel said. "I'll let you know."

Their waitress came over and they each ordered one of the local beers. Lisa looked at Rachel after they were alone again. "I need to get your opinion on something."

"You know I love to give my opinion," Rachel said with a smile. "Let me guess. There's drama going on with Toni? You can always count on drama when Toni's involved."

"Actually, Toni's been fine. She's awesome, actually, but I'm not sure if I should keep seeing her, which is really surprising, don't you think?"

"I'm shocked. I thought she'd break your heart again. I didn't think you'd be the one who wasn't interested in her."

"I should be slightly insulted by that comment, but you're right. She was my dream girl for so long. Although, just to get this straight, I did not follow her around like a puppy."

"Yes, you did. How come you don't want to keep seeing her?"

"Remember my friend Carrie?"

"The woman from the café." Rachel grinned at her. "I knew it. I knew from the way you kept talking about her there was something going on."

"Unfortunately, there really isn't anything going on. I wish there was, but she isn't interested in me."

"I don't get it. If there's nothing going on with Carrie, then what does this have to do with Toni?"

"That's why I need your advice. I've had an amazing time getting together with Toni, but I confess, the more time I spend with Carrie, the more I want to be with her and not with Toni. Deep down, I'm worried Toni is still a player and I'm just a passing fancy. When I'm with Carrie, it's a completely different feeling. She's loyal and caring, and we can talk about anything."

"But you said Carrie isn't interested in you." Rachel paused as the waitress brought over their drinks.

"Right." Lisa took a sip of her beer. "Am I being completely stupid? Should I just keep seeing Toni and not take it all so seriously? I'm really attracted to her and she's been great. I just don't have feelings for her like I do for Carrie. She's the one I have on my mind all the time. I keep wishing it was Carrie who wanted to be with me, and it seems unfair to treat Toni this way."

"Now this is some drama," Rachel teased. "My life is suddenly looking so boring."

"Oh, be quiet. Your life is not boring. Actually, don't be quiet, and tell me what you think I should do."

"Does Carrie know how you feel?"

"It's been pretty noticeable. I don't want to get on her nerves, so I haven't come out and said anything, but I'm sure she can tell."

"Don't assume she knows. Even if she has noticed, she might be holding back because you're involved with someone else."

"I really don't think so," Lisa said. "She never acts like she cares when I mention Toni."

"You deserve to be with someone who is going to make you the center of their universe. I didn't know Toni very well, but she never struck me as the sort of person who would be happy to settle down. She was always moving on to the next adventure and the next love."

"It's been a long time since you've seen her, and she's had plenty of time to change."

"That's possible, but I think you've made up your mind about Toni. It sounds to me like you wouldn't be happy having a fling with her if your heart's not in it."

"I guess you're right. I just needed to talk it over with you. I can't believe I'm even thinking of doing this. I could have a really fantastic time with Toni. She keeps inviting me to stay over with her."

"Oh my, that does sound exciting. You must have it bad for Carrie."

"It looks like I'm going to end alone, as usual." Lisa took another sip of her beer. "Carrie isn't interested in me and I'm thinking of ending things with Toni. It really makes no sense."

"Well, let's try to think of something positive." Rachel paused. "At least you're making some new friends since you moved to Maine."

CHAPTER TWENTY-TWO

Lisa pulled into the parking lot at the restaurant in Rockland a little earlier than she had originally planned. She took a look around and was glad to see Toni's car was already there, so it wasn't too early to meet her. She was hoping to talk with her before Toni started playing. The restaurant was on Main Street near the waterfront, which was a busy area in the summer, especially on a Friday night.

It was still early enough that it wasn't too crowded when she walked in. The band had set up their instruments in the corner, but she didn't see Toni anywhere. She walked past the bar which ran along one side of the main dining room and into an adjoining room which overlooked a deck stretching across the back of the restaurant. Lisa spotted her across the room. She was sitting at a table facing the deck with a familiar-looking man. Lisa tried to remember where she might have seen him before.

Toni and the man were eating dinner together and Lisa hesitated in the doorway, not wanting to interrupt them since

Toni wasn't expecting her to be here this early. As she approached the table slowly, she could hear their conversation.

"I had a blast the other day," the man said. "I want to see you again. Can we get together tonight?"

"I told you," Toni replied, "I'm meeting a friend tonight."

"What about later?" the man asked. "My friends are coming to hear your show and we could all hang out after. You know you're welcome at my place any time."

Lisa remembered where she had seen the man. He was one of the guys who had come over to talk to Toni after her set at the restaurant last weekend. Apparently, they had spent time together at some point afterward, which was interesting.

Lisa walked over to the table. "Hi there."

Toni turned around in surprise. "Oh, hi Lisa. I wasn't expecting you so early. Come join us."

Toni and the man were at a table for two. Lisa looked around awkwardly for a moment, not sure where she should sit. "Are you sure? I don't want to interrupt."

"Pull up a chair and sit down, please," Toni said.

Lisa pulled over a chair from a nearby empty table and sat down. Toni's dining companion did not look thrilled to see her.

"Lisa," Toni gestured to the man seated next to her, "this is my friend, Mark."

Mark nodded.

"Hello. I remember you from the other night at the High Tide." In spite of the uncomfortable situation, Lisa tried to be polite. "It's nice to see you again."

"Have you eaten?" Toni asked. "We're just about done here, but we can call the waiter over and order something for you."

"No, thanks." Lisa hadn't eaten yet, but she didn't want to sit there any longer than she had to with the two of them. "I'm fine. I had something before I left."

Mark looked at Toni and back at Lisa, apparently trying to size up the situation. The waiter saw Lisa and came over to their table. "Would you like to see a menu?"

"No, thank you." Lisa didn't think she'd be staying very long. It was fairly obvious what Mark had meant when he said Toni was welcome at his place. It confirmed she was doing the right thing by breaking things off with Toni. She wasn't feeling as upset about it as she would have expected. Part of her had known their connection wasn't meant to be a long-term relationship. It was somewhat of a relief to know Toni was seeing other people because she didn't want to hurt her.

"Can I get the check?" Mark asked.

"Yes, I'll be right back." The waiter picked up the empty plates from the table and headed toward the kitchen.

"Thank you for dinner, Mark," Toni said.

"My pleasure," Mark replied. "Hopefully we can get together again soon. If you change your mind about tonight, let me know."

Lisa looked at Toni and raised her eyebrow in question. Toni touched her hand. "I'm glad you came to see me. It should be a good show tonight."

"I can see that," Lisa said.

The waiter returned with the check. Mark left some money on the table and stood up. "I'll see you a little later."

Mark gave Toni's shoulder a squeeze as he walked away. She looked at Lisa and shrugged. "He seems like a nice guy. He looked me up and came by on Sunday. We ended up hanging out for a while."

"He looked you up and came over to your house? That sounds a little close to stalking. Please be careful. I know it's really not any of my business, but where was your daughter?"

"She was feeling better and she wanted to go over to her father's house for the night on Sunday, so she wasn't home. Don't worry, I don't have strange men around my daughter."

Lisa wanted to ask why she would want to have a strange man around herself, but she didn't want to argue. Her original intention had been to let Toni know she didn't want to keep seeing her anyway, so it wasn't her place to tell Toni who she should or shouldn't spend time with, but she couldn't resist asking one more question.

"I didn't realize you still dated men."

"Well, now you know." Toni reached for Lisa's hand. "I didn't think you and I were involved in anything exclusive just yet. I really like spending time with you, and I hope we can keep getting to know each other. I've missed you."

Lisa wasn't falling for it this time. She knew Toni meant what she was saying, but she knew she needed more out of a relationship than she would be able to have with Toni. She hadn't changed. She was still charming her way through a string of admirers, and it wasn't in Lisa's nature to share her lovers.

She had almost been swept away by the heady mix of sexual attraction and nostalgia between them, but Toni's capricious nature was not what she wanted in her life. The days when she longed for Toni's attention were in the past. They may be able to be friends again, but Lisa wasn't interested in anything more.

"I've really had a good time getting to know you again," Lisa said. "You're gorgeous and talented and you light up a room. I just don't think you and I are meant to be together as anything more than friends."

Toni looked at her in surprise. "Why not?"

Lisa didn't want to hurt Toni's feelings, so she avoided saying anything negative. "I just don't think I can handle an open relationship. I need more. I think I'll take a lesson from this, and I hope we can still be friends."

"You're taking this all too seriously. Mark doesn't mean anything to me. If I had known it would upset you, I wouldn't have given him the time of day."

"I probably shouldn't take things so seriously, but I can't help it." Lisa pulled her hand back from Toni's hold. "It was really wonderful to be together with you after all those years, and I'm glad we crossed paths."

"I don't want us to lose touch again. Your friendship means a lot to me. I wish you would think about this some more."

"Goodbye, Toni." Lisa stood up and walked out, feeling a deep sense of relief she had made the right choice.

CHAPTER TWENTY-THREE

The door opened, and Carrie looked up from the counter where she was busy chopping up the ingredients for the appetizers. Lisa walked into the entryway and smiled at her. In spite of Carrie's determination to take a step back and stop caring so much, her pulse quickened, and she couldn't keep the smile off her face. She set down her knife and walked over to the counter.

The café had been in a state of controlled chaos all morning. Between the breakfast rush and getting all of the food prepped for the party, the entire staff was busy with more than they could handle, and Carrie was grateful for any extra help she could get. She was planning to have Lisa assist her with some of the appetizers, not that she was looking for an excuse to be near her.

"Good morning," Lisa said. "It looks pretty busy around here. I hope I can help and not be in your way."

"I'm glad you're here," Carrie said. "I've got plenty of things you can do, believe me. I really appreciate that you came in."

"Are you kidding? You're always helping me, and I'm glad it's finally my turn."

"Come on back here." Carrie led her into the kitchen.

"This is the first time you've let me in your domain. It's kind of exciting."

"Hold on to that thought. In an hour or two after you've been chopping all morning, you may feel differently." Carrie handed her a knife. "It's pretty hot back here. We've got the air conditioner cranking, but it's not going to be able to keep up today."

Carrie tried to not to stare at Lisa as she started chopping the stack of peppers and tomatoes piled on the counter. Lisa's blond hair was curling in the heat, and Carrie could see a drop of sweat at the base of her neck by the collar of her T-shirt. She swallowed and went back to chopping the pile of vegetables on the counter in front of her.

She continued working while she kept an eye on everyone bustling around her. Lisa was focused on her task and making good progress. Carrie had assigned a few servers to stay out front and wait on tables in the dining area. Ryan was working the counter. The kitchen area was full, with two people preparing breakfast while Angie and Lisa helped her with the party prepping. Everything was on track for now.

Carrie and Lisa finished chopping and transferred the diced vegetables into storage containers. With those out of the way, it was time to start on the onions, which was never a pleasant task. Carrie felt a little guilty asking Lisa to help her with it. They moved over to the counter near the deep double sinks where Carrie had the onions in two large bowls.

"I had these in the freezer for a little while," Carrie said. "It makes them easier to chop without having your eyes water. I don't want to make you cry."

"I've never heard of that, but I hope it works."

They started chopping. The freezer trick helped, and Carrie got through most of the pile in front of her. Her eyes were stinging a little and she opened them wider to try and blink the tears away. Looking over at Lisa, she saw her head was down, and she was focused on her task. Carrie turned back to the onion she was holding and continued chopping, determined to finish without complaining.

A little while later, Carrie scooped the last of the diced onions into the nearby container. She looked over at Lisa and did a double take. Tears were streaming down Lisa's face as she resolutely kept chopping at the onions on the cutting board in front of her. Her eyes were red and puffy, and she looked miserable.

"Hold on there," Carrie said. "God, I didn't realize you were having such a tough time. I'm sorry. Go run your hands under some water. That will help."

"I'm fine." Lisa stared down at the cutting board and kept chopping.

"Stubborn is what you are." Carrie slid the cutting board away from Lisa and toward herself. When Lisa finally looked at her, Carrie struggled not to laugh. She bit her lip as Lisa started chuckling through her sobs.

"I'm a mess." Lisa finally relented and went over to the sink. "Now I remember why I never want to cook."

Carrie couldn't help but laugh. "Why didn't you say something? You didn't have to torture yourself."

Carrie finished the onions and went over to wash up next to Lisa, who was still splashing cold water on her face. "Wow, your eyes are pretty swollen."

"Thank you for letting me know. I smell like an onion too."

"Very sexy," Carrie teased. She looked into Lisa's reddened eyes and the rest of the room disappeared for a moment. She shook her head and turned away to dry her hands. So much for forgetting about her feelings for Lisa.

"How was Rockland last night?" Carrie knew hearing about Lisa's date would be a sure way to strengthen her resolve to stay away.

"I wanted to talk to you about that."

Carrie really didn't want to hear any details about Lisa's date.

"Hey Carrie," Angie called. "Can you come here for a minute, I need your help with this order."

"Be right back." Carrie turned away quickly, grateful that Angie had saved her.

Lisa dried off her face and looked around. She had been hoping for a chance to talk to Carrie, but it looked like it would have to wait until later. They were caught up on chopping vegetables, and she wasn't sure what to do next. Carrie and the other cooks were busy at the grill and Lisa didn't want to bother her. There was a door near the sink, which led to another room in the back, so Lisa decided to take a look around. The back room was apparently a storage area, full of shelves and supplies. It was also really hot. She opened the exit door and stepped outside. There was a picnic table sitting on a small stretch of lawn behind the building overlooking the lake. She looked around the corner and saw a set of stairs leading to the apartment above the café. The backyard was peaceful and quiet after the noise of the restaurant.

Lisa stood outside for a minute and let the breeze coming off the lake cool her down a little before heading back to the kitchen. She reached for the knob and began to turn it when the door suddenly swung open into the building. Caught off balance, she stumbled and began to fall forward. Strong hands grabbed her, and she found herself in Carrie's arms with their bodies pressed together in the doorway.

Lisa couldn't stop herself. The way Carrie was looking at her and the feel of her body was too much. Lisa's heart pounded as her self-restraint fell away. She reached up for Carrie's shoulders, bringing their faces together and kissing her lips. Lisa closed her eyes as a rush of desire washed over her. She opened her mouth as Carrie slid in her tongue and wrapped them in a breathtaking embrace. She didn't want this moment to end. Lisa ran her fingers through Carrie's soft, silky hair. Lisa let out a moan that was interrupted by the sound of footsteps entering the storeroom.

Lisa pulled away quickly and looked up at Carrie to see if she was upset. She knew Carrie had never wanted to be anything more than friends. "I'm sorry, I shouldn't have done that."

A look of anger crossed Carrie's face and she turned away. "Forget it."

Carrie walked into the storeroom and toward the kitchen. Lisa followed after her and nodded to Angie who was retrieving some ingredients from a rack of shelves in the corner.

Back in the kitchen, Carrie was all business. "Let's get going on the appetizers."

Lisa listened closely as Carrie explained how to prepare the different appetizers she had planned for the menu. They were going to assemble them on trays at the café and bring them over to heat up at the party. Carrie listed the steps and lined up the ingredients, avoiding Lisa's eyes the entire time. Lisa's heart dropped more by the minute.

Lisa waited for Ryan to pass by, then stepped closer to Carrie. There were tears in her eyes as she spoke to Carrie softly, "I'm really sorry. I know you didn't want me to touch you. I know you're not attracted to me and I promise it won't happen again. I don't want to lose your friendship."

"Wait, what?" Carrie stared at her. "I thought you were feeling guilty because of Toni."

"No," Lisa said. "That's what I wanted to talk to you about."

Two women came in through the backdoor and waved to Carrie. "Hey, Carrie. Help has arrived. We're here to save the day!"

"Hi there. Hold on a minute," Carrie called over to them. She turned to Lisa. "My friends are here. I called them in to work with us tonight. I do want to talk to you, but it's going to be crazy around here for the rest of the day. I'm going to have to deal with all the party prep and I probably won't have a free minute."

"It can wait," Lisa said. "I just don't want you to be mad at me. I promise I'll be more respectful of you."

"Listen, I'm not mad because you touched me. That kiss was awesome." Carrie looked into Lisa's eyes. "As soon as things settle down we can talk, okay?"

Lisa nodded and Carrie went to greet her friends. Lisa tried to focus her attention back on the food she was preparing. She needed to make it through the day and hope she could straighten things out with Carrie.

CHAPTER TWENTY-FOUR

Carrie stood in the spacious kitchen and ran through her checklist, making sure all the tasks were completed. It was time for guests to start arriving and everything was in place. The dishes for the main course were ready to be heated up and the appetizers were in the oven. The bartenders were at their stations. She looked over at Lisa and the four other women who were going to serve. They looked professional in their white shirts and black pants. She noticed Lisa looked particularly good.

Carrie took a deep breath, praying everything would go smoothly. She looked over at Lisa again and thought about their kiss. When Lisa had pulled her down and kissed her, Carrie thought she was dreaming. She felt terrible that she had made Lisa cry. It had surprised her to see how upset Lisa was.

Her mother's words had come back to her, and she realized she might have hidden her feelings too well. It seemed unlikely, but maybe Lisa didn't realize how she felt about her. She clearly wasn't good at analyzing love situations. Look at how she'd misread Lisa's relationship with Rachel. For some reason, she couldn't read Lisa correctly. Maybe it was time to admit to herself and to Lisa how much she cared about her.

She wished she had time to talk to her about everything, but she had been insanely busy all day. She was going to make sure they had a chance to get together tomorrow so she could try to figure out what was going on.

Leanne Mills appeared, wearing stiletto heels and a red cocktail dress. Her hair was carefully styled, and her makeup had been applied with a heavy hand. Carrie looked up from the trays she was arranging with the cold appetizers.

"Hello, Leanne."

"Please call me Mrs. Mills in front of the rest of the help," Leanne said. "What's going on in here? People are beginning to arrive, and I don't want any mishaps."

The most difficult part of the evening would be dealing with her. Leanne was one of the most pretentious people Carrie knew, and Carrie often had to fight to stay calm when she talked with her. Leanne had moved to Winchester after marrying Bruce, so Carrie didn't know her very well, and she had no desire to get to know her any better.

"We're ready to serve appetizers whenever you like, Mrs. Mills," Carrie said. "The bartenders are also ready to start making drinks."

Leanne gave an imperious nod. "Start circulating the appetizers now."

Carrie watched her walk out of the kitchen and then turned to Lisa and the other servers. "All right, let's get started. I'm going to have two of you take cold trays and two take trays with some hot apps."

Lisa was the last server to get a tray. She waited next to Carrie for the hot appetizers to be ready. "I'm hoping I can hear something interesting while I'm serving. I'll let you know."

"Just be careful," Carrie warned. "Also, don't forget to focus on serving the appetizers."

"Don't worry. I can feel all my old waitressing skills coming back to me."

"I thought you said you weren't very good at it."

"True. But I'm going to try really hard tonight. I promise."

Carrie passed her the serving tray. "Here you go. Just be sure to walk slowly and offer one to everybody you see."

"Got it." Lisa held the tray carefully and she walked out of the kitchen into the enormous living room overlooking the lake.

Carrie glanced up occasionally from her vantage point in the kitchen to watch as Lisa made her way slowly through the living room and out onto the patio, offering food to the arriving guests. She was trying to keep an eye out for Senator Lawrence. She hadn't yet seen him among the guests, but people were still arriving.

The servers' trays were emptied quickly and Carrie kept a steady supply prepared as they came back into the kitchen for refills. Lisa reappeared and approached the serving area near the oven, ready for another tray.

"You know what I just realized?" Lisa looked behind her to make sure no one was nearby. "I've seen pictures of Michaud and Senator Lawrence, so I'll recognize them, but I don't know what Bruce Mills looks like. I think he was the man I saw leaving Don's office, but how am I going to know which one is Bruce?"

"You're living a detective show in your mind, aren't you?" Carrie lowered her voice as she filled Lisa's tray up with fresh appetizers. "I know you want to try and find out some information tonight, but just make sure you don't bring any attention to yourself. These are not nice people."

"I just want to know what they all look like, so I can keep an eye on them and see if they start talking together or doing anything suspicious. I'll be very discreet."

Carrie sighed. Lisa was determined to observe the Mills family and their guests. She wondered how she would be able to keep watch over her while she was cooking. It wasn't going to be easy.

"Bruce Mills looks like his brother, but he's better looking," Carrie said. "Now tell me, how does the party seem to be going?"

"Everyone loves the food, of course. The appetizers have gotten lots of compliments and I made sure to smile gracefully while I served them."

"Good. Remember to focus on serving food, not investigating the guests."

"Yes, boss."

The house was stunning, with banks of glass doors in the living room leading out to a stone patio. A white tent had been set up in the yard as a dining area and people were strolling around both inside and outside.

Lisa carried her tray amidst the growing crowd of people. Leanne Mills stood with a group out on the patio. Lisa made her way over to them. As she drew closer, she noticed they were gathered around a distinguished looking older gentleman. He turned his head in her direction and she saw it was Senator Lawrence.

"Thank you so much for coming, Senator," Leanne Mills gushed. "We're honored to have you here."

"My pleasure," Senator Lawrence said. Many of the men in the crowd wore lightweight summer suit coats on this warm evening, but the Senator was dressed more formally, wearing a full suit and tie.

Lisa noticed a man standing next to Leanne and realized he must be Bruce. He was definitely the one she had seen leaving Don's office. Carrie was right. He looked a lot like his brother, but better looking. He was slimmer than Don and appeared to be in much better shape, with an athletic build and a thick head of hair.

She approached the group with her tray. "Would anyone care for an appetizer?"

Leanne gave her an irritated look at the interruption.

"Those look good. Don't mind if I do," Senator Lawrence replied. He helped himself to one of the scallops wrapped in bacon on her tray and turned back to speak with a man standing next to him.

Lisa lingered near the group while several people enjoyed the appetizers. Feeling more confident about her waitressing abilities, she went back in for another refill. Carrie was busy replenishing trays for the other servers, which gave Lisa a minute to stare freely.

Carrie's face was flushed with exertion from the pace she was keeping for herself. Lisa hadn't seen her sit down or take a break all day. Her short, dark hair was tousled, and Lisa thought she looked especially beautiful. She had learned her lesson this morning. Even though Carrie said she wasn't angry earlier, it wasn't worth risking their friendship to give in to the temptation to touch her again.

When Lisa's turn to replenish her tray arrived, she filled Carrie in on the party guests. "I saw Bruce Mills, and you're right, he is a handsomer version of Don. I still think they're both pretty repulsive."

"How does everything look out there?"

"The guests all seem very happy with the food, which isn't surprising because your food is always fabulous."

"Thanks." Carrie smiled and replaced Lisa's empty tray with a full plate of grilled asparagus wrapped in phyllo dough.

"I also saw Senator Lawrence. He was talking with Bruce and a group of other people. I'm going to head back over there and keep an eye on them. Maybe I'll overhear something good."

Another server handed Carrie a tray, and Lisa headed back out to the patio. Senator Lawrence was still speaking with Bruce, so she moved closer. As she approached the group, Lisa saw a man she recognized as Joe Michaud. He was standing near Bruce and speaking with another man who looked familiar.

Holding the tray carefully as she walked toward the senator's group, Lisa made her way through the crowd, taking her time to serve everyone who stopped her along the way. She found an inconspicuous position near Bruce Mills and tried to listen to his conversation with Senator Lawrence.

"I had expected to hear something on the school contract by now," Bruce said.

"These things take time," Lawrence replied.

Lisa held up her tray with a smile and saw Joe Michaud join the two men. She missed their conversation for a few minutes while she spoke with a couple who had questions about the ingredients in the appetizers. The couple thanked her politely and walked away, and she was finally able to listen again.

"We've worked well together, Bill," Bruce said. "I appreciate your assistance and I think we can continue our support for your next campaign as long as the assistance continues."

"I'm doing what I can," Lawrence said quietly. "I can't be overly blatant about awarding two big contracts in a row to your company. It could raise some concerns on the procurement committee and that's the last thing any of us wants."

"Make sure you find a way to take care of it without raising concerns." Joe stared at the Senator menacingly. "Another thing you wouldn't want is to have anyone find out about what happened last year."

"I'm well aware of that. I'm working on your proposal, but I don't believe this is the appropriate time or place for a detailed discussion." Lawrence nodded toward the bar. "Now if you gentlemen will excuse me, I think I'll go get another drink."

Lisa's head was spinning from what she had just overheard. The conversation had confirmed exactly what she and Carrie had suspected. Senator Lawrence was crooked, and the contracts were being awarded illegally.

Her tray was almost empty, and she knew she shouldn't hover in one place too long. Turning to walk back toward the door, she spotted Don Mills in the living room. He was standing with his wife and speaking with the familiar-looking man who Joe had been talking with earlier. Lisa considered trying to avoid him entirely but decided she might as well say hello since he was bound to see her when they started serving dinner. This could give her the chance to find out who the other man was.

Walking over to where Don and his wife were standing, Lisa greeted them, "Hello, would you like some fresh roasted asparagus?"

"Hello, Lisa." Don looked at her in surprise. "Are you moonlighting this weekend?"

"I'm helping out a friend." Lisa turned to Don's wife. "It's very nice to meet you. I work for Don."

Don's wife was a petite woman with graying hair. She looked at her husband quickly before answering. "Hello, it's nice to meet you, too. I'm Jean."

The man standing next to Don helped himself to the last of the asparagus on Lisa's tray. "These look tasty. The appetizers have been very good. I'm looking forward to dinner."

"I'm glad you're enjoying everything, sir," Lisa said.

"Make sure you stay on his good side," Don said with a hearty laugh. "You wouldn't want to upset the head of the Maine State Police."

"No, I certainly wouldn't." Lisa nodded with a smile. Returning to the kitchen with her empty tray, she was disappointed to see two of the other servers were there and Carrie was too busy to talk.

Leanne Mills strode into the room and spoke to Carrie, "It's time to have your people start seating guests. I trust that the dinner will be ready on time."

"Yes, everything is ready to be served," Carrie replied.

Leanne left, and Carrie turned to Lisa and the other servers. "All right, that's it for appetizers. You're all doing a great job so far, ladies. I'm going to start getting salads ready while you let the guests know dinner will be served shortly in the tent."

CHAPTER TWENTY-FIVE

Time flew by as Lisa and the rest of the crew served the courses Carrie had prepared. They brought out tray after tray of plated meals and picked up the stacks of empty dishes from the tables. Finally, dinner was over, and everyone was satisfied for the moment. Luckily, Leanne had decided to go with a buffet for dessert, so the guests were helping themselves from a table with an assortment of pies, cakes, and other sweets.

Torchlights glowed around the perimeter of the tent and the contented guests were relaxing, enjoying the summer night. A band had set up on the patio and music drifted across the lake. The bartenders had opened stations at either end of the tent and they showed no signs of slowing. Lisa was relieved to be able to take a break. She went in to check on Carrie and found her near the sink helping the two high school boys she had hired to wash dishes.

"I guess I passed, huh?" Lisa asked. "You're not going to make me help with the dishes, are you?"

"You did great and the dishes are all set." Carrie walked over to her. "No one had any mishaps at all, so hopefully Leanne will be happy."

"Thank God," Lisa said. "I'm beat, and you must be totally exhausted."

"I'm not tired yet, but I'm sure I'll crash later."

"I'm not used to this manual labor." Lisa groaned and leaned on the counter. "I don't know how you're still standing."

"Caffeine helps," Carrie said with a grin.

"You really throw an awesome party." Lisa lowered her voice. "Everyone looks stuffed and happy out there for the time being. I was thinking this might be a good time to look for Bruce's office."

Carrie looked around nervously. "I don't know if that's such a good idea. What if someone sees you?"

"You could be my lookout. We may not get another chance, you know."

"You're crazy and the worst part is, I'm listening to you."

"I heard Bruce and Joe talking to Senator Lawrence. There's definitely something going on. It's like we thought. They're holding something over him and using it to force Lawrence to award contracts to Bruce's company."

"You heard them say that?"

"Yes. They were talking about contracts, but they didn't give many details. They're trying to get a contract for a school, and Joe mentioned not wanting anyone to find out about something that happened last year."

"All right. This is way too risky, but I don't want you to get caught, so I guess I'd better help. Did you come up with any sort of plan about how to do this?"

"My plan is to head straight for his desk and look through the drawers. I'll get in and out of there quickly. If the drawers are locked, I'll look for a key like I did in Don's office."

"What if someone sees us?"

"We'll tell them you came looking for me and that I was looking for the bathroom."

"That's not a very good excuse. There's a bathroom right off the kitchen."

"Well, I'll tell them the one near the kitchen was occupied. Don't worry."

"You say that a lot." Carrie shook her head. "It doesn't stop me from worrying."

"Let's get going." Lisa headed out of the kitchen and into the living room. The Mills's home had two stories with a large staircase in the foyer off the living room. The living room was deserted, and everyone was outside enjoying the party.

Lisa looked around to make sure no one saw them before walking quickly toward the foyer and turning down the adjoining hallway. Carrie followed closely behind. She slowed as her footsteps echoed on the hardwood floor. Lisa made her way cautiously down the hall, hoping Bruce had an office on the first floor of the house. She opened each of the doors and peeked in to see what was inside. The third one opened to an office, and she gave Carrie a thumbs-up.

"Okay, I'll be as quick as I can," she whispered. "Just whistle if you hear someone coming."

"Why don't I hoot like an owl?"

"That works too." Lisa peered over Carrie's shoulder.

"Listen, crazy woman, I'm not going to whistle or hoot," Carrie whispered urgently. "I'm going to tell you if someone's coming, and then I'm going to drag you out if you don't get out quickly."

"That's a good plan, too."

Lisa eased the door open and walked as quietly as she could to the desk. The room was dark and there wasn't enough light from the hall to see well, so she switched on the desk lamp. Opening the top drawer, she took a quick look around and didn't see anything interesting. She rifled through the file drawer on the left side but all she saw were bills and other personal paperwork, nothing related to Senator Lawrence or to Mills Building Construction.

She turned to the right and pulled on the last remaining drawer, breathing a sigh of relief when it slid open. Kneeling down, she began to page through the files. The labels on most of them didn't mean anything to her. They looked like project names. As she reached the halfway point, she bit back a shout of delight when she saw the name Lawrence. Opening the folder eagerly, she flipped quickly through the pages. They looked similar to what she had seen in Don's file, with an assortment of spreadsheets and contract information. Near the back of the file was a copy of a report.

Lisa pulled the report out of the file just as she heard Carrie's urgent whisper, "Lisa, hurry up. I think someone's coming."

Folding the papers in half and stuffing them down her shirt, she closed the drawer and switched off the light. Running over to the door as quickly and quietly as she could, Lisa slipped out into the hallway and eased the door shut. She heard voices in the foyer and looked at Carrie, whose eyes widened in panic as the voices came closer.

Moving quickly, Lisa grabbed Carrie's shoulders and pushed her against the wall next to the office door. She whispered in her ear, "I know I promised I wouldn't touch you again, but this is strictly for our investigation. We want them to think we just came here to make out."

Before Carrie could answer, Lisa pressed her lips into a deep kiss. Carrie kissed Lisa back, pulling her closer. Lisa couldn't tell if her heart was pounding from terror or from her reaction to finding herself in Carrie's arms again. She had no idea what they should do next, but she didn't care at the moment.

"What's going on here?" Bruce Mills demanded as he entered the hallway. "What are you doing in this part of the house?"

Lisa and Carrie jumped apart and looked up to see Bruce glaring at them with Joe by his side.

"Sorry, it's my fault," Lisa said. "The bathroom near the kitchen was full so I went looking for another one and she came to find me. I thought we were alone. I'm really sorry."

"Looks like these ladies need a moment alone." Joe smirked at Bruce.

"Why don't you get back to the kitchen," Bruce said. "I'm sure you have a lot of work to do, and we aren't paying you to fool around."

"I apologize." Carrie nodded to the men and walked back toward the living room, pulling Lisa along with her. They didn't speak until they were back in the kitchen doorway.

"I think you just took ten years off my life," Carrie whispered angrily, glancing at the workers across the room. "I can't believe I let you talk me into doing that. Do you realize what would have happened if they caught you in Bruce's office? Not only would we have been in danger, but my business could be ruined if word ever got out I was trespassing into a customer's private rooms. No one would ever trust me again."

Lisa was stricken with guilt. In her eagerness to get more evidence against Don and the other men, she had selfishly forgotten to consider Carrie's feelings. It was completely thoughtless of her to jeopardize Carrie's business while she was supposed to be helping her with the party.

"I'm so sorry. I never should have put you in that position. I got caught up in trying to find proof and I didn't think of all the implications," Lisa said softly.

"I never want to be that close to being caught again. My nerves are shot."

"Mine, too. I really am sorry."

Carrie's glare faded, and she nodded at Lisa. "It's okay. You didn't force me to do anything. It was my choice to help you try and find more information. I don't want them to keep getting away with their sleazy deals."

"Do you think they suspected anything?"

"I don't think so or they wouldn't have let us leave," Carrie answered.

"I found a report." Lisa tapped the front of her shirt. "I didn't get to read it yet, but it could be something good."

"I certainly hope so after all that. We'll have to take a look later. I've got to get back to work and try to get us out of here as soon as possible."

* * *

Several hours later the last of the dishes, glasses, silverware, and other pieces of equipment which had been brought over for the party had been loaded into Carrie's Jeep and her friend's van. They were all set and could finally leave. The last of the guests had gone home hours ago.

There had been some uncomfortable questions from Leanne when she had come into the kitchen earlier. Bruce had told her about finding their caterer fooling around with one of the servers during the party and Leanne wasn't pleased. She had accused Carrie of being inattentive and wanted to know why she was wandering around the house instead of tending to the guests. Carrie apologized, but Leanne had used it as an excuse not to give her a tip.

Carrie and the remaining workers walked out to their vehicles in the driveway where Carrie thanked everyone profusely. "Thank you so much, everyone. I really appreciate all of your help tonight. You did a great job."

Two of her friends got in the van and the other one got into Carrie's Jeep. Carrie walked to Lisa's car with her to say goodbye.

"I wish you'd let me pay you," Carrie said. "I paid everyone else and you worked hard."

"I was helping a friend and I don't want to be paid." Lisa opened her car door and got in. "I feel terrible Leanne found out what happened and didn't tip you. You put in so much time and effort to make sure the party was perfect, and I messed it up for you."

"Leanne was probably looking for any excuse to screw me out of a tip. I'm just glad they don't know we went in the office. Now go home and get some sleep."

"I hope you do too. You've been working nonstop."

"My adrenaline is still pumping from before." Carrie smiled at her. "I'll try to catch up with you tomorrow and see what you found."

"I'm dying to look at the report." Lisa glanced at the bag on the seat next to her where she had put the papers for safekeeping. "Call me tomorrow when you get a chance. I don't want to bother you if you're sleeping."

Carrie was ready to give in to what she had been wanting to do all day. Just as she began to lean in the car window to kiss Lisa, the lights in the Jeep next to them flashed, and she heard her friend calling for her to hurry up.

Pulling back, Carrie stared into Lisa's eyes. When she kissed Lisa, she wasn't going to hurry. "You would never bother me. Call me any time."

CHAPTER TWENTY-SIX

Daisy nudged Lisa with her nose and woofed at her. Lisa opened her eyes to look at her alarm clock and was surprised how long she had slept. No wonder Daisy wanted her to get up. She pushed back the sheets and got out of bed, stretching her arms before patting Daisy.

"Poor girl. You must need to go out. Hold on one more minute."

She walked to the door and held it open for Daisy. Bright sun shone through the leaves on the trees overhead. It was going to be a beautiful day. Rachel was planning to stop by later, and she was looking forward to her visit. The weather would be perfect for kayaking. The lake was calm and it wasn't supposed to be too hot.

Hopefully she would be able to spend some time with Carrie today too. She couldn't wait for her to call so they could figure out when to get together and go over everything that had happened yesterday. Lisa still hadn't had a chance to explain to her how she had ended things with Toni.

The first time Lisa kissed Carrie at the café yesterday, she had felt sick with regret when Carrie had been angry with her. In spite of the craziness of the situation with Bruce Mills, she really shouldn't have kissed her again, but it was a desperate situation. Lisa had been worried Carrie might be upset about it, but the way Carrie had looked at her when she was leaving had given her a spark of hope that they had a chance together.

Lisa needed to talk to her about the report she had found in Bruce's desk. She had glanced at it the night before when she got home, but she was too tired to decide what they should do about it. It was a police report of an accident in Winchester during the previous summer. The report described an accident involving a young girl named Michelle Nelson who had been killed by a hit-and-run driver. The report had been filed by Sheriff Joe Michaud himself, and it stated there was no evidence found to help them identify a suspect.

This was what she and Carrie had been looking for. Senator Lawrence had to have been the one who hit and killed Michelle Nelson, and the Mills brothers must have helped Joe Michaud cover it up. It had occurred around the same date as when the senator's car had been repaired by Carrie's brother.

Lisa remembered Rachel pointing out Michelle's parents at the café and telling her about the accident. The question now was, what would be the best way to get this information to the right people without having it covered up again?

Lisa heard a car approach and looked out the window. She was surprised to see Daisy greeting Toni out in the driveway. Lisa thought back to their phone call the other day and remembered she had mentioned getting together on Sunday to Toni, but after their conversation she had assumed Toni wouldn't want to come by and she had forgotten all about it.

"Hello, Toni." Lisa opened the door and stepped outside. Toni had driven a long way to visit, and Lisa didn't want to be rude. "This is a surprise."

Toni gave her a long hug. "Hi there."

Lisa backed up. "Let's go hang out by the water where it's a little cooler."

"That sounds great."

Lisa led the way down to the dock and tried to think of what to say. "It's nice to see you, but I didn't think you were coming. Rachel should be stopping by soon, too."

"I wanted to talk to you because I didn't like how we left things the other day."

Lisa sat down in one of the chairs by the dock and Toni took the seat next to her. Lisa wasn't sure how to begin. She should have been clearer with Toni the other night. She didn't want to hurt Toni's feelings, but she needed her to understand she wasn't interested. After kissing Carrie yesterday, she knew she had made the right decision to end things with Toni.

"I've been thinking about what you said the other night," Toni said. "You said you needed more from our relationship and I wanted to see if you'll give me another chance."

"Toni—"

"Wait, just listen." Toni held up her hand to stop Lisa. "I know you were upset about seeing me with Mark, and I wanted to explain. I told you he doesn't mean anything to me. I don't need to see him again. If you want us to be more exclusive, I'm willing to try."

"You don't have to explain. I'm not upset." Lisa searched for the right words. "I've had a really good time with you, and it's been great to get to know you again. I just don't think you and I are right for each other."

Toni reached for Lisa's hand. "Why aren't we right for each other?"

"I need to tell you something. I've met someone else, and I didn't think it was fair to keep seeing you."

"What?" Toni dropped Lisa's hand and shook her head with a sarcastic laugh. "I guess I didn't need to feel guilty about Mark after all."

"I'm sorry. It took me a while to figure it all out. I really like spending time with you. I've always thought you were amazing and you know I had the biggest crush on you."

"I guess not so much anymore." Toni buried her head in her hands and began to cry. "It was really stupid of me to come here."

Lisa felt awful. She hadn't wanted to hurt her, but she had to be honest. She put her hand on Toni's back comfortingly. "You're too much of a free spirit to be tied down for long. I think we both know you and I are better off as friends."

"You're right. I don't like to be tied down, and I try to live in the moment, but I still wish things had worked out for us. I feel like we share a special connection."

"Things did work out for a little while. I still can't believe I finally got to kiss you after all these years. I hope you'll let me come hear you sing sometimes. Our connection doesn't have to end if we stay friends."

Toni smiled through her tears. "I would love to have you come to my shows."

"That sounds good."

Daisy ran toward the driveway at the sound of a car approaching. Expecting to see Rachel, Lisa turned to look and was surprised to see Carrie's Jeep pull in. Her arm was still around Toni as they sat by the water together. Lisa knew what it must look like to Carrie. She quickly pulled her arm away and watched in dismay as Carrie shook her head. The Jeep backed up and drove off before Lisa could move.

"What was that all about?" Toni asked. "Wasn't that your friend Carrie from Harvest?"

"Yes." Lisa stood up. She needed to figure out what she should do next. She didn't want to blow things with Carrie before they even got started. She was obviously upset to see her sitting with Toni. She'd never shown any reaction when she'd mentioned Toni before, which was one of the reasons Lisa had assumed she wasn't interested in her. Everything had changed when they kissed yesterday.

"Is she the one you were talking about when you said you met someone?" Toni asked.

"Yes." Lisa started pacing along the shore. "My life has gotten way too complicated."

"It looks like I got you in trouble. She wasn't happy to see us together."

They heard the sound of a car coming down the road again. Lisa looked over, hoping to see Carrie coming back. Instead, Rachel pulled into the driveway and parked next to Toni.

Rachel waved as she got out of her car. She took a beach bag out of the backseat and walked to the waterfront. Lisa was still trying to figure out what to do next while Toni lounged in the chair by the water.

"Hi there," Lisa greeted her. "You're just in time. Things are getting crazy around here."

"Hi Rachel," Toni said. "How are you?"

"Toni?" Rachel glanced with surprise from Toni to Lisa. "Wow, it's nice to see you."

"Carrie was just here, but she left. She wasn't happy said Lisa."

"She saw me," Toni explained. "Apparently I'm the other woman."

"All right then. I'll just sit back and watch you guys." Rachel put her bag down and sat in the empty chair next to Toni. "Lisa's made my life a lot more interesting since she moved to Maine."

"I've got to do something about this," Lisa said. "Do you guys mind if I take off for a few minutes? I need to try and find Carrie."

"No, it's fine." Rachel relaxed back in her chair. "Toni and I can catch up. We'll keep an eye on Daisy."

"Thank you," Lisa said. She headed toward her car. "I'll be back soon."

* * *

Carrie pulled into her driveway and turned off her Jeep. She sat still for a moment, thinking about Lisa and trying to figure out how she'd let herself get into this mess. She had known from the start that she didn't want to be involved with someone who was seeing someone else, but she'd let her guard down last night. It wasn't worth it. No matter what her mother said.

She walked down to the water. Angie and Ryan were covering the lunch hours at the café, so she'd been able to leave early. It had been a really late night and she'd gotten up at dawn. All she wanted to do at the moment was lay back on a comfortable chair and forget about everything. The sight of Lisa's arm around Toni had surprised and hurt her more than she wanted to think about. Yesterday she had thought Lisa really cared about her, but if that were the case, then she wouldn't be spending the day with Toni.

Carrie stretched back in the lounge chair and closed her eyes, letting the sound of the water soothe her. Just as she was starting to relax, she heard a car pull into her driveway. She turned to look and saw Lisa walking toward her.

"Carrie, we need to talk."

"I'm kind of tired right now." Carrie lay back down. There wasn't any point in trying to discuss things at the moment. She kept her sunglasses on and avoided Lisa's gaze.

Lisa sat next to her. "This is important. Can you please listen to me for a minute?"

Carrie sighed and looked up at Lisa. "What do you want to talk about?"

"When we kissed yesterday, it was an amazing experience for me, and I think you were feeling it too. At least I hope you were. Then today, when you saw Toni at my house, you jumped to conclusions and drove off, and I want to explain what was going on."

"Why did you kiss me in the first place?" Carrie was starting to get angry. "You're still involved with Toni, so why would you do that?"

"I'm not involved with Toni."

"What do you call it, then? I know what I saw."

"I told you yesterday I wanted to talk to you about her. You might not even care, but I told Toni on Friday I didn't think we should see each other anymore."

"That didn't last very long," Carrie said tersely.

"I wasn't expecting her, but she showed up at my house today to talk, and that's all we were doing." Lisa hesitated a moment. "I told her I'd met someone else."

"You did?" Carrie looked at Lisa. "Who was it you were talking about?"

"Please take off those sunglasses so I can see your eyes. It's hard enough to say it without feeling like I'm talking to the Terminator."

Carrie took off her sunglasses and sat up, looking into Lisa's eyes.

"It's you," Lisa said. "You're the only one I care about, and I hope I'm not making a mistake saying this to you."

Carrie's heart was pounding. She needed to make sure she understood Lisa correctly. "Why would it be a mistake?"

"Because you've never shown any interest in me. I've been attracted to you since I met you, but I didn't want to do anything to risk our friendship."

That was all she needed to hear. Carrie moved over to Lisa's chair, sitting beside her. She brushed Lisa's hair back from her cheek and slipped her hand behind Lisa's neck, pulling her close and kissing her gently on the lips. Carrie looked into Lisa's eyes. "I've wanted to do that from the minute I met you."

Carrie kissed her again, deeper this time. Her lips opened, and their tongues entwined. She pulled her close and felt Lisa's arms go around her. All the frustration she'd felt for the past weeks melted away. A warm breeze blew across the water, and their kisses grew more intense. Carrie traced Lisa's face with her fingers and slid her hand down Lisa's chest, savoring the taste and feel of her.

Lisa kissed her way to Carrie's ear and whispered, "Why did you wait so long?"

Carrie leaned back and looked at her. "I'm not good at sharing. I wanted to wait until you were all mine."

"I'm all yours now."

Carrie pulled her close again and kissed her while she slid her hands under her shirt. She ran her fingers along the soft skin on Lisa's back. Then shifted her hands to the front of Lisa's shirt and caressed her breasts, while stroking her mouth with her tongue.

Lisa groaned and shifted. "Lie down with me."

Moving together until they were lying back in the lounge chair, Carrie pulled Lisa on top of her. Lisa looked down into Carrie's eyes and smiled. "Hi there."

Carrie leaned into her for another kiss and Lisa pressed their hips together. Carrie drew Lisa closer and slid her hands along her sides.

"It feels so good to have you against me like this," Lisa said. "I've been wanting this since I met you."

"I've thought about you all the time. I wanted to lick strawberries out of your hand after we picked them that day."

"I think we need to go picking again some time."

"Mmm." Carrie licked Lisa's lips as she kissed her again.

The sound of a car pulling into Carrie's driveway pulled them out of their trance. Carrie looked back and saw her mother's car.

"Sorry. It's my mother," Carrie said.

"It's okay." Lisa gave her a quick kiss before sliding off and standing up. "We have plenty of time and I don't like to rush."

Carrie stood up and quickly straightened her shirt before taking Lisa's hand and walking toward the driveway.

"Hi Mom," Carrie said.

"Hello, Susan." Lisa gave her a wave with her free hand.

"Good afternoon." Susan raised an eyebrow to Carrie and smiled. Carrie smiled back and squeezed Lisa's hand.

"I don't want to interrupt anything," Susan said. "I just stopped by to ask how the party went last night."

"You're not interrupting anything," Carrie replied. "We were just hanging out. The party went pretty well but I'm kind of tired."

"The party was flawless," Lisa chimed in. "Carrie did a fantastic job with all the food and created a perfect atmosphere. She worked very hard."

Carrie looked at Lisa. "You did a great job serving too."

"Thanks."

"It's great to see you both looking so happy," Susan said with a pleased smile. She looked at Lisa. "We don't often get to meet anyone Carrie is dating."

"That's what I've heard." Lisa nudged Carrie. "I'm glad she's not hiding me."

"Maybe you two can come over for dinner some night?" Susan asked. "We could all get to know each other better."

"That would be really nice. I'd love to," Lisa said.

"All right then," Susan said. "I'd better get going. I have some errands to run. Glad to hear everything went well last night. Not that I had any doubts."

They waved goodbye as she drove off and Lisa turned to Carrie. "I probably should get back home soon. I kind of ran off and left Rachel and Toni sitting there. Do you want to come over with me?"

"You know what I'd like?" Carrie gripped Lisa's waist and pulled her close for a kiss. Lisa opened her mouth and stroked Carrie's tongue with hers before leaning back and pausing to catch her breath.

"Tell me what you'd like," Lisa said.

"I'd like to have you come back over later and I'll make you a special dinner. How about if you hang out with your friends this afternoon and then we spend the evening relaxing together?"

"That sounds fantastic." Lisa looked into Carrie's eyes. "I'm still trying to get used to the fact we're actually together."

"I'm really glad you came over and told me how you feel. I'm going to try not to hide my feelings from you. My mother says I do that too much, and I know I need to put myself out there more."

"She's right." Lisa ran her hands through Carrie's hair. "Now I see what you've been hiding from me, I don't want to lose you."

"You won't." Carrie kissed her. "As frustrating as it was at times, I'm glad we got to know each other as friends first. I feel comfortable talking with you about everything."

"Good." Lisa gave her another quick kiss. "Hearing your mother ask about the party reminded me I need to talk to you about the document we found in Bruce's office."

Carrie leaned into her and kissed her ear. "I want to hear all about it."

Lisa's expression turned serious. "It was a copy of a police report for the hit-and-run accident last year that killed Michelle Nelson."

"What?" Carrie couldn't believe it. The hit-and-run was a tragedy that had shocked the entire community when it happened. "Do you suppose Lawrence was the one who hit her?"

"That has to be it. I think the Mills brothers and Joe Michaud covered it up for him, and now they're forcing him to make sure Bruce Mills's company gets awarded some big state contracts."

"This is bigger than I thought. We have to tell the police."

"I know, but who do we tell? Michaud runs the sheriff's department and the head of the state police was at the party schmoozing with Don."

"Yeah, you're right. We'll have to be careful about who we bring this to. Do you have any ideas?"

"I'm kind of worried we still won't be able to prove anything. I mean, what if Joe Michaud says we made the whole thing up?"

"No way." Carrie shook her head. "My brother can be a witness too."

"I still need to check Don's emails. I want to see if we can find any conversations he might have had with his brother or the other two. Then we'll have to figure out the best way to get the information to someone in the state police who we can trust."

"I guess you're right. We may need more proof. I just don't want you to get caught. You don't seem to have a normal level of caution."

"Believe me, I'll be extremely careful. We need to stop these guys."

"I agree. Michelle Nelson deserves justice and I want to see this through, but the people we're dealing with are scary. We've got to go the police with this as soon as you get a chance to check Don's emails, okay?"

"Okay." Lisa kissed her again. "It's sweet how you worry about me. I'm not used to it."

"Get used to it." Carrie looked into her eyes. "I'm going to be here to look out for you."

"All right." Lisa gave her a last hug. "I guess I'd better go. I can't wait to see you later."

Carrie held her close. "I remember the first time you hugged me at your house. I didn't want to let you go."

"Well now you don't have to."

* * *

Daisy greeted Lisa happily when she returned. She saw Toni's car was gone and Rachel was relaxing in a chair by the waterfront. Lisa hurried over to join her.

"I'm really sorry I took so long. I didn't mean to leave you sitting here alone when you came all the way here to visit," Lisa said. "Did Toni get sick of waiting?"

"We chatted for a little while, and then I think she got bored," Rachel said. "I've been happy to sit in the sun and enjoy the peace and quiet. Now I want to hear what's going on with you and Carrie."

"I'll fill you in on everything but first I'm going run inside and get us some snacks. You must be dying of thirst. I'll be right back."

Lisa returned a few minutes later balancing a tray. She placed it on a side table near Rachel. "Not sure what you wanted to drink."

"Thanks," Rachel reached for a bottle of water. "Okay, no more stalling."

"I caught up with Carrie and everything is great. I can't believe how great." Lisa flopped down in the chair next to Rachel. "Toni was really upset I ended things. I wasn't expecting her to be here, and then Carrie stopped by and saw us. It was a big misunderstanding."

"Toni didn't seem very upset when she was talking to me," Rachel said. "I think she was hoping you were going to come back brokenhearted and she could be here to pick up the pieces."

"She came over to see if I'd give her another chance, and I told her it wasn't going to happen. She was crying before you got here, and I felt terrible about hurting her."

"I'm sure she's fine. From what she was telling me, she has a very full social life, so don't feel guilty. She's always gotten a kick out of stirring up drama. She was laughing about how quickly you took off after Carrie."

"It's so clear now Toni was never the right one for me."

"Tell me about Carrie. I'm dying to hear what happened. She sounds really sweet."

"She's very sweet, unlike the two of us," Lisa teased with a smile. "I'm going back over for dinner tonight. I told her how I feel, and she feels the same way about me. It's almost too good to be true. I could go on all night about her. She's really special and I want you to meet her."

"Going over for dinner?" Rachel asked. "Now what exactly does that mean? Are you going to spend the night?"

"I don't know," Lisa admitted. "I guess it all depends on how the evening goes. God, now you're making me nervous."

"I'd be nervous too. I know you really care about her. I don't remember the last time I heard you talk about anyone like this."

"You're not helping my nerves. Let's go kayaking."

* * *

Lisa waved to Rachel as she drove away. She turned to go into the house and called to Daisy, who chose to ignore her until Lisa offered her a piece of cheese from the tray she was bringing inside.

They went upstairs, and Lisa fed Daisy before going down to get some things together just in case she did stay over at Carrie's. She wasn't sure how the night would go, and she didn't want to make assumptions. The best thing to do would be to pack a few things, but leave them in the car.

No one other than her nurses and doctors had seen the scars from her cancer treatment. It might be difficult to show Carrie. She didn't want to worry about it too much, but Lisa hoped the scars didn't disturb her. That could change everything. Carrie had responded so well when Lisa told her about having breast cancer, maybe it boded well for how she would react to seeing her?

Images of Carrie filled her mind and her heart raced when she thought about spending the night. The sound of her phone ringing brought Lisa back to her senses. She reached into her pocket and saw it was Rachel on the line.

"Hi. What's up?" Lisa answered. "Did you forget something?"

"I wanted to tell you there's a sheriff's car watching your road, so be careful if you go anywhere," Rachel said. "I had just gone around the corner from your place when he pulled me over."

"Why did he pull you over? Were you driving fast?"

"He said I was speeding, but I wasn't. He was obnoxious. It's a good thing I only drank water this afternoon and didn't have a beer."

"Did you get a ticket?"

"Yes, can you believe it? I'm livid because he made the whole thing up. He kept asking me questions about what I was doing there."

"Did you tell him you were visiting me? I don't think he knows who I am."

"He knew your name when I told him where I was coming from, which surprised me. I guess since it's a small town, he probably knows everyone."

"I guess." Lisa wasn't sure what to think about this. "Where was he exactly?"

"He was down around the corner where your road joins the other one. I don't know why in the world the sheriff would be parked out there pulling people over. There isn't any traffic. It makes no sense, which is why I called to let you know."

"That is weird," Lisa agreed. "I'm really sorry you got a ticket."

"Me, too. It was very aggravating. All right, I've got to go. I'll talk to you later."

"Thanks for the warning."

Did this have anything to do with last night? Had Joe Michaud found out her name and decided to target her?

CHAPTER TWENTY-SEVEN

Carrie looked out the kitchen window as Lisa pulled in and parked next to the Jeep. She went out to the screened porch to greet her and Daisy. Lisa's blond hair was shining in the sun and Carrie couldn't help but notice how good her legs looked in her shorts.

"Hi there. I'm glad you're here."

"I'm glad you asked me to come over." Lisa joined Carrie on the porch. "I really wanted to see you tonight."

"I want us to spend some time together. I'm going to cook dinner and we can have a nice, romantic evening, just the two of us." Carrie slipped her hands around Lisa's waist. "I know you have to work in the morning, so I'll try to make sure not to keep you out too late."

Lisa kissed Carrie's lips gently. "Are you going to make me go home?"

Carrie's body responded as she kissed Lisa back. She pulled Lisa close and kissed her way to Lisa's ear. She sucked on her earlobe and whispered, "I'm not going to make you go anywhere. You can stay as long as you like."

Lisa shivered and smiled. "Can Daisy stay too?"

"Daisy is always welcome." Carrie continued to kiss the tender place behind Lisa's ear while Lisa's hands wrapped around her.

"It feels so good to touch you. I don't want to stop."

"I don't want you to stop." Carrie slid her hands down Lisa's back. "Let's go inside."

Carrie followed Lisa and Daisy into the house and watched as Lisa looked around and turned to her with a smile. "The flowers on the counter are so pretty."

"They're for you. I stopped over at my parents' house this afternoon and picked them from their flower gardens."

"Thank you. Everything looks beautiful." Lisa kissed Carrie as they stood by the table. It was set with Carrie's favorite dishes and she had candles ready to light. Their dinner was ready to be taken out of the refrigerator. The fruit she had chopped up for an appetizer was sitting on another table out on the deck.

"Let me get us a couple drinks and we can sit outside." Carrie headed to the refrigerator and took out two bottles of cold beer.

"That looks like a good drink for a hot night. What can I do to help?"

"I'm all set."

They walked out to the deck and sat down together on the couch where they could relax with a perfect view of the sun beginning to set over the still waters of the lake.

"What a gorgeous night." Lisa looked into Carrie's eyes.

"It is." Carrie didn't take her eyes off Lisa as she set her bottle on the table. Reaching for her waist, she slid Lisa closer to her. "Come sit a little closer."

"I need to touch you right now." Lisa reached for Carrie and pressed their mouths together, kissing her and tasting her with her tongue. Lisa traced the side of Carrie's cheek with her hand and ran her fingers gently through Carrie's hair.

Carrie responded immediately, lifting Lisa up and sliding her onto her lap.

"You feel so good." Carrie closed her eyes and kissed Lisa while she slipped her hands under Lisa's light cotton shirt and felt the smooth skin of her stomach and sides. Moving her hands up to Lisa's breasts, she began to caress them.

"Hold on a second."

"What's wrong?" Carrie suddenly realized what Lisa was concerned about. "Are you worried about your scars?"

Lisa nodded. "No one's seen me without my clothes on."

Carrie kissed her gently. "I think you're beautiful. A few scars aren't going to make any difference."

"I can't help it. I'm nervous about showing you. I don't want you to be grossed out or feel sorry for me, and I'm not sure which is worse."

"Nothing about you would ever gross me out." Carrie paused. "At least nothing physical. You may have some habits I don't know about."

Lisa laughed. "I may."

"Seriously, though, I don't want you to worry about showing me anything. I have plenty of my own flaws and I don't know anyone who's perfect. Why in the world would I feel sorry for you? I admire how well you've handled everything, and I'm grateful you're healthy now."

"Okay. Is it all right if we go inside?"

"Whatever you want to do is fine. Why don't we have dinner and relax for a little while?"

Lisa slid off Carrie's lap and held out her hand. "I don't think I can wait that long. I just want to be with you."

Carrie took Lisa's hand and stood up. They walked into the house together and Carrie led her up the stairs to her bedroom.

"Can I take your shirt off?" Carrie asked.

Lisa nodded, and Carrie gently lifted her shirt over her head, dropping it onto the floor. Carrie pulled her own shirt off next and tossed it aside. She kissed Lisa and reached behind her to unfasten her bra and slide it off. Keeping her eyes fixed on Lisa's, Carrie unfastened her own bra and took it off. She put her arms around Lisa and kissed her lips, pulling back the covers as she guided her down onto the bed.

She lay next to Lisa and began leaving a trail of kisses along Lisa's exposed skin. She began by kissing the scar near her right shoulder and continued her way over to Lisa's left side. Carrie glanced up at Lisa and smiled before running her tongue all along her left breast and kissing it gently and thoroughly.

Carrie paused for a moment. "Honey, you're beautiful."

Lisa closed her eyes. "I knew you would never say anything unkind, but I was still a little worried about how you would respond when you actually saw me without my clothes."

Carrie moved back up next to Lisa. She wanted to say the right thing and alleviate all of Lisa's doubts. "You have nothing to be worried about. It's hardly noticeable and I've never seen anyone I wanted as much as you."

Lisa's gaze traveled down Carrie's body and back to her face. "I was just thinking the same thing about you."

Carrie slid her shorts and panties off and knelt beside Lisa on the bed, kissing her stomach. She reached for Lisa's shorts and unbuttoned them before gently pulling them off and tossing them to the floor. Smiling at Lisa, Carrie slipped her fingers into Lisa's panties, sliding them down carefully until finally they were both naked.

Lisa sat up on her elbows as Carrie kissed her way up her inner thighs until she was between her legs. She lay back with a moan as Carrie's tongue went inside her. Carrie delighted in discovering Lisa's unique taste and letting her tongue explore her special shapes and folds. She took her time, enjoying the responses she could feel coming from Lisa. Carrie felt her own arousal grow and she experienced a surge of desire that shocked her with its intensity. She wanted nothing more than to make Lisa happy and she was filled with pleasure when Lisa finally lay still and contented.

"Oh my God," Lisa panted.

Carrie slid up next to her and kissed her. "Did you like that?"

"I had no idea you were hiding such a skill." Lisa rolled over on top of Carrie. "Now it's my turn."

She pulled Lisa's hips closer, craving her touch. Lisa kissed Carrie's mouth and continued pulsing against her hips. Rising up on her hands, Lisa kissed her way down Carrie's neck, finally reaching her breasts.

Carrie moaned as Lisa circled her nipples with her tongue and kissed her way down Carrie's stomach. She couldn't keep her hips still as Lisa moved between her thighs. Her body was combusting with desire when she felt the warmth of Lisa's mouth between her legs.

Her brain felt like it was exploding with desire and she couldn't process a clear thought. She let her mind go blank, allowing herself to enjoy the waves of pleasure that were passing through her. Nothing distracted her from the intensity of the moment. She gasped with pleasure as Lisa brought her over the edge, leaving her speechless and exhausted.

Running her hands through Lisa's hair as she slid up next to her, Carrie kissed her lips and lay back with Lisa's arm around her. It was too soon to feel this way. They had only known each other for a few weeks, but she had never felt this close to anyone before.

"I can't think of anything better than being here with you right now," Carrie said.

"Me either," Lisa said. "It seems so sudden, but I've been falling for you for weeks now."

"Have you?" Carrie smiled at her. "I remember you said you thought I was intimidating."

"I also said you were gorgeous like your brother."

"That's right, you did say that."

"I was dying to get your attention, but you never seemed interested."

"I've been alone for a long time, but I've never felt lonely until I met you and I thought you were with someone else. I wanted you from the start and I didn't want to share you with anyone."

"I had no idea you felt that way. I thought you just weren't interested. That's why I tried to make it work with Toni, but my heart wasn't in it. I only wanted to be with you."

Carrie rolled over to face Lisa. "I'm going to make sure you know how much I care about you."

"Show me." Lisa pulled her in for another kiss.

Carrie slid her leg between Lisa's as she kissed her back.

* * *

Carrie chuckled at the sight of Daisy jumping down from her spot on the couch when she heard their footsteps coming down the stairs. "I guess someone is feeling right at home."

They walked into the kitchen together, finally ready for something to eat. Lisa let go of Carrie's hand and leaned on the counter while Carrie opened up the refrigerator and took out the dishes she had prepared earlier.

"I can't wait to see what you've made for dinner," Lisa said.

"I've got a couple types of salad ready. Does that sound all right?"

"I'm sure it will be delicious. I'll get our drinks."

Carrie put the serving bowls on the table and lit the candles while Lisa retrieved two fresh bottles of beer for them. They sat down together, and Lisa moved her chair closer to Carrie's. The sun had long since gone down, and the table was lit with the soft glow of candlelight.

"This looks really good." Lisa ran her hand along Carrie's bare leg and ignored the food.

Carrie swallowed the bite of pasta salad she was eating and tried to sit still. Lisa was making her want to go back to bed. "I thought you said you were hungry?"

"I thought I was," Lisa shrugged, still stroking Carrie's leg. "I can't seem to think of anything but you at the moment."

Carrie leaned forward and kissed Lisa, sliding her own hand up Lisa's leg. "It's too bad you have to work in the morning, but at least I'm going to get to have you for the night."

"Maybe I'll go in late. I'm sure no one at work would care."

"I don't want to get you in trouble."

"Speaking of trouble, Rachel got pulled over by the sheriff when she left my house."

"That's an odd place to get pulled over."

"I know. He gave her a ticket for speeding, even though Rachel said she wasn't driving fast. Luckily, he was gone by the time I left to come over here."

"What did he say to her?" Carrie asked, growing concerned.

"He asked what she was doing there and where she was coming from. It's funny, but Rachel said he knew who I was when she told him she'd been visiting me."

"Michaud must have decided to keep an eye on you after seeing us together at Bruce's last night. This is not good."

"I don't think they know I was actually in Bruce's office. I think they would have done more than just keep an eye on my house if they knew."

"I hope they don't notice the police report is missing from Bruce's desk. We have to get all of your information to the police. This is getting out of hand."

"I still wish we had more proof, but you're right. If the sheriff is starting to notice us, then we've got to report what we know. The question is, who should we call?"

"I've been thinking about it and I know a guy who's a state trooper. His name is Luke and he's one of my regulars. I'm pretty sure we could trust him. I also know a woman named Anna who works for the newspaper. She'd be a good person to contact."

"Those are both good ideas. Let's do it."

"The problem is, I don't have their private numbers. I only see them at the café and I don't really know them personally. I could look up their work numbers tomorrow morning and try to call them both during business hours."

"That's a good plan." Lisa put her hand back on Carrie's leg and slid her fingers up her inner thigh, squeezing gently. "Now I've got some plans for you that are going to keep us both busy tonight."

CHAPTER TWENTY-EIGHT

Lisa looked up from the file she was working on to see Mary standing in the doorway of her office. She had been daydreaming about Carrie and thinking about the night before. They hadn't slept much but she had gotten up early enough to make it in to work on time after all. Daisy was going to hang out with Carrie for the day, lucky dog.

"Hi Mary," Lisa said. "How was your weekend?"

"Pretty good," Mary replied. "Are you going to the company picnic on Friday?"

"Yes. After you told me Don would be expecting us all to be there, I realized I should plan on going." Lisa lowered her voice. "Hopefully we don't have to spend any time with him."

"No, don't worry. All of the partners will be there, and he won't bother with us. The picnic usually consists of everyone gathered around awkwardly trying to socialize for a few hours while they serve food and drinks. Most people take off as soon as the meal is over."

"Sounds like a blast."

"Keep your fingers crossed they don't make us do any team building exercises. One year we had to spend time visualizing our places in the organizational structure."

Lisa laughed. "I'm glad we don't do that every year."

"Hopefully this year we'll have lunch and be able to leave." Mary left with a wave and Lisa turned back to the numbers she was working on.

Her attention began to wander and she glanced down the hall. The office was quiet today, which could give her a good opportunity to try and get into Don's email account. She had written down some of the passwords she had found on the notes in his office. Now that they knew about the police report and had decided to go to the authorities, she had to quickly get as much information as possible.

Logging out of her own email account, Lisa clicked the login button for the company's intranet. When the company login screen came up, she entered Don's email address for the username and tried the first password on his list, *Jean1960*. An error message popped up. Knowing the site would automatically lock her out if she made three unsuccessful attempts, Lisa looked the list over carefully before choosing a second password to enter, *MillsMillionsXX*. Once again, an error message appeared. Holding her breath, she tried the last password on his list, *IlikeT1Ts00*.

The home screen opened, and Lisa watched as the page loaded. She was inside. Now to access his email. Clicking on the email link, she entered Don's login credentials again and her excitement grew as his inbox opened on the screen in front of her. There were several other folders listed along with the inbox, and she wasn't sure what to look for. As she had said to Carrie, there may not be anything of interest to them in his work emails. He probably had a private email he used for personal correspondence, but it was still worth checking here.

He had organized his folders into categories for the various areas of operations he oversaw. There were headings for audits and other types of projects, which contained multiple folders with related correspondence. She looked through some of the messages, trying to find anything related to Senator Lawrence. Spotting a folder named "Contracts," she clicked on it, hoping to find information like she had previously. There didn't appear to be any emails related to the Lawrence contract in that location, so she changed directories and kept looking.

Unable to find anything useful from the various email folders, she decided to do a search for Bruce Mills to see if there were any messages containing his name. A list of possible emails scrolled up on her screen. Lisa scanned the subjects, hoping to see some mention of Senator Lawrence. A message Don had received from his brother Bruce on a date shortly after Michelle Nelson's accident caught her eye.

"Don, I heard from Joe and he confirmed the report has been corrected and submitted. Repairs should be completed within the next day or two. We need to get together and discuss the next steps. I have some ideas about a contract I want to talk to you about. Let's get things going while he's still feeling grateful."

Lisa forwarded a copy of the email to her personal account and then deleted the copy from the folder which listed all email sent by Don's account so he wouldn't notice. She sat back and thought for a moment. While the message didn't actually give any specific information about the accident or William Lawrence's involvement, it implied confirmation about what she and Carrie had suspected. The accident report and vehicle repairs were directly related to a contract Bruce Mills wanted, which had to be the one Lawrence had helped him to secure. She looked through the other emails in her search results and didn't find any other direct references to the accident.

Trying another search, she looked for messages that contained William Lawrence's name. Again, a list of results displayed and she started looking through them. The contents once again failed to mention any specifics, but there was one message Don had received from Senator Lawrence, which Lisa thought might give them additional evidence, if they ever needed some way to prove Lawrence's involvement with the Mills brothers.

"*Good morning. As I am sure you are already aware, the procurement committee has agreed with my recommendation, and I will soon be announcing publicly that the contract for the new Augusta business park has been awarded to Mills Building Construction. This endorsement is a gesture of my faith in Mills Building Construction and allows me to show my appreciation for your continued support.*"

She forwarded the email to her account as well and was trying to think of other possible searches she could do when her desk phone rang. She looked at the number and saw it was Don on the line. She quickly clicked on the link to log off his account on the company intranet as she picked up the phone.

"Hello, Don," Lisa answered.

"I need to speak with you for a moment. Please come down to my office."

Lisa tried not to panic. There was no way he could have known she was logged into his account. It had to be something else. She took some deep breaths and tried to stay calm as she walked down the hall toward his office.

The door to Don's office was closed. She knocked once and waited. She heard his muffled voice. "Come in."

She opened the door and stepped into the office. Not wanting to be alone with Don, she left the door ajar.

"Close the door." He fixed his gaze on her from behind his desk. "Take a seat."

She reluctantly closed the door behind her and walked over to the chair in front of the desk, being careful to angle herself away from the hidden camera. His demeanor was much different than usual, and she wasn't sure what was going on. Reassuring herself again that there was no way he could have known she accessed his email account, she forced herself to sit quietly and wait to find out what he wanted. It didn't take long.

"I'm very disappointed in your performance lately," he said. "When we hired you, I had high expectations and I'm afraid you aren't meeting them."

Lisa looked at him in shock. She knew her work was always first rate, and she had never heard a complaint about her job performance in her life.

"I don't understand. What do you mean my performance? What have I done that you aren't happy with?"

"I had hoped you'd be able to step up and assist with audits, but I'm afraid your work just isn't good enough. We require our staff accountants to be more than competent. We need people who are going to excel, and I'm sorry to say you're not up to par."

"But what exactly did I do wrong?" Lisa was unable to process what was happening. "I got an excellent review after my first six months."

"I'm afraid your services will no longer be needed."

Lisa was shocked into silence. She hadn't imagined she would be fired. Her competency had never been called into question. She knew she did excellent work and had always taken great pride in how well she did her job. Clearly Don had made up his mind and there was no point in arguing.

"My brother tells me you're on remarkably friendly terms with the woman who runs the café in Winchester. The one who catered his party." He leaned back and folded his hands across his bulging stomach. "Perhaps you should speak with her about finding a new line of work better suited to your abilities."

Suddenly, she realized what was going on. Bruce must have told Don about finding her and Carrie kissing in the hallway at the party. Her temper ignited. She was being fired because Don had found out she was a lesbian. He wanted the women working for him to feed into his sexual fantasies and now she didn't fit that role.

"Do you have a problem with my personal life?" Lisa demanded angrily. "Perhaps a problem with lesbians?"

"That's not what I said at all." He winced at the word and avoided her eyes. "Obviously you're not a good fit for this office."

"You know damn well my work was beyond reproach." Lisa clenched the sides of her chair, trying to reign in her response. She ached to blast him with her knowledge of the secret files and pictures, but she couldn't tip her hand at this point.

"You're not a team player. We need to give our customers a certain level of service and someone like you just isn't going to cut it."

"Let me get this straight, or as straight as I can get it." Lisa stood and put her hands on his desk, leaning toward him. "Do you mean a lesbian isn't going to cut it?

"Bruce mentioned they found you wandering around in places where you shouldn't have been." Don's face was starting to sweat. He rolled back in his chair, putting space between them. "It's just another example of how you don't meet company standards. You've brought this upon yourself."

"You know what, Don? You think you have all the power here, but you don't. To tell you the truth, I'll be happy to leave. You have not gotten the best of me."

The only thing holding her back from losing her cool completely was the satisfaction of knowing she and Carrie were going to be bringing him down very soon.

He picked up his phone and dialed the receptionist's number. "Please escort Miss Owens to her office and help her clean out her desk."

Don hung up the phone. "We'll give you two weeks' severance pay. I can't allow you to have access to client records from this point on. I'm sure you understand."

Lisa turned to leave. "I understand exactly what's going on here."

Lisa left his office and stormed back to her desk. The receptionist hurried after her, carrying a cardboard box.

Though she had been there less than a year, there were books, pictures, and a few other items in her office she didn't want to leave behind. She wanted to get out of the building as quickly as possible, but she took her time looking through her desk and gathering up her things. She powered down her laptop and left it on her desk. After one last look around, she nodded at the receptionist and headed for the door.

Fortunately, she had made a habit of backing up important files on her laptop to a personal external hard drive. A former coworker had advised her to do this several years ago, and she was glad she had listened. She kept the drive in a small compartment in her work bag which was an oversized leather bag containing her wallet and other personal items. It hadn't drawn the attention of the receptionist who was monitoring her, and it was a relief to know she wouldn't lose anything important.

Lisa's face burned with shame as she walked down the hallway carrying her things in a box with the receptionist following close behind her. She saw her former coworkers looking at her from their desks with curiosity. She had seen this happen to other people in the past, but had never dreamed it would happen to her.

CHAPTER TWENTY-NINE

The drive home passed in a blur. Still not sure how she had gone from having a secure job to being unemployed so quickly, Lisa couldn't think clearly. Her identity had always been tied to her job, and she was doing her best to hold back tears. The more she thought about what had just happened, the angrier she got.

It was ironic how careful she had been to find a job with a reputable firm, only to discover her boss was sexually harassing multiple women. Don was truly a pervert, and he had the audacity to fire her without a moment's notice because of her sexual orientation. There was no other reason that made sense. Nothing in her work performance had given him any basis for firing her.

The turnoff to her driveway came into view and she debated between going home and thinking things over or going to Carrie's. The thought of being able to talk to Carrie won out and she kept driving until she made it to her house. Pulling into the driveway next to the Jeep, she got out of the car and looked out at the lake for a moment while she tried to calm down.

"Hey there." Carrie came out of the screen porch door and down the steps, followed by an excited Daisy. "What are you doing here so early?"

She was suddenly filled with embarrassment at the thought of telling Carrie what happened. She bent down to pet Daisy for a minute then straightened up to face her. She still couldn't look her in the eyes and she gazed back down at the ground. "I got fired."

"What?" Carrie closed the distance between them and pulled Lisa into her arms. "Honey, what happened?"

Lisa tried not to cry while Carrie comforted her, but she couldn't stop herself. Tears fell as Carrie held her close. After a few minutes, she trusted herself enough to speak. "I'm still so shocked I can barely process it. I got called into Don's office and he told me I wasn't meeting expectations and they weren't satisfied with my performance. He said I wasn't a good fit for the company."

"I'm so sorry. I know you didn't like working for him in the first place, but I'm sure you wanted to leave on your own terms."

"I'm good at my job." Lisa wiped her eyes. "I've always gotten excellent reviews. My performance wasn't the real reason. He fired me because he found out I'm a lesbian."

Carrie's jaw dropped. "What did he say?"

"At first I couldn't figure out why he was saying I wasn't meeting company standards. Then he started taunting me about his brother finding us together at the party and how I should talk to you about finding a new line of work. That's when I knew what was going on and I went off on him."

"I don't blame you. I'd like to kick his sleazy ass."

"He denied it had anything to do with my personal life, of course, and told me I brought it on myself."

Carrie gave her a worried look. "Did you tell him you know about the files and the pictures he has?"

"I really wanted to, believe me. It took every shred of my self-control to hold myself back. I just kept telling myself how great it was going to be when we expose him and the others. It was the only thing that got me through this humiliating day."

"I'm really sorry. I feel terrible seeing this happen to you. We never should have gone snooping around Bruce Mills's house."

"You have nothing to be sorry about." Lisa looked at Carrie. "I was the one who made you come with me to Bruce's office, and I was the one who kissed you. I'm definitely not sorry about that."

Carrie leaned down and kissed her gently. Lisa slid her hands around Carrie's neck and pulled her closer, kissing her back.

"I must look like a mess," Lisa said.

"No, you don't." Carrie kissed her again. "I think you're beautiful, but I hate seeing you so upset. Let's try to figure out what we can do about all this."

Carrie took Lisa's hand and they walked into the house together. Lisa sat down at the table and tried to sort out her thoughts.

"It's good that I've already been putting some résumés out. I've got a decent amount of savings, so I should be fine for a while. I wish I could talk to Rachel, but she's gone on vacation for a week. She has a lot of contacts and she might have some job leads for me."

"I'm sure you'll find something you like better." Carrie walked into the kitchen to get them each a glass of water. "In the meantime, maybe this will give you a little time to relax and enjoy the summer."

"Yeah, I need to keep a positive outlook. I just wasn't expecting this."

Carrie sat next to her. "We've got to hurry up and do something about Don. First the harassment, now this."

"Yeah. Obviously we need to turn him in because he helped cover up Michelle Nelson's death, but I also want to make sure he doesn't get away with firing me because of my sexual orientation. That's illegal in Maine."

Carrie leaned toward Lisa and put a comforting hand on hers. "Do you think you should contact an attorney?"

"Again, I don't have any solid proof. I could show there was nothing wrong with my job performance, but all Don would have to say is I'm not a good fit for the company and there wouldn't be any way to prove otherwise. I wouldn't want my job back at this point anyway, but I don't want him to be able to do this to anyone else."

"Is there anyone in the company who oversees Don?"

"There are some other partners in the firm, but they're in a different office. I don't know if it would do any good to talk to them or not. Right now, I think getting the information we've gathered about the accident to someone who can help us is more important. We need to focus on making sure none of those guys get away with what they've done. Don's harassment charges will be icing on the cake."

"That's true. I tried to call Anna and Luke earlier, the reporter and the state trooper I told you about. They were both out of their offices and I couldn't get in touch with either of them. He's on vacation until Saturday and she's out until Friday."

"What do you think we should do?"

"I guess we should keep quiet and wait a couple days until we get a chance to talk to people we can trust. We'll tell them everything we know and hand it over to them. Then I think you should talk to a lawyer about the way Don Mills treated you."

"Oh, I almost forgot. I was able to get into his email before he called me in to his office and fired me."

"Did you find anything?"

"Nothing new, but there were a couple messages that backed up our theories about the police report and the contracts. Luckily, I had a chance to save copies. They'll help us tie everything together when we turn our information over to the police."

"Every bit helps. I think there's enough evidence now that we should be able to get people to listen to us. I just hope Don, Bruce, and Joe don't find out we know anything."

"I'm glad we've been able to work together on all of this. I don't know what I would have done without you." Lisa squeezed Carrie's hand. "I've been alone for so long, it really makes me appreciate having someone I can count on."

Carrie smiled at her. "I'm glad you know you can count on me."

"Same here."

"I don't have to go in to the café since it's Monday, so we've got the whole day to spend together now. Let's do something that'll take our minds off everything for a while. What do you feel like doing?"

"Let's take the kayaks out for a little while." Lisa leaned forward and kissed Carrie's lips. "Maybe later we can think of some indoor activities."

CHAPTER THIRTY

Carrie pulled out of the driveway at the café and headed toward Lisa's place. The past few days had been stressful while they waited for Anna and Luke to return Carrie's calls. Carrie thought she was more upset than Lisa about the way Don Mills had fired her. She couldn't wait to see him get caught and finally have to face the consequences for all the nasty things he'd done.

In spite of their worries about Michaud and the Mills brothers, they had found time to relax and enjoy each other's company. Carrie usually liked to spend as much time as possible at the café, keeping an eye on things and making sure all her customers were happy. Today she couldn't wait for the lunch rush to be over so she could leave and go see Lisa. They were both used to living on their own and each valued their autonomy, but she was finding it was nice to have someone to go home to.

She reached Lisa's place and pulled in. Daisy came running up with her usual happy greeting as Carrie reached for her gym bag and got out of the Jeep.

"Hi, girl." Carrie knelt down to give her an ear rub as Daisy's tail wagged madly.

"Hi there. Are you ready for a run?" Lisa stood in the doorway in her running clothes.

"Only if we get to jump in the lake afterward." Carrie walked over to Lisa and kissed her gently on the lips. "I probably smell like lunch, so I shouldn't get too close."

"You smell delicious." Lisa pulled her close for a deeper kiss. "Maybe that's why Daisy's especially happy to see you today."

Carrie laughed. "I'd better hurry up and change my clothes. We need to get a good run in before we go to my parents' house for dinner. Less than two weeks to go for the 5K."

"At least I have plenty of time to train these days."

Carrie set her bag down and paused in the entryway. "I know you're not going to have any trouble finding another job, and I hope you can enjoy having a little time off without worrying too much about work. You know I'll help you if you need anything."

Lisa put her arms around Carrie's waist. "That's very sweet, but don't worry. I'm all set financially for now while I look for a new job, if that's what you're talking about."

Carrie shrugged. "I just wanted you to know I'm here if you need any help."

"Thank you." Lisa gave her a hug. "I was thinking about something along those lines today. I was wondering if you'd like me to help out while I have some free time."

"Help me out?" Carrie leaned back and looked at her. "What do you mean?"

"I want to keep busy. I'm going to get bored really quickly with nothing to do all day. Why don't I give you a hand at the café?"

The café was in the middle of its busy season and she could always use an extra set of hands. Plus, they'd get to spend more time together. "You know, that's a good idea."

"I have them every now and then."

"What about the fact you don't like to cook, and you didn't like being a waitress?"

"Hey, I was good at serving for the party."

"I know you were, and I really appreciated it. I just wouldn't want you to do something you didn't enjoy."

"I'd enjoy being with you while I have a little extra time on my hands." Lisa slipped her hands under Carrie's shirt and caressed her skin. "I know something else we could enjoy together. Why don't you let me help you take a nice shower and get cleaned up?"

"What about our training run?"

"Who says we can't go for a run after we take a shower?" Lisa took Carrie's hand and led Carrie to her bedroom and the master shower.

"How can I argue with that?" Carrie grabbed her gym bag and followed Lisa.

* * *

Lisa walked into the café and stopped to inhale the delicious smells of breakfast coming from the grill. Her empty stomach immediately started to growl. She stood by the counter and looked into the kitchen. Carrie had her back to the door and was busy cooking eggs and sausage. The case in front of Lisa was full of fresh muffins and scones along with packages of Carrie's homemade granola. She had come here to help, but it smelled so good she had to eat some breakfast first.

It was midmorning and there were only a few people sitting at the tables in the dining area. The sky was cloudy with rain in the forecast, and the water on the lake was dark and choppy. Summer vacationers would probably find it a good day to go out to eat. Lisa hoped it didn't get too busy. She remembered all too well from her days waiting tables in college how easy it was to get overwhelmed, and she wanted to impress Carrie on her first day.

Leaning on the counter, Lisa called back into the kitchen. "Hi there."

Carrie turned and saw her. "Good morning. How are you?"

"I'm ready to get to work as soon as I have one of those pumpkin muffins. They look so good I can't resist."

Carrie put the eggs she was cooking onto a plate with some toast and sausage. "Let me deliver this meal and I'll be right back. We can talk about how you can help." On her way to the dining room, she whispered, "You look so good I can't resist either."

Lisa smiled as Carrie placed the dish in front of a waiting customer and returned to the counter. They walked into the kitchen area and stopped next to the center counter where Carrie was getting ingredients ready for the daily meals.

"Are you working by yourself today?" Lisa asked.

"Angie was here earlier and now I've got you."

"You certainly do." Lisa slipped her arm around Carrie's waist and kissed her. "What would you like me to do? I can help here in the kitchen or wait on people in the dining room."

"We usually have counter service for breakfast and lunch. We only wait on tables during dinner hours. I was hoping you might want to run the counter for me and help deliver orders to tables when we get busy."

"That sounds fine." Lisa was relieved. She would much rather take people's orders and run the register than wait on tables and worry about keeping everyone happy.

"Thanks, honey." Carrie waved her hand at the array of food on the workspace in front of her. "I'm going to get busy making some things for lunch."

Lisa took a look at the cash register. She familiarized herself with the controls and located the order pads in their location under the counter. Everything was neatly organized, and she was hoping she'd get the hang of it quickly.

She took a muffin out of the case and ate it while she waited for customers. She was going to have a hard time staying away from all of the delicious temptations right next to her in the bakery case. There were some cinnamon rolls that were calling to her.

Fortunately, the café was fairly quiet for the rest of the morning. Lisa was able to build up her confidence as a few customers came by and she successfully took their orders. Eventually, lunchtime approached, and the number of customers increased. She started to get busy and she wondered if she should ask Carrie for help. The café was full and there was a line of people waiting at the counter.

Taking a deep breath, she tried to stay calm while hurriedly writing down orders and ringing up customers on the register. She jotted down all the sandwiches and other items for the family that was currently at the front of the line and rang up their order. Turning around quickly, she placed the slip in front of Carrie.

"How are you doing up there?" Carrie looked up from the wraps she was preparing.

"You know I'm not used to a lot of public interaction, but I think I'm doing all right." Lisa didn't want to admit the line of people was intimidating her. "As long as people aren't in too big of a hurry, we should be okay."

Lisa hurried back to her spot behind the counter and took the next order. She had just finished filling out the slip for a mother and her two children when she looked over to see Carrie's mother walk in the door. Lisa waved hello and Susan bypassed the line and walked behind the counter to join her.

"Hi there. This place is certainly busy today," Susan said. "Can I give you a hand?"

"That would be fantastic," Lisa answered with a sigh of relief. "We can get through this line a lot quicker, and then I can see if Carrie needs any help in the kitchen."

Lisa began writing down people's requests on the order slips and passing the papers over to Susan to ring up on the register. The line dwindled quickly, and they were soon caught up.

"Thanks for the help," Lisa said. "You're a lot faster at running the register than I was."

"Don't worry. You'll get the hang of it," Susan said. "I help out every now and then, so I know most of the prices. That makes it easier."

"Thanks again for dinner last night. I had a great time and now I know where Carrie learned some of her cooking skills."

"You're very welcome. It's nice to see Carrie so happy."

"She's a really special person and I'm lucky I met her." Lisa turned around to look at the kitchen behind them. "She's working on a bunch of orders. I'd better go see if I can help her."

"I'll join you and we can keep an eye on the counter."

She followed Susan to the sink where they washed up before joining Carrie at the prep counter. Carrie looked up from the row of plates she was working on.

"Hi, Mom. Thanks for stopping by. It's been busier than I expected today, and I was feeling bad about leaving Lisa all by herself up there."

"Lisa was doing a great job. I'm sure she would have been just fine," Susan said. "Now how about you let me take some of those slips?"

Susan grabbed the top one and began working on the orders with Carrie. Several plates were ready and waiting, so Lisa delivered them to their hungry customers.

The lunch hour passed quickly as she balanced her time between taking orders and delivering meals. Normally a quiet person, she found she was enjoying having a chance to meet and talk with customers. There was a good mix of locals and tourists. She didn't know many people in town and this was turning out to be a good way to meet some of them.

By midafternoon, the café was quiet again. Susan had gone home earlier, and Carrie was busy prepping for the dinner hour with Angie. Lisa finished wiping down the tables and walked back into the kitchen, carefully avoiding the bakery case.

"Is there anything you need me to do before I go?" She was planning to leave shortly and go home to check on Daisy. Carrie was going to stay for a little longer and make sure things were running smoothly for dinner.

Carrie looked up from the vegetables she was chopping and smiled at her. "I really appreciate your help today, honey."

"I had fun, actually, and I met some nice people. It was good to stay busy and keep my mind off other things for a while."

"We can definitely keep you busy here," Angie said, putting a tray of bread loaves into the oven. "It's a fun place to work and there's always something that needs to be done."

"I'll be back tomorrow." She realized she probably shouldn't make assumptions; Carrie might not need her tomorrow. "I mean, if it's all right with you and if you want some extra help."

"It's more than all right." Carrie resumed chopping while she spoke. "It was great having you here and I'd love to have you come back tomorrow. I don't want to take up all your free time, though, so we'll have to figure out a schedule."

In spite of the fact she had lost her job and was trying to uncover her former boss's illegal activities, she felt a surge of pleasure and contentment. It was amazing to reflect how the choices she had made lately had changed her life so completely. If she hadn't chosen to end things with Toni and let Carrie know how she felt, she would not have been able to experience this incredible happiness.

As far as her career went, it may not have been the safest choice to dig deeper into Don's shady dealings, but she didn't have any regrets. She and Carrie were going to follow through and make sure he and the other men didn't get away with covering up Michelle Nelson's accident for Senator Lawrence.

"Could you do one favor for me before you go?" Carrie asked.

"Sure."

"My hands are covered with tomatoes and we're out of paper towels. There's a case of them in the back room. Would you mind bringing some in, please?"

"I'll be right back."

A wave of stifling heat hit her when she opened the door to the back room. The air-conditioning system kept the kitchen fairly comfortable, but the closed door prevented the cool air from reaching this area. She turned on the light and started looking through the cans, boxes, and other items on the shelves until she spotted a large cardboard box containing paper towels on a rack in the back corner.

Before taking the rolls back to Carrie, she decided to look around and familiarize herself with the layout and location of the various supplies. The walls were lined with shelving racks packed with everything from canned goods to paper products.

In spite of the quantity of stock, everything was organized into neatly stacked rows. The food items were stored in the racks on the left side of the room along with two large refrigerated cases. The shelves on the right side of the room had cleaning materials and paper goods in the back area. The pots, pans, dishes, and utensils were all put away on the racks in the front area. An industrial-sized freezer took up the back wall under the lone window.

She picked up the paper towels and paused to look out the window. It had started to rain, and the wind was kicking up whitecaps on the lake. There were no boats in sight. She turned to head back into the kitchen when the door opened, and Carrie came into the storage room, closing the door behind her.

"Hey there." Carrie walked over and looked outside at the rainy weather. "I started thinking about the last time you were back here, and I decided to come see what you were doing. I was hoping we could step outside for a minute, but I guess we'd better stay in."

She dropped the paper towels and clasped Carrie's waist. "The last time I was back here I couldn't keep my hands off you."

"I remember. You almost fell when I opened the door and I caught you." Carrie reached for her shoulders and gently pressed her back against the wall. Her lips met Lisa's in a slow, intense kiss.

She relaxed into Carrie, pulling her closer. Her tongue met Carrie's as she slid her hands up Carrie's lower back, feeling the firm muscles under her soft skin. Carrie's hands stroked her hair as their kisses deepened.

Lisa wanted to feel more of Carrie's skin against hers, but she knew they could be interrupted at any moment. The thrill of illicit sex in the storeroom tempted her for a moment, but she reluctantly ended the kiss and looked into Carrie's eyes. "You need to get back to work. Let's hold this thought until tonight."

"I'm planning to hold you tonight, not just this thought." Carrie stepped back and released her. "You're right, though, I should get back to work. I want to get things squared away so I don't have to stay too late."

"Don't forget your paper towels." Lisa passed the rolls to Carrie and gave her another quick kiss. "I might as well go out this way."

"I'll call you when I leave. Still want me to stop by after dinner?"

"Of course. See you later."

She went out the back exit and closed the door firmly. The wind blowing off the lake drove the light rain down briskly as she hurried around the corner of the building toward the side lot where her car was parked.

She stopped short as she realized she had left her bag and her car keys inside the café. She jogged back around the corner and reached for the rear door, only to find it had locked behind her. Giving a groan of exasperation, she ran for the front door.

Her bag was where she left it behind the counter. Thoroughly wet now, she picked it up and waved to Carrie.

"Did you forget something?"

"Yes. I can't get too far without my car keys. I realized I forgot them right after I left, but the door locked behind me."

Carrie came to the counter. "Sorry you got so wet. If you ever need to come in the back way again, there's a spare key hidden underneath the picnic table in the yard."

"Good to know, thanks."

Lisa dashed to the parking lot and got into her car. Giving her head a quick shake to dry off, she started the car and turned on the windshield wipers. It was close to the time she normally came home from work, so Daisy would be expecting her and would need to go outside soon.

Pulling out of the parking lot, she headed down Main Street and turned down one of the roads that ran parallel to the lake. She turned right when she reached another road that branched off along the cove to the area where she lived on East Ridge Road. The more extravagant lakeside houses, such as Bruce Mills's house, were on Lakeshore Drive, which branched off to the left. The area in town where Lisa's and Carrie's houses were located was a more natural and private setting, which Lisa much preferred to the pretentious spot where Leanne and Bruce lived.

She passed Sawyer Road and approached the corner before her turnoff. Suddenly the sheriff's car appeared in her rearview mirror and accelerated quickly until it was a hair's breadth from her bumper with its blue lights flashing. She came to a rapid stop on the side of the road and the sheriff pulled up behind her.

Her heart pounded with nervousness and an unfounded sense of guilt. Surely she hadn't done anything wrong, so why was she getting pulled over? Rachel had warned her to be careful, but there was no way to avoid driving down her own road. She reached into the glove compartment to pull out her registration and insurance card. When she straightened up, she could see Joe Michaud walking toward her. She rolled down her window.

Michaud strolled slowly over to her car door. He was wearing his uniform hat and he had sunglasses on in spite of the rain, so she couldn't see his eyes. "Give me your license and registration."

She passed the papers through the window and Michaud examined them closely. She didn't want to appear confrontational, so she stayed quiet for a few minutes, but her curiosity eventually won out. "Could you please tell me why you pulled me over?"

"Step out of your vehicle."

Cold fear began to wash over her as she opened the car door and stepped out. Michaud put a firm grip on her arm and forced her to turn and face toward her car.

"Put your hands on the vehicle."

No houses were in sight and there was no one to call to for help. She realized she was completely at Michaud's mercy. She placed her hands on the wet roof of her car and waited for him to pat her down. She kept her face turned to the car, not wanting to antagonize him.

"I could do anything I want to you right now," Michaud growled in her ear. His hot breath smelled like stale coffee.

Lisa stared at him as the light rain soaked through her shirt.

"You need to realize I can come after you or your girlfriend at any time. I may decide to teach you a lesson one of these days, and I can make sure it's your word against mine."

"Why are you doing this? You don't even know me."

"I know you used to work for Don. You got fired and you tried to blame it on the fact that we caught you with your girlfriend. I want to make sure you understand this doesn't go any further. Don't even think about making up some sort of claim that you were fired unfairly."

So that's what this was all about. Don had sent the enforcer of the group to intimidate her. Unfortunately, it was working at the moment. There was no way she was going to drop any of the things she had learned about Don, but Michaud was doing a good job of scaring her. He held all the power at the moment and this could easily turn into an ugly situation if she didn't handle it carefully.

"I understand." Rainwater was dripping into her eyes, but she didn't dare move. "I'm looking for another job and I won't say a word about this to anyone."

"That's right. You won't. If I find out you've done anything otherwise, I'll make sure you regret it."

Michaud stayed silent and she could feel him watching her. The rain continued to soak through her clothes and her hair was dripping wet, but she kept still, with her hands on the car roof. Finally, he turned and walked back to his vehicle. She lowered her arms to her sides and watched as he drove past her and disappeared around the corner.

CHAPTER THIRTY-ONE

Carrie paced across the kitchen floor and into the living room. She tried to collect her thoughts as she looked out the glass doors to Lisa's deck and the lake beyond. Yesterday when Carrie learned Joe Michaud had pulled Lisa over, she was furious. She'd wanted to go find Michaud and confront him, but she knew that would be a stupid thing to do, so she'd left Angie and Ryan in charge at the café and rushed over to Lisa's to make sure she was all right.

She turned to Lisa, who was sitting at the kitchen island eating a bowl of cereal for breakfast. Thankfully Lisa was doing just fine, and Carrie was grateful she had been able to handle the encounter with Michaud so well. It had shaken her up, but it hadn't lessened her resolve to go after Don and the other men. Carrie was glad she wasn't intimidated, but the situation was escalating and they had to do something.

"We need to figure out the best way to handle this so Michaud can't come after you again," Carrie said. "I don't want anything to happen to you."

"One good thing is that Michaud and the others don't realize we know what's going on with Senator Lawrence."

"I don't want to think about what he would have done to you, if he knew you'd seen their files." Carrie sat on one of the stools next to Lisa and shook her head. She kept recalling the stories she had heard about Michaud's retaliation against people who crossed him. "He's got the law on his side."

"I was thinking about that too." Lisa pushed her empty bowl away. "He's counting on intimidating us into silence and that isn't going to happen."

"We'll need to be especially careful from now on. I'm worried he's going to find a way to go after you again."

"Where are the police body cams when you need them?" Lisa said. "If he does go after either of us, it will come down to his word against ours."

"That's why we need to get in touch with Anna, the reporter. She's supposed to be back to work today and we have to talk to her. If we give her all the information we have, at least there'll be some record to back us up."

"Do you really think we should we tell a reporter before we have a chance to tell the police?"

"As long as she keeps it quiet until we can talk to the police, I think it would be fine."

"Okay. I have another idea. The annual company picnic is today. I think I should go and talk to the other partners at the firm. I want to expose Don publicly in a way which can't be swept under the rug. There are three other men who started the company with Don and they work in the Portland office, so I don't know them. They may be just like him and may not want to hear what I have to say, but almost everyone from the company should be there. If I show up and tell people what happened, at least they'll have to listen to me. They may all say I'm crazy or try to find some other way to dismiss what I'm saying, but I want to try."

"Are you sure you shouldn't talk to a lawyer first?"

"I thought about that, but I think it would give Don a chance to come up with a way to discredit me with the notes he saves from conversations. He's always come up with a way to stop anyone who has accused him in the past, and I don't want to let that happen this time."

Carrie leaned back in her stool and thought about Lisa's plan. She didn't like the idea of confronting Don publicly. He would never allow Lisa to threaten his career without trying to retaliate or discredit her. Carrie knew she was determined to stand up to Don and there was no stopping her, but she wanted her to be cautious.

One good thing about Lisa's plan was there would be too many witnesses for Don to do anything to her at the picnic, so she shouldn't be in any immediate danger. They had to get the rest of their information to the police as soon as possible and put an end to all of it.

"Are you sure you want to expose Don's harassment before we go to the police?" Carrie said. "I thought you wanted to wait and bring all the evidence at once."

"I'm not going to put up with his intimidation tactics. First he harassed me and now he's got the sheriff bullying me. I'm going to tell everyone exactly what's been going on at the office. I think I should bring copies of the files and pictures I found. What do you think?"

"Yes, you should take the copies with you. Otherwise they might think you're just out for revenge because you were fired." Carrie reached for Lisa's hand on the table. "I'm proud of you, and I'm glad you're trying put a stop to Don's behavior, but your plan scares me."

"I'll be fine." Lisa rubbed Carrie's hand. "He won't be expecting it and I'll be surrounded by people."

"I still don't like it, but this might work out better than hitting him with everything at once," Carrie said. "Don and the others will have no idea we know about the cover-up and this can buy us some time to get everything to the police."

"We'll still have the element of surprise when we expose them."

"I guess you're right, but I want to come with you today."

"I appreciate it, but I think it will be easier for me to slip into the picnic if I'm alone. They probably won't notice me if I walk in with some other people from work. I think it would draw attention if you were with me and it might stop me from getting in."

She wasn't happy about that. "I don't like the idea of you going anywhere by yourself if Joe Michaud is after you. Once he hears from Don, he may try to pull you over again and who knows what he'll do next time."

"I'll stay on the main roads and come meet you at the café when I get back, okay?"

She leaned toward Lisa and kissed her. "Please be careful. Call me if there's any trouble and come straight back. After this I don't think either of us should go anywhere alone."

* * *

The annual summer picnic was held each year at a waterfront restaurant on the coast. The facility offered outdoor dining along with a recreational area that had badminton nets and horseshoe pits. The tables had a picturesque view of the adjoining marina, which was busy with fishing boats and pleasure crafts coming in to the docks.

Lisa had never been to this particular spot, but she hadn't had any trouble finding it. She waited in the parking lot until a group of people arrived, and then she casually walked to the dining area with them, hoping to blend in.

She caught sight of Don standing near the outdoor bar area. He was speaking to a group of men who were gathered near him with drinks in their hands. She had pulled up pictures of the other three partners on the company website before she left home to remind herself what they looked like. She thought she recognized all three of them in the group that was standing with Don.

A few women were sitting at the table to her left. She didn't see anyone from the Augusta office, so she sat down in one of the empty chairs. The copies of the files and pictures from Don's desk were safely tucked away in her bag at her side.

She turned to the woman in the seat next to her. "Hi, my name is Lisa and I'm from the Augusta office."

"Nice to meet you, Lisa." The woman smiled in greeting. "I'm Charlotte from the Portland office."

Charlotte introduced Lisa to the other people at the table. They were a friendly bunch who had traveled together from Portland. Most of them had been with the company for several years.

"This is my first time at the annual picnic." Lisa didn't want to reveal too much and was careful not to say anything that was untrue. "I started working for the company last fall."

"They usually have an excellent meal at these things. People are supposed to socialize, but no one really does except for the bosses. Still, it's good to get out of the office for the day."

"I don't know anyone from Portland, so it's nice to meet all of you. Other than Don Mills, I haven't met any of the partners. Are they here today?"

"They're all standing over there with Don." Charlotte pointed to the bar area. "See the man in the blue polo shirt next to Don? That's Tom White. The one next to him is Steve Dawson. I think that's Jon Andrews in the striped shirt with his back to us."

Charlotte's description verified the men Lisa recognized from the website. Now she had to figure out the best way to approach them. She didn't want anyone from Augusta to see her before she got a chance to talk to the partners. It would be extremely embarrassing to be thrown out for crashing the party before she had a chance to speak. This could be her best shot to confront Don. There would be plenty of witnesses and the other partners would be forced to hear what she had to say. They may try to discredit her, but the pictures would speak for themselves.

She scanned the crowd for faces she recognized. She spotted Mary sitting with some of the Augusta people a few tables away. Luckily, she had her back to Lisa and no one else at the table had noticed her. It was time to make her move. She stood and took a deep breath, gathering her courage before she headed to the bar.

"Have a nice lunch," she said to Charlotte and her companions. "Hopefully we'll get a chance to speak again later."

She made her way through the rows of tables and walked up behind Don. She tapped on the shoulder of the man next to him and he turned to look at her.

"Hello Mr. White. My name is Lisa Owens and I need to talk to you, along with Mr. Dawson and Mr. Andrews, about some things that have been going on in the Augusta office which you may not be aware of."

"What are you doing here?" Don had a shocked look on his face. He turned to the other men. "This woman was fired earlier this week and she is mentally disturbed."

"I thought your partners would want to know what's been going on in Augusta." Lisa spoke quickly before he could stop her. "Were you aware that Mr. Mills has been sexually harassing his female employees for years?"

"You're obviously retaliating because I fired you." Don waved his hand dismissively at her. "You're making this all up." He called over to the bartender, "Will someone please call security? This woman is not an employee and should not have been allowed on the premises."

The crowd had gone silent. Everyone was watching the confrontation at the bar with rapt attention. The bartender looked around for help—to no avail—before hustling toward the restaurant for backup.

Lisa turned to one of the partners. "Mr. Andrews, are you aware of the legal definition of sexual harassment? Don has created an intimidating and offensive work environment and initiated contact that a responsible person would consider to be unwelcome. The hostile work environment in Don's office consisted of a pattern of sexual remarks and physical contact of a sexual nature. That, sir, is the definition of sexual harassment."

"She is out of her mind," Don protested. "I had to fire her because of her poor job performance and now she's looking for payback."

"Actually, Don fired me due to my sexual orientation when he found out I'm a lesbian." Lisa looked at the third partner. "Mr. Dawson, would it surprise you to hear Don keeps a folder in his desk full of revealing photos of the women who work in the office along with notes about his sexual fantasies with these women? That's not something you would approve of, is it Mr. Dawson?"

The bartender returned, accompanied by a group of employees. She knew it was only a matter of minutes before she would be escorted out. Pulling the copies from her bag, she quickly handed a set to each of the three partners. The pages included many of the crotch shots from Don's hidden camera along with the notes detailing his lascivious comments about his employees.

"What are those?" Don began to panic when he saw the pages his partners were looking at. His face flushed, and he pointed a finger at Lisa. "She broke into my office. Breaking and entering is a felony. I want her arrested."

Steve Dawson held a hand up to stop the men from the restaurant who were approaching Lisa. He stepped in front of Don. "These came from your office? What the hell is going on here, Don?"

"He has a hidden camera near his desk." Lisa looked out at the women in the crowd. "Anyone who wore a skirt in Don's office should probably be concerned."

She turned to the partners. "I'm not the first person this has happened to. There have been several other women who Don targeted over the years. I'm not sure if this something you knew about or not, and I want to give you the benefit of the doubt. I hope you don't find Don's behavior acceptable, because I do not want to see this happen to anyone else."

"You're lying," Don said. "You were fired because you weren't good at your job."

"We both know that's not true," Lisa answered. "I'm not going to be intimidated into silence, so it's not going to do you any good to send Joe Michaud after me either."

Lisa was done talking. She watched as the three partners gathered around Don and began conferring in lowered voices before moving away toward a more private spot. She could see Don's face continue to redden as he shook his head vigorously.

One of the men in the group of restaurant employees stepped in front of her. "Ma'am, we're going to have to ask you to leave."

Lisa raised her hands obediently. "Of course. I'll be happy to go."

She held her head high and didn't look back as she walked away. Never in her life had she made such a scene, but she didn't regret it. She had to make sure Don didn't get away with the way he treated women.

* * *

It was midafternoon, and the café was quiet when Lisa arrived. The ride back from the coast had taken an hour and she had kept a close eye out for any police cars. She was still shaking with adrenaline from the confrontation. Carrie greeted her with a hug and they found a private spot to talk at one of the tables in the dining room.

"How did it go? I've been thinking about you all day."

"I did it. I stood up to Don," Lisa said. "I was really nervous about making a scene, and I was worried I was going to get thrown out before I had a chance to say anything, but it all worked out, and I ended up telling the other three partners what was going on. Everyone was watching, and Don couldn't do a thing to stop me."

"That's amazing, honey. I wish I could have seen you. He must have been furious."

"Oh, he was. He accused me of making the whole thing up in retaliation for being fired. Thanks to the pictures and his files, they had no choice but to believe me."

"I'm incredibly proud of you." Carrie reached for Lisa's hand and squeezed it.

"You should have seen his face when I pulled out those pictures. The cool thing was, he started shouting that I had broken in to his desk, so everyone knew they really were his."

"Wow, he's really going to be screwed. What do you think is going to happen to him?"

"The last I saw, the partners were talking with him. I didn't stick around because I figured I would deal with all the legalities later. They certainly won't be able to cover it up. They'll have to fire him, and his troubles will just be starting."

"Now you have to promise me you'll be careful. Like we talked about earlier, we've got to make sure we don't go anywhere alone until we know it's safe."

"You're right." Lisa nodded. "I told him not to bother sending Michaud after me again."

"Now he knows you broke into his desk. Let's try to think if there was anything else there that might tip him off that we know about the Lawrence cover-up?"

"I don't think he'll know we've figured it out." Lisa thought back to the photos she had taken. "There was the garage receipt along with some spreadsheets and a memo, but nothing that would draw attention if we weren't looking for it specifically."

"It might be enough to make him worry."

"The other evidence comes from the files I found on the company network and the police report. He won't know we found those things."

"I bet his suspicions have been raised, but he won't be sure how much we know at this point." Carrie motioned toward the kitchen. "Let's go out back and I'll try to call Anna again. I called her office earlier and left a message, but I haven't been able to catch up with her yet."

Lisa followed Carrie behind the counter and kept an eye on the front entrance while Carrie dialed Anna's number. The customers were eating their meals and didn't need anything at the moment. Carrie hung up and Lisa turned her attention to her.

"She still isn't answering her phone at the office," Carrie said with a frown. "I've left two messages and hopefully she'll call back soon. We may not be able to catch up with her today."

"Shoot, we really need to bring someone else in on this."

"I know. I don't think we can afford to wait much longer. Meanwhile, Luke should be back from vacation tomorrow. I'm going to try to get in touch with him first thing."

"That will be good. We can finally report everything to the state police."

"Now I've got to get back to work and get ready for dinner. Are you okay with hanging out here? I don't want you to drive home alone tonight."

"I'm glad you said that because I want to hang out here with you. I can help out at the counter or wherever you need me. The only thing I'm worried about is Daisy. It's a long time for her to be stuck in the house."

"Do you want me to ask my father to go over and check on her? He could bring her to my place and you can stay there tonight if you wanted."

Lisa pulled Carrie in for a kiss and tried to forget her worries for the moment. She drew back and looked at Carrie. "That sounds like a great plan. I would love to stay at your place tonight and it would be very nice of your father to help with Daisy."

Carrie smiled. "Good. Now let's get busy."

CHAPTER THIRTY-TWO

The next day was a long one and Carrie was glad to be done with work. Weekends were always extra busy. She and Lisa had been at the café since early that morning and they were finally headed back to Lisa's place. Together they had handled both the breakfast and the lunch shifts, and they hadn't had time for many breaks. They had just come from setting up for the evening meal, which was also the café's weekly music night. Fortunately, Angie and Ryan were going to cover for Carrie and she was able to go home early for a change.

Carrie didn't want to leave Lisa alone while the threat of Joe Michaud hung over their heads. Now that Lisa had confronted Don, there were sure to be some major repercussions. Anna, the reporter, had finally returned her messages from the previous day. Unfortunately, Anna had called during the lunch rush, and Carrie hadn't had time to go into much detail about what was going on.

"I am completely exhausted," Lisa said. "I don't know how you do this every day."

"It's not always this busy." Carrie glanced over at Lisa in the passenger seat. "I'm glad I could get the rest of the night off. We can just relax and hang out."

"It would be a great night to go out in the kayaks, don't you think?"

"That sounds perfect." Carrie reached over for Lisa's hand.

They went home to Lisa's and were greeted at the door by Daisy, who was anxious to get outside.

Lisa held the door for Carrie. "It's so nice of your father to help me with Daisy. I really appreciate him coming by to let her out. We brought her home at the crack of dawn this morning when we left your place, and I wouldn't have been able to leave her alone all day like this."

"He doesn't mind at all and I appreciate your help today, too. Let's get changed and go out on the lake."

"Let me grab us a couple drinks and I'll be ready in a flash."

A short time later, Lisa and Carrie headed down the rocky path to the dock. They had changed into T-shirts and sandals with their bathing suits on underneath. Carrie looked out at the lake and saw the water was smooth as glass. The heat of the sun had passed, leaving the evening air warm and comfortable. She could hear a motorboat off in the distance, but the cove was empty.

Together they carried the kayaks to the dock. Lisa passed Carrie a paddle and a life jacket. Carrie stowed her life jacket behind her seat and slid the kayak into the water. Balancing on the dock ladder, she climbed in and sat down carefully.

Lisa joined her a moment later, her kayak rocking gently in the water. "Here we go."

They paddled in comfortable silence, watching for fish rising to the surface and listening to the sounds of the lake. A pair of loons swam ahead of them as they made their way along the shoreline. Carrie felt the stress of the day dissipate as they took in the serenity of the evening.

"This was a really good idea," Carrie said to Lisa.

"It's the perfect time of day to be out here. It's not too hot and the lake is nice and calm."

The boat Carrie had heard in the distance drew closer. She looked over her shoulder to see it come around the point and into the cove. She and Lisa continued to paddle and reached the point at the opposite end of the cove. They turned the corner and the boat disappeared from view. Most boaters kept a good distance from kayakers and made sure their wakes were small when they passed by, but it was always preferable not to be too close, so Carrie was happy to have the boat out of sight.

"Want to head out to the island?" Carrie pointed to a small, uninhabited island that was several hundred yards from shore. The rocky piece of land was covered in pine trees and blueberry bushes and was a favored habitat for the eagles that lived in the area.

"Sure," Lisa agreed, plunging her paddle into the water and turning toward the middle of the lake. "So, what did you tell the reporter when you finally spoke to her today?"

"I was really busy, and I didn't have a lot of time to talk privately, so I only gave her the bare details. I told her a friend had come across information that implicated her boss, along with two other men, in a plan to cover up an accident involving a state senator in exchange for political favors. She wants to find out more, of course, and I told her we wanted to discuss it in person. She's going to meet with us at the café tomorrow morning."

"That's good. We can get all of our information organized and ready to present to her." Lisa looked back over her shoulder. "What about your state police contact?"

"I called Luke this morning and he called me back this afternoon. I didn't give him many details either because I want us to talk to him in person. I was hoping we could tell him about everything tonight, but since he just got back from vacation, he's busy on another case and he wants to come see us tomorrow."

"We only have to hold on for one more day. We can do that."

Carrie paddled with smooth, even strokes, matching Lisa's pace as they moved across the water. They lapsed into silence and made their way closer to the rocky shore of the island.

Carrie pointed to a stand of tall pine trees growing along the water's edge. "I saw an eagle's nest in one of those trees this spring."

Lisa peered toward the trees, letting her kayak glide slowly.

Carrie noticed the distant buzzing of a motor coming across the lake in their direction. She looked toward the sound, trying to tell if it was the same boat that had been back in the cove. An uneasy feeling came over her as she saw it was indeed the same one. Hopefully whoever was steering would turn away before it came closer.

The boat continued to head toward them. She glanced at Lisa, who hadn't noticed anything yet and was still looking for the eagle's nest.

"Lisa, I think that boat is coming at us a little too fast."

Lisa turned to look quickly, and her eyes grew wide. "What should we do?"

"Paddle hard toward shore."

They both dug their paddles into the water and raced for the island.

As the boat drew near, Carrie realized they were still about fifty yards from shore and there was no way they could outrun it. She slowed her pace and let Lisa get ahead of her. Moving to position her kayak between Lisa and the oncoming watercraft, she looked back over her shoulder and let herself glide. She felt time slow down as the looming bow headed directly toward her. Taking a deep breath, she dropped her paddle, grabbed the sides of her kayak seat opening and launched herself into the water. Seconds later, she heard a resounding crack as the boat smashed into her kayak. She could feel the vibrations from the motor in the water and braced herself for impact as she swam away frantically. Instead, the engine slowed, and the driver turned and began to steer away in a looping arc.

Carrie treaded water for a moment and wiped drops from her eyes. Scanning the surface of the lake for Lisa, she heard her before she saw her.

"Carrie, no!" Lisa screamed. She stopped paddling and stared in horror at Carrie's damaged kayak. "Oh my God."

Carrie realized Lisa hadn't seen her jump out. She waved her arm. "Lisa, I'm over here. Keep paddling!"

Carrie saw Lisa's face collapse in relief as she looked over and saw her. There was no time to spare as the driver circled back toward them. The engine began revving up and Carrie started swimming rapidly toward the island.

Instead of coming back to Carrie, she watched in alarm as the boat sped toward Lisa, who was still several yards from shore. She stopped swimming and shouted, "Lisa, jump!"

Lisa looked back at the oncoming boat and threw her paddle, struggling to get out of the kayak. She flipped over and disappeared from view just as the bow collided with her kayak's hull.

Carrie froze in shock. Her heart filled with dread as she watched the kayak bounce off the bow of the boat. The driver was traveling much too quickly this close to shore. Momentum carried the boat forward and there was an earsplitting crash an instant later as the boat collided with a group of rocks in the shallow water near the edge of the island. The impact lifted the back of the hull cleanly out of the water, twisting and turning until it flipped over and landed on its side in the rocks with the damaged propeller grinding noisily for a few seconds before coming to a halt.

The force of the collision had flung the driver from the boat. He had flown through the air and come to rest on the nearby rocky shore, where he lay facedown and motionless in the bushes.

Carrie swam as fast as she could toward Lisa's battered kayak. She heard a gasp and looked to see Lisa's head pop to the surface a short distance from the kayak. Relief washed over her as she swam even harder toward the rocky shore.

Moments later Carrie felt her feet touch bottom as the water became shallow. She quickly made her way to Lisa and they fell into each other's arms. Carrie kissed her and pulled her close, reassuring herself that Lisa was all right.

Lisa gripped Carrie's waist tightly. "When I heard the crash and turned around, I couldn't see you and I thought you were gone. It was horrible. Please don't ever scare me like that again."

"I was petrified when you didn't come up right away after your kayak got hit." Carrie ran her hands down the back of Lisa's soaked shirt. "It all happened so fast and there was nothing I could do to stop it. I'm so thankful you're okay."

Lisa studied her face. "Why were you so far behind me? Did you slow down so the boat would go after you? You did, didn't you?"

"I thought you had a better chance of making it to shore than I did. I'm not going to let anything happen to you."

"You tried to save me." Lisa kissed Carrie. "I've never met anyone like you."

Carrie looked over at the man lying on the rocks. "We should probably go check on him."

"I really don't want to check on him. What if he's faking it and he tries to attack us?" Lisa looked out across the water. "The crash should have caught someone's attention. I wonder why no one seems to be coming?"

"Maybe no one saw or heard anything. There's a good-sized marshy area directly across from here with no houses, so there aren't many people with views of this part of the island." Carrie gave Lisa a comforting hug. "We're safe now. He doesn't look like he's faking it."

Carrie made her way across the rocks until she reached the man. Lisa followed a short distance behind her. The man's body was sprawled in an unnatural position with his legs hanging into the water. Waves washed gently around his feet.

Carrie pushed the blueberry bushes aside and bent over him, putting two fingers on his neck. "I don't feel a pulse and he's not breathing. I don't think there's anything we can do."

"I know we shouldn't move him, but we need to find out who he is. It all happened so fast I couldn't get a good look." Lisa bent down to join Carrie and gently turned his head until they could see his face.

"Bruce Mills," Carrie gasped. "I knew Don and his cronies would come after us, but I was expecting harassment from Joe Michaud. I didn't think they'd try to kill us."

"We've got to get out of here and go to the police. I wish we had our phones with us."

"Okay. We need to get going before it starts to get dark." Carrie stood and looked around at the lake. "Both of our kayaks are damaged. I saw a big crack in yours and mine isn't even floating anymore. It looks like we'll have to swim."

Lisa let out a sigh. "That's a long way across."

"We could stay here, and someone will eventually rescue us, but I'm worried about what Don and Joe might be planning."

"I don't want one of them to be the first to find us."

"Do you think you can make it?" Carrie decided to appeal to Lisa's competitive nature. "How about we have another contest? The first one to reach the other side gets to pick where we go for our vacation next winter."

"We're going on a vacation next winter?"

"Remember I told you how I close Harvest for a month and go somewhere warm?"

"Are you going to take me with you next winter?"

Carrie put her arms around Lisa. "I want you to come with me. What do you say?"

"I would love to go with you." Lisa kissed Carrie. "Let's get going. I need to get across the lake first so I can pick where we go."

"Even though it will slow us down, I think we should each wear a lifejacket, just in case."

They stripped off their soaked T-shirts and sandals and left them on the shore. Wading out across the slippery rocks, they made their way to the spot where Lisa's kayak had washed ashore. Lisa slipped her lifejacket from the bungee cords holding it in place and put it on.

They waded over to the upended boat and Carrie looked into the jumbled interior. She spotted a lifejacket among the debris floating on the waves and pulled it out. Carrie put her arms into the jacket and secured it in place.

"Ready?" Carrie asked.

Lisa nodded. They headed for deeper water and began the long swim back across the lake. Carrie tried to keep a steady pace. They had plenty of adrenaline-fueled energy now, but they had almost a half-mile to go. She didn't hear any boat motors and she had mixed feelings about that. It would be nice if someone in a boat came along and gave them a ride to shore, but it could be Don Mills or Joe Michaud. She was fine with swimming.

Carrie took the lead. After a time, she paused to tread water and check in with Lisa. "How are you doing?"

Lisa swam up beside her. "I'm feeling pretty good. My arms are tired, but not too bad. How about you?"

"I'm doing all right, honey. We should take a break every now and then."

They started back up and Lisa swam alongside Carrie as they moved steadily closer to the cove. Carrie was getting tired, but their 5K training had stood them well. They both managed to keep going and soon they had Lisa's home in sight.

The night sky had grown dark and the rising moon lit their way as they approached the dock. Lisa suddenly switched into high gear and pulled ahead. Carrie couldn't help but laugh as she watched her slice through the water and swim to the dock ladder. She followed her at a slower pace and finally reached the ladder.

She climbed wearily out of the water and Lisa held out her hand at the top. Carrie reached for her hand and they fell into an embrace on the dock. Carrie's energy was completely drained.

"How about the Florida Keys next winter?" Lisa asked.

CHAPTER THIRTY-THREE

"Did I say I was exhausted earlier?" Lisa leaned on Carrie's shoulder. "I had no clue what exhausted was. I am beyond tired."

"Me too," Carrie said. "We've got to call the police but I'm too tired to move. I left my phone inside with my clothes."

"Hey, where's Daisy? She usually waits and watches for me when I go out on the lake." Lisa looked around the deserted shoreline. Daisy was nowhere to be seen.

"We've been gone a long time. I hope she didn't run off."

"Daisy, come here girl." Lisa walked along the path to the house. "Daisy, come get a treat."

Carrie followed Lisa. "Let's get some shoes on and we can search around a little better."

Lisa began to grow worried. "She's a little naughty and she doesn't come half the time I call her, but I'm surprised she isn't near the house. It's past her dinnertime."

The motion sensor light in the driveway came on as they approached the house. Lisa still didn't see any sign of Daisy. She gave one last call before going inside with Carrie. "Daisy, come get your dinner."

The cool air of the entryway hit them when they walked in. Lisa shivered and turned to Carrie. "I've got to put on some dry clothes then go find Daisy. Do you need anything?"

"No. I just want to get the call to the police over with. I can't say I'm sorry about what happened to Bruce. After all, he was trying to kill us. But it's going to be hard to explain."

Lisa nodded. She was worried about the state police commander she had seen at Bruce's party. "How do we know we won't reach a friend of Joe Michaud's when we call the state police?"

"Luke gave me his cell number when I talked to him today. I'm going to call him directly."

Hopefully nothing would get back to Michaud until they had a chance to explain the situation and present the evidence they had been putting together. Lisa wanted to get her files ready for the police so she could explain everything clearly. First, she needed to get changed.

Suddenly, they heard a yip from the door. Lisa's face lit up with a smile. "Daisy's back."

Carrie reached for the doorknob behind her. She opened the door and Daisy bounded in, wagging her tail happily as she greeted them.

Lisa knelt down. "Daisy, where have you been?"

"She must have wandered off a little and heard you calling."

Lisa rubbed Daisy's chin and started patting her. "Hey, her collar is missing."

"That's very strange." Carrie knelt down next to Lisa and patted Daisy. "Was it a plastic clip that could have sprung open or did it have a buckle?"

"It was a sturdy buckle. She would have had to wriggle out of it or else someone took it off her, which wouldn't make sense." Lisa gave Carrie a perplexed shrug. "We'd better hurry up and make the call to the police. This whole situation is getting more suspicious by the minute."

Lisa followed Carrie into the bedroom where she had left her phone next to her overnight bag. While Carrie looked up Luke's number, Lisa rinsed off quickly and changed. Carrie was sitting on the bed when she came out. Lisa sat down next to her and slid her arm around her waist.

"How did it go?"

"Luke is on his way and should be here in about half an hour. Meanwhile, he sent out a team to go check on Bruce. I told him what was going on and asked him not to let the sheriff's department know yet, so he's going to try to have the rescue squad keep it quiet while they go out to the island."

"Do they need to have us go back out there?"

"He didn't mention it. Hopefully not tonight."

"You should take a quick shower and get some dry clothes on." Lisa tucked Carrie's damp hair behind her ear. "I'm going to feed Daisy and then I'll get the files ready for the police."

Lisa walked upstairs with Daisy at her side. Once the dog was happily eating her dinner, Lisa turned her attention to organizing the files she wanted to show to the police.

She looked on the table where she kept her laptop and was startled to see it wasn't in its usual spot. It took her a moment to realize she hadn't moved it; the laptop was missing. She looked around the kitchen and living room, trying to tell if anything else might have been taken. Her phone and pocketbook were on the side table where she had left them when she got home earlier. Nothing appeared to be out of place.

She ran downstairs and into the bedroom to tell Carrie. The bathroom door was open, and Carrie was brushing her hair.

"My laptop is gone," Lisa said. "I don't know if it was here when we got home from the café, but I think I would have noticed if it wasn't in its usual place. I haven't used it all day."

"Is anything else missing?"

Lisa looked through the case she kept on top of her bureau. All of her jewelry was still there. She couldn't think of anything else of significant value she kept in the house. The laptop was the only item that was unaccounted for.

"Everything else seems to be here."

"You must have had all the files you found from Don's office on your laptop and he wanted to make sure you couldn't do anything with them."

"Yes. I bet Don sent Joe here to get it." Lisa began to pace the floor. "When do you think he broke in?"

"You haven't been home for more than a few minutes since yesterday. He could have come any time."

"How would he have gotten in without breaking in?"

"You leave a key under the doormat." Carrie shrugged. "I'm sure it's the first place someone would look."

"Good point. I need to find a better spot."

"Let's go upstairs and wait for Luke."

"Hold on, I need to get something." Lisa opened up the top drawer of her bureau and pulled out a flash drive and held it up. "He didn't check my underwear drawer."

"You backed up all of the files?"

"Of course, and I always keep my backup in a separate spot."

Lisa followed Carrie upstairs. "I wonder if Joe had anything to do with Daisy's missing collar. Maybe he came over while we were kayaking and tried to grab her, and she slipped away."

They sat down on the couch together. Carrie rested her arm on the back of the couch and looked at Lisa. "That could have been what happened. I saw Bruce's boat go into the cove when we were kayaking, and it took a while before he came back out. Maybe he stopped here."

"For all we know, Bruce met Joe here." Lisa leaned against Carrie. "They were probably trying to hunt us down. Joe and Don must be wondering where Bruce is."

Carrie sat up. "You know what, I was just thinking about what Angie and Ryan told me about their friend who ran into trouble with Joe Michaud."

"Yes, you warned me about how Michaud goes after people. You were certainly right about that."

"He planted drugs on Angie and Ryan's friend. What if he did something like that here?"

"Oh my God. What if he hid something and is planning to report me?" Lisa started to panic. If the police came and found drugs in her home, she could be thrown in jail. No one would believe it was a setup because she would have no proof. "We've got to search the place before the police get here."

Carrie jumped up and started looking through the bookshelves in the living room while Lisa ran toward the kitchen area. Daisy yawned at all the commotion.

"Why didn't I get a dog with tracking skills?" Lisa opened drawers and searched through cupboards in the kitchen with mounting anxiety. She opened the refrigerator and looked inside. As far as she could tell, there was nothing inside other than groceries.

"I can't find anything in the living room," Carrie said. "I didn't notice anything downstairs in the bathroom or the bedroom, but I'd better go check again."

Lisa opened the freezer and started moving containers around. She picked up a bag of frozen peas and spotted a foil-wrapped package. "What's this?"

"Carrie, come here. I found something."

Carrie ran back up the stairs and looked at the package in the sink where Lisa had placed it. "You'd better open it and check."

Pulling the foil open carefully, Lisa found a plastic baggie filled with fine white powder. "What do you suppose this is? It looks like cocaine."

"I have no idea, but thank God you found it."

"Now what?" Lisa wrapped the foil back around the bag. She didn't want to deal with this at all. "Should we tell the police, or should I just go throw it away somewhere?"

"Luke should be here any minute. I think you should tell the police everything; your laptop is missing, and you found this powder planted in your freezer."

"I'm scared that they won't believe me, and I'll get arrested." Lisa looked at Carrie, hoping she would know what to do. "This is all getting to be too much."

"Yes, it's getting crazy." Carrie wrapped her arms around Lisa. "That's why we have to tell the truth about everything. It's all too complicated to try and hide any of it."

A knock sounded at the door and Daisy ran to the top of the stairs. Carrie sprang up from the couch anxiously and looked out the window. "The police are here."

They walked down to the entryway together and Lisa opened the door. "Hello. Please come on in."

A gray-haired man dressed in street clothes accompanied by a clean-cut young man in a state trooper's uniform entered the house.

The older man extended his hand to Lisa. "Hello, I'm Detective Luke Hodgton and this is Officer Baker."

Carrie stepped forward. "Hi Luke. Thank you for coming all the way out here tonight. This is my girlfriend, Lisa Owens, and this is her house. Why don't we go upstairs to the living room and we can fill you in on everything that's been going on."

Carrie followed Lisa up the stairs and took a seat next to her on the couch. Luke and Officer Baker sat in two adjoining chairs. Carrie glanced over at Lisa, who was holding the flash drive she had retrieved earlier from the bedroom.

"As you know, we have a team at the scene of the boating accident," Luke began. "Carrie gave me a brief overview of the situation earlier. Let's go over the whole story from the beginning and you can both fill me in on exactly what's been going on."

Carrie listened while Lisa described the events at her office. She described Don's harassment and explained how she had stumbled across information about his involvement in engineering the cover-up for Senator Lawrence along with help from Bruce Mills and Joe Michaud.

"Do you have any proof Senator Lawrence was responsible for the accident that killed Michelle Nelson?" Luke asked.

"I have the original accident report and I've made an electronic copy of it." Lisa passed the drive to Luke. "I have it here, along with a repair receipt for Senator Lawrence's car after the accident. We also have a copy of a contract that was awarded to Mills Building Construction. That ties in with several spreadsheets detailing payments between Don, Bruce, and Joe. There are also memos and emails giving additional corroboration of how the contract was awarded to Bruce Mills's company in exchange for their silence about the accident. It's all on the flash drive."

"How did you get this information?" Luke asked.

"I found some of it on the computer network at the office."

Carrie didn't want Lisa to implicate herself in any unlawful activity. She interrupted before Lisa gave any details about breaking into Don's desk or trespassing in Bruce's office. "We were planning to show you all of the files, but we just found out Lisa's house was broken into and her laptop has been stolen."

"Your home was broken into?" Luke sat forward in his chair. "Was anything else taken?"

"I didn't find anything else missing," Lisa answered. "After Bruce ran over our kayaks, we had to swim back, and we called you as soon as we got here. I went to get my laptop ready so I could show everything to you, and that's when I discovered it was gone."

Carrie put a reassuring hand on Lisa's knee. "While we were kayaking, I noticed the boat Bruce was driving was here in the cove. He may have stopped here looking for Lisa."

"You believe Bruce broke in and took the laptop?" Luke asked.

"I told you about Joe Michaud's earlier threats and how Lisa reported Don's sexual harassment," Carrie answered. "Don knew Lisa had information related to the harassment and he may have sent Joe and Bruce over to get her laptop. We believe they were here earlier this evening and we believe it was one of them."

Luke exchanged a glance with Officer Baker. "I'm sure you both know how serious these accusations are. We're talking about a young girl and a prominent local businessman who have both been killed. You're telling me a state senator and the sheriff are involved. This situation will require extraordinary care."

Carrie was relieved Luke was taking them seriously. She knew he could have dismissed their information as pure conjecture and arrested them. There was one more hurdle to overcome. She caught Lisa's eye and looked toward the kitchen. Lisa nodded.

"Luke, there's one more thing," Carrie said.

Luke looked up from the notes he was taking. "More?"

"We believe Sheriff Michaud broke in and planted evidence. He must have been planning to have Lisa's house searched so she'd be implicated in a drug charge."

"How did you find the evidence?"

"Michaud has a reputation for doing this to people," Carrie answered. "When Lisa found out her laptop was missing, we looked around to make sure he hadn't hidden anything. That's when we found it."

"Let's see what you've got." Luke stood up.

Lisa led Luke and Officer Baker into the kitchen and showed them the packet she had left in the sink. Luke pulled out a pair of gloves while Officer Baker took a photo. Luke carefully peeled back the foil, revealing the white powder.

"You've never seen this item before?" Luke asked.

"No," Lisa answered. "All I know is it's a good thing Carrie thought of searching the house. I would have had no idea how this got here or where it came from."

Carrie and Lisa stepped back into the living room while Luke and Officer Baker bagged up the packet of drugs. They waited quietly until Luke finished taking notes.

"All right, ladies." Luke closed the folder he was holding. "This is quite a situation. Officer Baker and I need to check in with the rest of the team. We're going to take the evidence to the lab and get everyone else up to speed. I'm sure we'll talk again soon, so don't go too far from your phones."

"We really appreciate your help, Luke." Carrie stood up. "We'll wait to hear from you."

Lisa stood next to Carrie. "Thank you for listening to us. I know it's hard to believe Senator Lawrence and the others are involved in a conspiracy like this."

"I learned long ago that people do some crazy things regardless of how much money or prestige they have."

They walked the men downstairs and let them out. Lisa closed the door and leaned back against it with a tired sigh. "This day feels like it will never end."

Carrie pulled Lisa close. "Let's try to get some sleep. I'm sure they'll be back with more questions."

Lisa wrapped her arms around Carrie's shoulders and kissed her. Carrie closed her eyes and breathed in Lisa's scent. The kiss intensified as their tongues found each other and Carrie responded in spite of her fatigue.

"Are you trying to wake me up?" Carrie whispered in Lisa's ear.

"Let's go into the bedroom and we'll see." Lisa took Carrie's hand and led her down the hallway and into the bedroom. She faced Carrie and slowly took off her shirt.

Carrie forgot about sleep and ran her hands across Lisa's soft skin, unhooking her bra and dropping it to the floor. She kissed Lisa's neck and worked her way down to her breasts. She traced her tongue lightly along Lisa's fading scars.

"You're so beautiful," Carrie whispered.

"I need to feel your skin." Lisa's hands found their way under Carrie's shirt and lifted it over her head. She moved to the bed and pulled Carrie down beside her, quickly shedding the rest of their clothes.

Carrie rolled on top of Lisa and her mouth found its way back to her breasts. Knowing how close she had come to losing her when her kayak was hit made her savor the moment. She could feel Lisa's hands awaken her most sensitive areas.

"I almost lost you in the lake. Don't scare me like that again," Carrie murmured as she shifted slightly to one side and slipped her fingers inside Lisa's wetness. "I've never needed anyone like this before."

"You saved me." Lisa pulled Carrie's head down into a deep kiss.

Carrie's mouth muffled Lisa's groans of pleasure as she began to respond to Carrie's thrusting fingers. Her legs tightened their grip around Carrie and they moved together as Carrie brought her over the edge.

They lay tangled together in the sheets, catching their breath. Lisa looked at Carrie. "There's something I've been wanting to tell you."

"Something good, I hope," Carrie said.

"I love you."

Her eyes grew wide with surprise and she leaned over to kiss Lisa. "I love you too."

"I've never given my heart to anyone like this before," Lisa said. "You said before that you needed me, and I want you to know how much I need you in my life too."

"I love you," Carrie repeated with a happy smile.

"One more thing before you go to sleep," Lisa said. "I think it's my turn now."

Carrie lay back on the bed, awash with pleasure, as Lisa slid under the sheets.

CHAPTER THIRTY-FOUR

The insistent ringing of her cell phone woke Carrie from a deep sleep. Reaching over to the bedside table, she picked up her phone and tried to focus her eyes on the screen. Expecting to see Luke Hodgton's number, she saw with alarm that the call was from Ryan. Sliding her feet over the side of the bed and brushing off the last of her sleepy disorientation, she sat up and answered, "Ryan, what's going on?"

"Hi boss. I'm sorry to call in the middle of the night, but I knew you'd want me to tell you someone tried to break in to the café."

Lisa gave a muffled groan beside her and rolled over. Carrie stood and walked into the bathroom in an attempt to make less noise.

"What happened?" Carrie asked. She was wide awake now and her mind was racing through the various possibilities. It may have been a simple break-in attempt, but more likely it had been Joe Michaud or Don Mills.

"Angie and I had finished closing and we'd gone upstairs. Music night was great, by the way. Anyway, we hung out for a little while and then we went to bed. I'm not sure what woke me up because we had our air-conditioner on, but I went into the living room and I could hear someone walking around outside. I heard them go out back and then I heard them trying to open the back door."

"Did you call the police?" Carrie had mentioned Lisa's incident with Michaud to both Ryan and Angie. She hadn't gone into any details about why he had pulled Lisa over, but she had warned Ryan and Angie about it in case Michaud started targeting any of them as well.

"No, not yet. I figured I'd check it out myself first. You know how I feel about Joe Michaud. I don't want him coming here and searching my apartment, if you know what I mean. He'd probably find a way to throw me in jail."

"Ryan, you and Angie need to be safe. I don't want you confronting anyone." Calling the police would definitely not help the situation if the intruder were Joe Michaud. "I agree with you about Michaud, though. I'll call someone I know who works for the state police. Did you see anything else?"

"I opened the back window and there was a man standing by the door. The motion sensor light wasn't on, so it was too dark to get a good look. I yelled down at him and as soon as he heard me, he took off toward the front. I went and looked out the front window, but I didn't see anyone, so he must have left. That's when I called you."

"So they're gone?" Carrie wanted to be sure Ryan and Angie weren't in any imminent danger.

"It's all quiet," Ryan answered. "Hold on, I see a car coming down Main Street. It looks like the sheriff's car."

That confirmed Carrie's suspicions. "Is he stopping at the café?"

Ryan paused for a moment. "No, he drove by and went around the corner."

"All right. I want you to stay put. I'll be there in a few minutes to take a look around."

Carrie hung up the phone and went back into the bedroom. Lisa was sitting up in the bed, waiting for her.

"What's going on at the café?" Lisa asked.

"Someone was trying to get in the back door and Ryan scared them off." Carrie pulled on her shorts and T-shirt while she explained. "Ryan just saw the sheriff's car go by, so I'm sure it was Michaud who tried to get in. I have to go check on things."

Lisa got out of bed and quickly began getting dressed. "I'm coming with you."

Carrie started to disagree, but then she realized she didn't want Lisa to be here alone. "Yeah, that's a good idea."

"Shouldn't you call Luke?"

"We can call on the way over. It will probably take a half hour for any help to get there, and I don't want to wait here for them. I want to make sure Ryan and Angie are all right."

Carrie brushed her teeth while Lisa finished dressing and soon they were ready to go. They got into the Jeep and started toward town, keeping a close eye out for any vehicles. She passed her phone to Lisa so she could call Luke while Carrie focused on the road. The last thing they needed was for Joe Michaud to spot them on one of the back roads.

"It went to voice mail." Lisa passed the phone back to Carrie. "If he doesn't call back in a couple minutes, I think we should call the main number for the state police."

"I agree. Ryan said whoever was there took off, but who knows if they might come back?"

Main Street was dark and deserted as they approached the café. The streetlight on the corner cast a pool of light on the nearby lake. They pulled next to the building and parked in a spot near the entrance. A light was shining in one of the windows of the upstairs apartment. Carrie picked up her phone to let Ryan know they were there.

"Ryan, I just pulled in. I'm going to take a quick look around, and then I'll come up and check in."

"Okay," Ryan answered. "Angie is a little freaked out, so I'll wait here with her."

Carrie hung up the phone and looked over at Lisa. "Honey, can you stay in the Jeep while I go check things out?"

"No way." Lisa shook her head. "You're not walking around a dark building by yourself and leaving me here alone."

Carrie put her hand on Lisa's leg. "I'm worried Joe or whoever was here before might come back and I don't want him sneaking up on us. One of us should keep watch for him."

Carrie watched Lisa consider this for a moment and was relieved when she nodded in agreement. She wanted to keep Lisa as safe as possible, and it would be better for her to stay in the vehicle in case anyone was lurking around the building.

"Luke hasn't called you back and we need to get in touch with the police," Lisa said. "I'll call while you look around, okay?"

"That's a good plan." Carrie leaned over and touched Lisa's lips with a brief kiss. "Thank you for keeping watch for me. Be careful and I'll be back in a few minutes."

"You be careful too." Lisa kissed her again.

Carrie got out and closed the door quietly. She scanned the side of the building and didn't see anything out of place. The front of the café had appeared fine when they drove in, but she wanted to take a closer look to make sure nothing had been touched. Before she did that, she decided to go check on the back door where Ryan had seen the man.

She was plunged into darkness when she went around the corner. Ryan had mentioned the motion sensor light wasn't working. Other than the sound of water lapping at the shoreline, the night was silent. Even the loons had gone to sleep. Carrie activated the flashlight app on her phone. It was surprisingly bright and illuminated the back of the building quite nicely. She cast the beam at the door while she tried the knob and made sure it was still locked.

She turned the light in an arc, shining it along the backyard and across the back wall, checking to see if anything was out of place. The beam revealed an odd red object sticking out from around the opposite corner of the building. She walked closer to investigate.

Shining her light on the corner as she approached, she suddenly realized what she was looking at and froze in shock. A red gas can sat on the ground, obscured by some bushes which were growing along the other side of the building.

Lisa put her phone away in annoyance. She had finally gotten through to someone at the Maine State Police communications center, but it hadn't been easy. Not wanting to alert Joe Michaud, she had decided not to dial 911. Since it was the middle of the night, it had been difficult to find a number that didn't go to a pre-recorded message. She eventually reached a dispatcher and reported the break-in and had asked that Luke Hodgton be contacted.

Movement near the side of the building caught Lisa's eye. Carrie walked rapidly around the corner and unlocked the front door of the café before she went inside. The interior was illuminated when Carrie turned on a light in the kitchen. The angle of the building obscured her view, so Lisa couldn't tell where Carrie went from that point.

Lisa settled back in her seat. Headlights from an approaching car appeared down the road. The thought of Joe Michaud discovering them here gave her a ripple of fear. It was also possible the car was a state police cruiser, but it was probably much too soon for them to get here. She took out her phone to warn Carrie when she saw the car pull off the road into a neighboring driveway.

Sighing with relief, Lisa set her phone back down. The lights were out in the nearby houses, and there were no signs of anyone stirring in the quiet darkness. Other than the car she'd seen a few minutes ago, there was no one on the roads.

She scanned from one side of the café over to the other and then looked in both directions down Main Street. It had only been a couple minutes since Carrie had gone into the café, but Lisa wished she would hurry. She was getting more nervous by the second.

Another movement caught her eye as she looked toward the road where the car pulled over earlier. A shadowy figure appeared and approached the front, creeping through the trees and bushes stealthily. As the person drew closer, Lisa could see from the light of the café's front window that it was a heavyset man and he was carrying something. She slid down in her seat and reached for her phone as she tried to get a better look. He paused on the front step to peer inside. His face turned in her direction as he reached for the knob and opened the door. Lisa saw to her horror it was Don Mills and he was holding a gun. He walked inside and closed the door behind him.

Dialing Carrie's number as quickly as she could, Lisa tried to think of what she should do. The police were on their way, but it could be a while before they arrived. Carrie's phone rang for several seconds and she didn't answer. It went to voice mail and Lisa hung up. She dialed it again and the phone rang unanswered again.

She couldn't sit here and do nothing. She slipped out of the car quickly and eased the door shut. Keeping an eye on the front of the café, she darted to the side of the building, hoping Don wouldn't look outside.

Ryan's light was still on upstairs, and Lisa wasn't sure if Carrie had spoken with him again. She didn't have his number and she didn't want Don to hear her knocking on Ryan's door for help. She had to find out what was happening to Carrie on her own.

Staying close to the building, she hurried along the side and out to the back. The storeroom light was off, and it was pitch dark. She could see the shape of the picnic table silhouetted in the light from the stars and she made her way over to it, trying to stay as silent as possible. Running her hand along the rough boards on the underside of the table, she felt for the hidden key and found it.

She ran over to the back door and unlocked it carefully. Slipping inside noiselessly, she closed the door gently. Her eyes took a moment to adjust to the darkness of the room. Luckily, she had a fairly good idea of the layout from her tour the other day.

Muffled voices sounded from the kitchen. She could hear Carrie talking, but couldn't tell what she was saying. The voices came closer. She wasn't sure how she could stop Don if he had a gun. She had to think of something, but meanwhile she needed to stay out of sight. There was a small space in the corner between the freezer and the wall which would be hidden by the shelves of canned goods. She quickly slid behind the rack next to the freezer, wedging herself into the corner where she could crouch down unseen.

The kitchen door opened, and the harsh glare of overhead lights filled the room. Lisa prayed Don wouldn't look closely at the corner where she was hiding. Peeking through the cans on the rack in front of her, she watched him push Carrie into the room with one hand while he kept the gun pointed at her with the other. Carrie tripped and stumbled into one of the racks of dishes. Don walked in, keeping the gun closely trained on her.

"Keep your hands where I can see them," Don commanded.

"Do you really think you can get away with this, Don?" Carrie stood up slowly, keeping her hands raised in front of her.

"That's the least of what you should be worried about." His back was to Lisa and she couldn't see his face. "I'm sure I can make this all look like an unfortunate accident or the work of an unknown intruder. After all, you're involved with a known drug dealer."

"We've talked to the police and they know you and your brother and Joe Michaud covered up Senator Lawrence's accident."

"The senator is a drunken idiot, and no one is going to be able to connect him with me."

"Was the senator drunk when he ran over Michelle Nelson?"

"Of course he was. It's common knowledge the man has a drinking problem. He was lucky Bruce happened to be on his way home and found him crying by the side of the road. Joe and I were able to help him clean things up and no further harm was done. There was nothing anyone could have done for the girl anyway."

"You're sick. That girl's parents have suffered all this time, wondering who killed their daughter. How can you possibly think the police won't connect you?"

"No one is going to consider either you or your girlfriend to be a credible witness. She's going to find herself in a world of trouble and you're going to die tragically in a fire that destroys a beloved local landmark. Joe should be back here soon, and we'll make sure all the loose ends such as yourself are tied up."

"You've always been a bully and gotten away with it, but not this time. Lisa found enough evidence to put you in prison."

"Lisa had no right to break into my desk. She's going to be sorry she didn't mind her own business. Soon she'll not only be jobless, but she'll be facing questions from the police. We'll make sure she's the prime suspect for the fire."

"That's laughable, you know. Lisa will make sure everyone finds out what you've done. You and Joe Michaud will be the ones facing questions. Of course, your brother has already gotten what he deserved."

He pointed the gun at Carrie's head. "What are you talking about? Where is my brother? We haven't heard from him for hours."

Lisa watched with alarm. She knew Don's temper was ready to blow, and she didn't have any way to stop him if he shot Carrie. He wasn't used to meeting with resistance to his authority. If Carrie continued to goad him, he was going to lash out at her. Lisa looked around for anything she could use as a possible weapon.

Carrie shrugged innocently as she used Don's earlier words against him. "Bruce met with an unfortunate accident."

"What accident?" His free hand came up and he struck Carrie in the face. Her head snapped back and hit the shelf behind her.

As he shouted at Carrie, Lisa stood and grabbed one of the large cans from the rack in front of her. She had to do something now or she might not get another chance. Holding the heavy can in both hands, she lunged to the side of the rack and leaped toward Don, bringing the sharp edge of the weighted can down on the back of his head with all her might.

The blow stunned him and he stumbled toward Carrie. Lisa lifted the can and struck him again as Carrie tried to grab the gun from his hand. The movement caused the already cocked revolver to fire with an explosive blast in the small room. Don collapsed to the floor, holding his foot and screaming in pain.

Carrie held on to the gun firmly and reversed their positions, training the gun closely on Don while she stepped back. Lisa dropped the can to the floor and wrapped her arms around Carrie's waist, careful not to block her view of Don.

"Thank God you're okay," Lisa said. "I thought he was going to shoot you."

"How did you get in here?" Carrie put her free arm around Lisa while keeping her eyes fixed on Don's writhing body on the floor in front of them.

"I saw Don go in the café and I tried to call you, but you didn't answer."

"I must have shut off the ringer when I turned off the flashlight."

"I saw he had a gun, so I knew I had to do something. The police are on their way, but there wasn't time to wait. I remembered about the hidden key."

"You saved me with a can of beans."

"I thought you'd appreciate that. Now we just have to hope the state police get here before Joe Michaud."

Footsteps came running through the kitchen and Ryan burst into the storeroom. "What's happening? I thought I heard a gun."

Ryan saw the gun in Carrie's hand and looked down at Don. He blinked in surprise.

"We have company," Carrie said.

"You shot him?" Ryan asked. "Remind me not to get on your bad side."

"Don was holding Carrie at gunpoint and it went off when she got it away from him," Lisa explained. "He was planning to burn down the café."

"What?" Ryan gave Carrie a stunned look. "With me and Angie upstairs?"

Carrie nodded. "I found a gas can out back and I came inside to check things out. He came in and jumped me in the kitchen."

"Sorry I didn't come help, boss. I didn't hear anything. I was in the bedroom with the air-conditioner blasting. I figured you were still looking around and you'd come up eventually."

"You found a gas can?" Lisa turned to Carrie. "I heard Don say that Joe should be back soon. We'd better make sure he can't get to it before the police get here."

"It must have been Joe outside earlier." Ryan looked down at Don who was glaring at them silently. "This one doesn't look like he'd be able to run off very quickly."

"I didn't want to get my fingerprints on it before," Carrie said. "But Lisa's right. Can you go get the gas can, Ryan? It's right around the corner out back."

Ryan nodded and turned for the exit door. He stopped short when blue lights illuminated the front of the café.

Carrie looked at Lisa. "I hope that's the state police."

Lisa froze with fear. The bakery case blocked their view of the front door from the storeroom and the glare in the front window prevented them from seeing if the car belonged to the sheriff or the state troopers. If Michaud was here, there was no telling how he would react if he came in and saw them holding Don captive with his own gun. He may decide to shoot them all and get away.

They heard the front door open. Footsteps crossed the entryway slowly and Lisa saw Luke Hodgton edge around the counter with his gun pointed defensively. "This is the state police. Nobody move."

"Luke, we're in here," Carrie called.

Lisa sagged against her in relief.

Luke rushed into the storeroom, closely followed by Officer Baker. Carrie lowered the revolver and set it down on the floor.

"What have you two been doing now?" Luke stared at Don Mills.

"I can't tell you how happy we are to see you," Lisa said. "Joe Michaud is out there somewhere, and we need to find him."

"You don't need to find anyone," Luke said. "We'll take things from here."

CHAPTER THIRTY-FIVE

Lisa found a reserve of energy when she came around the corner and spotted the finish line. She burst into a sprint and headed for the line.

"Hey, wait for me!" Carrie increased her speed and ran to catch up.

"Come on," Lisa called over her shoulder.

Lisa held out her hand to Carrie as they reached the finish and crossed together. She slowed and tried to catch her breath as they passed the people standing along the sides of the road, cheering on the runners. The heat had hit her hard and she was dripping with sweat.

"I need some water," Lisa gasped to Carrie.

They made their way through the crowd to a group of tables set up near the town beach. There were rows of bottled water along with an assortment of orange slices, bananas, and granola bars. Lisa grabbed a bottle and drank greedily. She watched with interest as Carrie opened a bottle and took a deep drink before letting the water spill over her face.

Lisa leaned close to Carrie's ear. "This is reminding me of how hot we got when we went strawberry picking."

Carrie smiled at her. "I remember."

Lisa leaned toward Carrie. She looked incredibly sexy with her dark hair framing her wet face. Lisa ran her fingers along Carrie's arm and was tempted to pull her close in spite of all the people around them. She looked over Carrie's shoulder to see her parents walking across the town park toward them. Lisa gave them a wave.

Carrie turned and saw them. "Hi Mom and Dad."

"Hello ladies," Susan said.

"You both had a good run today," David said. "I thought Lisa was going to beat you, Carrie."

Carrie nodded. "She had a strong finish."

"I had a great coach." Lisa said to David. "She held back the whole way. She could have left me in the dust any time she wanted to."

"We'll let you two catch your breath," Susan said. "We're going to go find a good place to watch the parade."

"We're planning to head home and take a quick shower," Carrie said. "Do you want to meet here for lunch around noon? We can get something from one of the food trucks."

"As long as you don't have to cook," Lisa said. "You need a break."

* * *

Lisa bit into one of the crispy french fries that accompanied their lunch. The food trucks parked around the town center served so many tasty offerings that it had been hard to choose. They were relaxing at one of the picnic tables near the beach.

"I'm just so relieved you two are all right," Susan said. "I still can't believe what Joe Michaud and the Mills brothers were doing right under our noses. When I think about how much danger you two were in, it absolutely terrifies me."

"I'm very proud of the both of you." David looked at them gravely. "Michelle Nelson's parents have told everyone in town how grateful they are to finally know what happened to their daughter. If you hadn't chosen to stand up to those men, no one would ever have found out how the Mills brothers and the sheriff covered everything up."

"The reporter who broke the story has written some fascinating articles about the whole scandal." Susan smiled at Carrie and Lisa. "I'm thankful you were able to explain everything to her so she could expose the truth about the accident and all the other corruption that's been going on around here."

"Anna has done a good job," Carrie said. "Senator Lawrence's career is finished, as it should be. I've heard he's facing a long jail sentence."

"Along with Joe Michaud and Don Mills," Lisa added. "Two men who couldn't deserve it more. I hope they never get out."

Carrie put her arm around Lisa. "Lisa got some good news yesterday."

Susan and David looked at Lisa expectantly.

"I got a call from one of the partners at the accounting firm where I used to work. They offered me my job back with a raise and a big promotion. I know they're scared of a lawsuit, but it was still nice to have the offer."

"That's wonderful," Susan said. "Do you want to go back?"

"I haven't decided. I'm going down to Portland to meet with the partners. I'm not sure of their involvement with Don's harassment, and I want to find out their level of awareness."

"That's certainly understandable," David said. "It makes me furious to hear about men treating women like that."

"Thank you, David. If I do go back, I'm going to ask that the company dedicates more resources to preventing sexual harassment. I also want them to reach out to the women Don targeted in the past and make sure they're compensated."

* * *

Carrie made sure Angie and the other cooks were all set in the kitchen before she walked out to the dining room to find Lisa. Harvest was packed with the summer festival crowd.

They had finished serving dinner for the night and people were relaxing with drinks and listening to Toni and her band, who were headlining this evening's music night performance. The annual summer fireworks were due to start soon, and people would be moving outside to find a good spot near the shoreline.

Carrie spotted Lisa sitting at their favorite table near the window. Rachel and her husband had joined Lisa for dinner that evening while Carrie worked in the kitchen. She paused to look at Lisa. Her face was lit up in a smile as she talked with her friend. Carrie's heart filled with love as she thought about everything they had been through together.

Carrie hadn't noticed feeling particularly lonely before, but now she realized how empty her life had been without Lisa. The courage Lisa had shown in facing Don and the other men had inspired Carrie to make sure she didn't hold back her feelings. She planned to keep showing Lisa how much she loved her. They shared a bond that was stronger than she could have imagined.

The last song of the night ended, and Carrie walked over to their table. She sat in the empty seat Lisa had saved for her and leaned over to give her a quick kiss. "How was everyone's dinner?"

"It was delicious, exactly like I knew it would be," Lisa said.

"I loved my meal," Rachel said. "I'm going to have to eat salad for the rest of the week after that giant piece of blueberry pie you gave me. We just got back from vacation and I was trying to be good. Oh well, it was worth it."

"Dinner was amazing," Rachel's husband Will said. "Rachel has been raving about this place and it's good to meet you, Carrie."

"Thank you, Will." Carrie extended her hand to him across the table. "It's nice to meet you, too. I'm glad you both came by to watch the fireworks with us."

"The music has been awesome tonight," Lisa said. "I'm so happy you got Toni to come perform. It's great that there isn't any awkwardness between us."

Carrie looked over to the corner where Toni was talking with her guitarist while they packed up their instruments. "It was lucky for me she had a free night. The musicians who were supposed to play couldn't make it and I would have had a hard time finding anyone nearly as good."

"We should go out and stake out a spot to watch the fireworks soon," Lisa said.

"Don't worry, I reserved the picnic table for us."

Lisa lingered behind when the others made their way outside to wait for the fireworks. She hadn't had a chance to speak to Toni, and she wanted to see how she was doing.

"Hello, Toni. You sounded great, as usual."

Toni gave Lisa a hug. "I'm glad there aren't any hard feelings with your girlfriend. It was quite the scene at your place when I showed up."

"Yeah, well, we worked everything out," Lisa said. "Are you sticking around for the fireworks?"

"Actually, I've got to run. I met the most amazing guy and I'm supposed to be meeting him. I guess it all worked out for the best between us, huh?"

"It certainly did." It was a relief to know Toni was obviously no longer upset. Her energy and passion were contagious, but that wasn't what Lisa was looking for. She thought of the trust she shared with Carrie, who she loved with all her heart. She knew she was the most important person in Carrie's life, and so much more than a passing fancy.

Lisa walked around to the backyard. People had set up chairs and blankets on the small lawn behind the café. Locals and summer residents had gathered at vantage points all along the shoreline for the festivities. The lake was scattered with boats that had anchored to watch the display from the water.

She sat next to Carrie on the picnic table bench. It was the perfect spot to enjoy the warm summer night. There was a cold drink waiting for her, and she reached for Carrie's hand.

Carrie leaned over to Rachel, who was sitting on the other end of table. "Did Lisa tell you about her job offer?"

"Yes, she did," Rachel said. "I'm not sure if I would want to go back to that company."

"I liked my job," Lisa said. "The other people I worked with were nice. It was Don who I had problems with."

"I'm still in shock about everything he did to you. I had no idea he was harassing you like that. You should have told me."

"I was going to tell you, but I was trying to figure out what to do."

"It must have been awful when he fired you," Rachel said.

"It was, but I knew I still had the power to choose what I wanted to do. I didn't let him take that away from me. I decided I wasn't going to let him get away with firing me because he found out I was a lesbian. It was time to put a stop to his harassment."

"I'm so proud of how you stood up to him," Carrie said.

"With your help." Lisa squeezed her hand. "I'm just glad it's over and everything turned out all right."

"You both could have been killed while we were away on vacation. I feel terrible I wasn't here to help." Rachel looked at Will. "See what happens when we leave town?"

"That's very sweet, Rachel," Lisa said. "I wouldn't have wanted you to get drawn into it and have Joe Michaud come after you again. It was bad enough he stopped you that afternoon."

"I never did like Sheriff Michaud," Will said. "I had a run-in with him myself once when he pulled me over for speeding."

"Thankfully he's never going to intimidate people like that again," Carrie said. "From what we've heard, he's going to be in prison for a long time, and I doubt he'll ever be back in Winchester."

"Winchester is such a great little town," Rachel said. "I'm so glad you moved here."

"It was one of the best choices I've ever made." Lisa smiled at Carrie. "That reminds me, I'm actually going to be moving again."

"What do you mean?" Rachel gave Lisa a startled look. "I thought you were happy here?"

"I'm very happy and I'm not going far." Lisa pulled her gaze away from Carrie and turned to Rachel. "I know it's a little sudden, but Daisy and I are going to move in with Carrie. We want to be together, and after everything that happened, I'm not as comfortable being alone."

Will leaned forward. "I think that's great. Let me know if you need a hand moving anything and I'll be there."

"Thanks, Will," Lisa said.

They heard the whistle and sputter of fireworks as the display began. Carrie put her arm around Lisa and held her close. They had a prime view as the colorful explosions lit up the night sky over the water. Lisa rested her head contentedly on Carrie's shoulder while they watched together.

"Are we still going to the Florida Keys this winter?" Lisa whispered in Carrie's ear.

"I wouldn't miss it for anything."

Bella Books, Inc.

Women. Books. Even Better Together.

P.O. Box 10543
Tallahassee, FL 32302

Phone: 800-729-4992
www.bellabooks.com